A Garland of Straw

A GARLAND
OF STRAW

Twenty-Eight Stories by
Sylvia Townsend Warner

Short Story Index Reprint Series

BOOKS FOR LIBRARIES PRESS
FREEPORT, NEW YORK

Some of these stories originally appeared in *The New Yorker*

INTERNATIONAL STANDARD BOOK NUMBER:
0-8369-4139-X

LIBRARY OF CONGRESS CATALOG CARD NUMBER:
75-38726

PRINTED IN THE UNITED STATES OF AMERICA
BY
NEW WORLD BOOK MANUFACTURING CO., INC.
HALLANDALE, FLORIDA 33009

CONTENTS

6 *Contents*

A Garland of Straw

A GARLAND OF STRAW

THE woman who had been introduced as Miss Woodley leaned forward and laid her hand on the newcomer's knee. One would not have expected so light a touch from so old and cumbrous an organism; the ugly hand with its lustreless nails and rather dirty knuckles came to rest as lightly as a butterfly.

"Insanity is a terrible thing, you know."

It was a large room, and cold, and furnished chiefly with wicker chairs and tables. On the mantelpiece was a large inaccurate clock. Grimy net curtains veiled the heavy sash-windows which looked into a heavily shrubbed suburban garden. All the room was rather grimy—grimy and tidy, a bleak dirt. The newcomer nodded.

"For insanity is a thing you can't wash out, it runs in the blood. Though you may be quite all right yourself, you may pass it on to your children, your children will be mad."

There were five other women in the room. One was making crochet lace, two were turning over the battered illustrated papers which lay on the wicker tables. They did not speak to each other, and when the crocheting woman crossed the room and pulled at the bell-handle by the fireplace she skirted women and wicker with a peculiar wary privacy. Goldfish in a bowl behave so, some hanging poised in aloofness, the others moving among them as impersonally as water.

"All my children," said Miss Woodley, "were mad."

The newcomer had been thinking, *that bell didn't ring.* Now she raised her eyes from Miss Woodley's ringless hand to Miss Woodley's dull face.

"Such beautiful children, too! My eldest was a boy. I shall

never forget the moment when they laid him in my arms, he weighed nine pounds and there was not a spot or a blemish on him. We could not make up our minds what to call him, he never really had a name, but my second boy was called Tristram Donald. Then I had three daughters—Armine, Felicity, and Rosemary Eve. Armine grew into a most beautiful child, olive complexion, tiny little hands and feet, long black eyelashes and a pink hat. You should have seen Armine dance! She won any number of prizes for dancing. Felicity was musical. She had chestnut hair and green eyes, and a little mole, a beauty-spot, high up on her left cheek. My Rosemary Eve was a cripple, she was dropped out of a window, and after that she could never walk again, she was always my baby in arms. Such a sweet nature! I used to hope that perhaps, as she was a cripple, she might be spared the other thing. But she went mad on her tenth birthday, just like all the rest."

Once again the crocheting lady slid across the room and rang the bell.

"Then I had twins," said Miss Woodley. "Daphne and Mezereon, a boy and a girl. They were born out of doors in a snowstorm, the easiest birth I had. They both developed insanity on the same day. Twins, you know."

She sighed, her clumsy massive bosom, cupped by old-fashioned stays, lifting the schoolgirlish tie of her woollen shirt. Then she turned her head and looked out of the window, as though, from the ungainly shrubbery, the coverts of lanky-stemmed lilac and spotted laurel, children might appear. Her face, so heavy and harsh, was almost youthful in profile—the broad forehead flowing gently into a mild snub nose, the full lips and rounded chin.

"We had any number of dogs and ponies," she continued on a more confident note. "Not cats. Cats are not safe with children. As we could only keep them for ten years we tried to make their lives as happy as possible. You never saw such happy children, singing and dancing the whole day through."

Rapidly and furtively one of the reading ladies tore an advertisement out of her magazine, folded it into a small square, and dropped it into her handbag.

"Then I had another boy, called Roderick. His god-father, who lived in the Highlands, left him a most beautiful collection of live humming-birds. They used to fly all over the house, and nested every spring. Then I had a daughter, Myrtle Irene. She was born in the first year of the war, two months after her father was killed in action. Do you remember the war?"

She leaned her head against the grimy curtain, the cold glass. Tears swelled out between her puffy eyelids, dripped off her chin on to the woollen shirt and the cheap tie.

"And then I could have no more children, you see."

Her hand groped in the pocket of her cardigan jacket, pulled out a handkerchief, spread it, neat and useless, on her knee.

"They wouldn't let me marry him!"

Her voice had gone thin. She whined, and dragged out the words with hysterical emphasis. The crocheting lady arose, this time with a frown, and pulled at the bell more vehemently.

"They wouldn't let me marry him! They said there was madness in his family, my sister Kitty kept on saying that if I married him my children would be mad. So they were! Nothing but mad children. And why? Because they wouldn't let me marry him!

"So I went mad myself," she said, as though it were the end of a song.

Her tears ran no longer, she folded up the handkerchief and put it away.

"What a pretty blouse you have! But very thin, I don't think it can be warm enough for this house. Sitting about so much one gets to feel the cold. You must be careful not to catch cold, my dear. You should have brought a little coat."

Absorbed in her own doubts, her own griefs, the newcomer had listened unmoved to Miss Woodley's weeping. But now she was ready to weep herself, to weep for self-pity. Those words, *my dear,* struck upon her as though they were an echo from an already lost world, an echo of a forfeited human kindness whose reality would never lighten upon her again.

The door opened. With a start, as though some electrified rod had been thrust into the goldfish-bowl, all the women looked round.

"Miss Woodley, dear. Here is your sister come to see you."

The visitor wore a fur coat, she was small, nattily elegant, her brilliant white hair was waved, she brought a smell of perfume with her, and with a bright false tooth she nibbled her scarlet lower lip. With unquenched hatred, with an insatiable ravening of triumph, she surveyed her sister, not even troubling to cross the room.

Miss Woodley rose, she lumbered her way among the women and the furniture, and held out her hand.

"It's their Aunt Kitty," she said.

SETTERAGIC ON

M R. PURVEY (Thomas A. Purvey, Tobacconist) laid down his penknife and held out a square of pasteboard at arm's length. At the same time, to get the maximum vista, he leaned his head back and half-closed his eyes.

"Pretty good. Pret-ty good. Not *quite* perfect, though."

He was a small man, and weedy. His hair was thinning on top, his ears were pale and unarticulated and suggested mushrooms. From head to foot he seemed to have been contrived thriftily, nourished sparingly. There was nothing abundant about him except his eyelashes, which were thick and even, like a doll's.

He gave the penknife a deft stroke or two over the carborundum, and went on picking at the lettered pasteboard.

"There, Doreen! How will that do?"

"Looks all right."

"Another advantage of doing it in stencil," he said, apparently continuing some private conversation, for to his wife he had not mentioned any previous advantages, "it will do just as well when the black-outs come round again. Six o'clock on a November evening, lights on in here, dark outside. They'll be able to read it without coming in. No draughts, you see. No wet umbrellas dripping all over the place. That is, of course, if it is still needed then."

"If *it* is, we shan't be," she said.

The words were like bubbles rising through stagnant water. They seemed to have no relevance to the woman who uttered them, a woman who sat behind the counter and knitted, her head with its elaborate top-knot bent over her

work, her lips continuously stirred as she registered stitch
after stitch.

When he had fixed the pasteboard on the glass panel of
the door he went out and examined it from the street. Returning, he went into the back of the little shop and began
to tidy some drawers. Only then did she raise her eyelids
and look at the stencilled pasteboard. Presently her lips began
to stir again, but this time to a different rhythm.

SETTERAGIC ON. OCCABOT ON.

Other words in that crow's language were TAM HTAB,
GNIKOMS, and MOOR TELIOT. Crow's language, crow's letter-
ing too, with the letters turned backwards, as children write
them, chalking on blank walls words they ought not to know.
Through the stencilled crannies she could catch minute
bright aspects of the world outside; and thus beheld, the sea
seemed bluer, and the billows of barbed wire more sharply
jagged and intricate than when seen through the rest of the
glass door-panel, or between the pyramids of dummy packets
in the shop-window.

Staring at these prismatic aspects of the July afternoon she
found herself hearing the wind.

At first she hardly knew that it was the wind. There was
nothing in the view, the blue sea and cloudless sky, the few
passers strolling hatless and in summer clothes, to suggest a
wind blowing. The noise seemed more like something mechanical, unrelated to weather. It was more like the noise
of a bomber than the noise of the wind.

Then, with no cadence, no diminution, it left off—left off
as though it had been turned off. If it had been a bomber,
she thought, I would have been under the counter by now.
But actually the houses along the sea-front were the safest
houses in the town, for the bombers waited to have their
target well under them before they let go.

The noise returned, pulsing and strident, and rose to the

former pitch, and continued for a while, and again seemed
to be turned off.

"Tom! Do you hear that? That's the wind."

"Getting up, isn't it? I say, Doreen, we've got another gross
of pipe-cleaners. What a pity we didn't know it when everybody was asking for them, and they were so short. And
seven more of those Jubilee cigar-cases."

"Bit late, isn't it?"

"No, why? I'm going to put them out, anyway. After all,
they're patriotic, that brings them up to date. Historic, too."

"Pity you can't find a fag, Tom. That would be historic,
all right."

He came out with a trayful of his oddments, and began
rearranging the glass show-case. She moved to one side and
stood watching him.

"Tom, Tom, what shall we do?"

"What do you mean, dear?"

"You know what I mean, all right. What shall we do if
this shortage goes on? We can't live by selling extras, even if
people are fools enough to buy them."

"S'only temp'ry," he said; and pulling out a silver lighter
he began to polish it on his sleeve.

"Temporary? And what did we hear six months ago? Do
you remember that evacuee woman from Sheffield, who said
you couldn't get any up in the north for love or money?
And what about all the Tommies, that lot from the Midlands, who used to buy fags to send home? That was soon
after Christmas, that was. And what about those letters in
the papers, round about Easter, saying that women ought
not to be allowed to smoke? Temporary? So's creeping pa-
ralysis."

His elbow knocked a display card. It fell with a clatter,
and brought down a structure of dummy cartons with it.
But listening to the wind she did not seem to hear.

"But you heard what it said on the wireless. There's never been so much tobacco let out as there is now. After all, you can't go against facts, Doreen."

A woman, passing, stopped and looked searchingly in the window. She came in.

"Good-afternoon. I want some cigarettes. I expect anything you have got will suit me, I'm really not a bit particular about the brand." She spoke jauntily, airily, and flipped a ten-shilling note on the counter.

"I'm sorry, madam. But we have no cigarettes."

"Goodness! Getting quite rarities, aren't they? Well, I don't mind rolling my own for a change. One must be adaptable, mustn't one, in war-time? What tobacco have you got?"

"We have no tobacco either, madam."

"No tobacco? Worse and worse! Well, I suppose you've got pipe tobacco, some sort of shag. I'm not particular. Or cigars, those little cigars?"

"No pipe tobacco either, madam. Nor cigars. No tobacco whatsoever."

Shrugging her shoulders she turned to go. Pausing, she turned back an altered face, and said humbly:

"I want it for my husband, you know."

After she had gone Doreen exclaimed: "Fool! Hasn't she got eyes in her head? *I* can read that board backside forward. Setteragic on! Occabot on!"

"What, dear?"

She pointed to the board on the door.

"So it does," he said with interest. "*Setteragic on.* Sounds funny, doesn't it?"

"Funny as the wind," she said. "What does it mean, howling its head off on a boiling hot day in midsummer, and not a cloud in the sky? Lunatic, I call it."

"It's past midsummer, though. The longest day was nearly three weeks ago."

"That's right! Now you tell me the days are beginning to draw in."

"I expect it means a change in the weather," he said. "It often does, a wind at this time of year. I do miss the weather forecasts on the wireless, I must say. Though of course we couldn't have spies reporting them to the enemy. I think I shall make one of those seaweed barometers. They're very good, I believe, very reliable. They get moist when it's going to rain."

All of a sudden she bowed her head, pressing her cheek to the glass top of the show-case.

"Oh God, Tom! I shall go mad if I can't get a smoke."

A shadow darkened the doorway, paused, and went on.

"It's a pity I'm such a fool, isn't it? But it's this silly wind, howling for no earthly reason, that gets me down. And the smell in this shop, and all the dummies grinning at me all round. And then what you said about the days drawing in, and the black-outs and the air-raids beginning again."

He put his arm round her waist, his glance meanwhile straying about the shop. "If we could sell the business . . ."

"If a bomb would fall on the business!"

"If we could sell the business, maybe we could move somewhere quieter. Plenty of jobs I could get now, you know, even with my feet. Maybe before the winter . . ."

"More likely I'll be called up by then. Well, they say making munitions takes your mind off it. Here's another fool that can't read."

This time the customer opened the door; but he had walked on again while the door-bell still jangled. Thomas shut the door and went to the back of the shop.

"Tom," she said, after a while, "I've been thinking. Isn't it funny?—if we were out in this wind, you know, we should say how refreshing it was. Blowing the cobwebs away, and all that."

"Talk of cobwebs, you ought to see this cupboard. It

must be a year since I gave it a proper turn-out. More. Here's one of those Munich mascots that were among the stock we took over."

"And if it were raining," she continued, "properly stormy, and one could see the clouds moving and the breakers out at sea, that would be all right, too. Sort of cosy and adventurous. But to sit here on a glaring fine afternoon listening to a wind that's doing nothing—I'd rather it blew the roof off. Tom! Do you suppose that what I'm really pining for is another go of air-raids?"

"I'm sure it's the very last thing."

His tone was kind and reassuring, and only slightly inattentive. And because his head was buried in the cupboard he sounded as though he were speaking from some religious compartment, a pulpit or a confessional. She looked at his dusty back, where a scrap of cellophane was poised like a butterfly.

Fossicking in that cupboard, she thought. Always busy, always inventing something to be busy about. Always about nothing. Make-believe. It's a spade and bucket he should have really.

She smiled, pinching in the corners of her mouth and nodding to herself. A spade and bucket was just what he had got, and some nice sand into the bargain. She looked at the ARP outfit, neatly grouped in the corner. Another poor fool had paused to contemplate the lying window.

"Strain," continued the voice in the cupboard. "Just strain. And one way or another way, we all feel . . . Good Lord! Doreen! *Doreen*! I've found a box of fifty!"

He hurried forward, shaking, but still remembering to blow the dust off the lid. She turned as though set on fire. And the door-bell jangled, and a second convulsion turned them, quietly attentive, towards the customer.

"Good-afternoon," he said. He smiled, and his voice was cordial. "It's all right, I'm not after fags. I believe what you say on the door, though I wouldn't in most establishments. But being back in the old place I thought I'd just look in, and ask how you're getting along."

He was a tall fellow, and one could see that even a little while before he had been dashingly handsome, with a swarthy satanic beauty; but now he looked a shabby Satan, at once aggressive and devitalized. And not even an expensive new suit could mask the sagging lines of his shoulders, the heaviness of physical strength going stale.

"You don't remember me, I gather."

"Yes, I do," she said. "You're Mr. Martin, you used to be at the Esplanade Garage."

"That's me. Nothing wrong with your memory, Mrs. Purvey."

He turned his dark gaze on her, a glittering broadside; but the effect was marred by a nervous twitch that closed up one eye.

"And now you're doing aircraft production, aren't you? What's it like, up there?"

"Well, some says one thing, and some says another. Yes, it's a Valley of the Shadow factory all right. But I don't mind it. Still, it's nice to be out for a bit."

"On a holiday?" asked Mr. Purvey.

"Well, I'm here and not there."

"What? You mean to say you just marched out? Will they take you back?"

He looked at his right hand, scarred and sinewy, with its short nails newly polished.

"They'll take me back all right, Mrs. Purvey. They aren't so straitlaced as some, they'll take me back."

"Absenteeism, eh?" said the tobacconist. "What they write about in the newspapers. Mind you, I can see your side of it too. A seven-day week and overtime. The human frame can't really stand it."

"But the money's good," she said.

"Money's all right. But what's the sense of having money when there's nothing to buy with it? What's the sense of it? All my life I've wanted to smoke cigars, and couldn't afford them. Now I can afford them with as much gold bandaging as an Admiral. And I can't get them."

"Still, it's our duty to save," said Mr. Purvey.

His face twitching, the young man looked round the shop. With every contraction the left side of his upper lip was pulled up as though he were about to snarl. The husband and wife exchanged glances, and Mr. Purvey pushed the box of fifty a little farther under cover.

After a long survey of the wares the young man bought a silver-hooped tobacco jar.

"Do to keep my ends in," he said. "When I've got ends." The wind, steadily rising to the same pitch, hung for a while on its shrill note and was shut off.

"Quite a storm getting up," she said.

"I should say so. I was passing the scenic railway on my way here, and saw it rip off a bit of canvas, the bit painted like rocks and a waterfall, easy as cutting butter. Poor old scenic! Nobody goes there now, I suppose?"

"No. It's been closed for a long while. No more holiday people now, you see. Not allowed."

"I used to enjoy the scenic," he said. "Like a kid, I did. It used to feel quite dangerous, too, didn't it, round the bends? I remember one day I was on the scenic, and a pansy in the seat in front of me he got so upset he fell on his knees and began to pray. Shut his eyes and prayed about the hour of his death to everything in heaven."

For a moment his laugh was genuine; but as they echoed it it became false as theirs.

"Roman Catholic, I suppose," said Mr. Purvey.

"Times are changed, aren't they? There was a lot of fun in those days, though. Everything was pretty pleasant. Fish and chips, and no particular hurry, and half-days regular, and the esplanade all lit up at night, and the band playing, and a fag whenever you wanted it. Well, half the time you don't know when you're lucky."

Her hand moved towards the box. Mr. Purvey shoved it a little farther away.

"Here for long?" he asked.

"Going back tomorrow like a good boy. Not taking any smokes with me either, though I hoped I would. I thought you'd still got them down here."

"They don't come in as they did," said the tobacconist. "And they go in a flash. Everyone's after them. I can't make it out. They said on the wireless there's never been so much tobacco let out as there is now."

"Somebody's getting them!" she exclaimed. "Stands to reason somebody's getting more than their fair share. What I'd like to know is, who?"

"Well, it isn't me, Mrs. Purvey, I know that. And it isn't you either, judging by that card in your door. I did see one packet of twenty up the town, but they wouldn't let me have it because I wasn't a regular customer."

"One has to do it that way," said Mr. Purvey, standing his ground between his wife and the shelf towards which her hand sketched a wavering movement.

"Hard on you folk too, I reckon."

"We must hope for better times," said Mr. Purvey. "And it's the people in your job who are bringing those better times nearer. Better times for all concerned. So you're going back tomorrow? Well, I'm sure we both wish you the best of luck."

"Stop and have a cup of tea. Do, Mr. Martin! I always make a cup about this time."

Her voice, at once urgent and hesitating, seemed to charge the words with a dare. He stared at her, blinking, as though she were a light suddenly turned on. Her face assumed an expression of desperation, of terror.

"Tom! Just go and put the kettle on the gas-ring."

Tom did not move.

"It's very kind of you, Mrs. Purvey. But I think I'd better be getting along, all the same. So here's Cheerio and Good-bye!"

When the door had shut, when the bell had rocked itself to silence, they turned and looked at each other.

"Oh God, aren't we awful? Why did you stop me?"

"Good thing if I did. You need them as much as he does. More. You know how you feel if you can't get your smoke, Doreen."

"You know what my temper's like if I don't, more like it."

He pulled out his handkerchief and began to wipe the tears off her cheeks. Having last been used in the cupboard the handkerchief was dusty. She sneezed.

"Oh Tom, you're worse than a mother, really you are."

"And it's my duty to look out for you," he continued. "That's how I look at it. You first, the rest nowhere. And if it was wagonloads of Martins, you'd come first. It's natural. Now why don't you have one now, slip away into the back, and have one?"

She opened the box, drew a deep breath, ran her finger delicately along the ribbed ranks under the paper bind.

"No. I'll wait till this evening, till I can give my whole mind to it. You must smoke some too, Tom. We must share and share alike."

"Well, just one to keep you company," he said.

APPRENTICE

THE front door, where the officers came in, was level with the street; but the house being built on a slope, from the narrow garden at the back one looked over a wall, and there, six feet below, were the heads of the passers-by. Not often, though. Not many people, and no officers, went down the narrow muddy lane, on the farther side of which was another wall, and another slope, and the upper boughs of an old pear tree.

Perched on the wall was a small stone summer-house, no bigger than a sentry-box. It had eight corners, a little spire, and a window like a church window, only the glass had been broken during the fighting. From the window one could look down into the lane, or across, over the roof-tops of the lower town, over the river and the forest, to the mountains. The mountains were stony and jagged. They were so close that one could imagine they echoed back the noises of the town— the jangling churchbells, the clear bugle notes from the garrison barracks, the cry of the goat that was tethered in the garden of the pear tree; though after a few weeks the goat cried no more, so someone must have eaten her.

"My house," said Lili. As the autumn was fine and warm they gladly allowed her to spend most of her time there. Lili was a sweet child, and Major von Kraebeck made quite a pet of her. Still, it was better to have her out of the way, for what is sometimes amusing is not always amusing.

Whoever Lili's father had been—and Irma honestly did not know—there could be no doubt that he had been all right. No Jewish blubber-lips had befouled a healthy German maiden on that occasion. Lili's eyes, set as closely in her face as the imbedded jewels in an old-fashioned ring, were flax blossoms to corroborate her flaxen hair. Her limbs were solid and straight, her flesh, as Anna remarked, was like the most expensive face-cream. Though she was only ten years old she was already rounded and womanly. She was a quiet child, quiet in a healthy un-morbid way, as though, without any break, she would develop from a model baby to a model woman.

So Lili kept house in the gazebo, sometimes eating a biscuit, sometimes thrumming on her guitar, sometimes inscribing picture postcards to send to her friends. For though Poland was a detestable country, it was rather grand to be in Poland.

As usual, all thanks were due to Major von Kraebeck. His interest in Irma extended to the whole establishment, to the three other doves and the dove-mother, and to Lili, who was his littlest dove. He managed everything; even the formalities of Lili ceasing to be educated he managed; and when they arrived he had a lovely house for them, victuals, bedding, clothes, cosmetics, everything of the best. He had even remembered to collect toys for Lili.

The people who used the lane were all Poles. They were poor and shabby, there was nothing interesting about them, except sometimes the extraordinary things they carried. They carried mirrors, saddles, gramophones, mattresses, statues, cooking-pots. Once an old man went by carrying a large gold clock that chimed in his arms. They went down the hill with their strange burdens; and after a while they would come back again, and sometimes they would have exchanged what they had taken for beetroots or cabbages, but sometimes they would bring back what they had carried down. They walked slower on the way back, because it was all uphill. Some of them looked at the mountains, but no one ever looked up at Lili.

A Polish woman came to the house to clean. She came at nine in the morning, and somebody had to get up to let her in. Quite often Lili did. Like a dead leaf the woman would whisk down the stairs, and then one would hear sounds of scrubbing, chopping wood, washing dishes. She was no fun at all, she was silent and looked cross, and she had a skin disease. Helge said that it was not wholesome that she should wash their dishes, but Madam Ulricke said it was nothing infectious, it was only because her blood was so poor.

One day there was a crash, and the noise of chopping ceased.

"Oh God, she's gone mad! She's begun to break things," cried Helge.

And Lili's mother said:

"Why on earth did we ever let her get hold of the axe?"

They clustered together at the head of the cellar steps, listening.

No sound came. They talked in whispers about barring the door, or sending for a Gestapo man. After a while came the sound of a heavy sigh.

"That's just a fit," said Madam Ulricke, and went down to the cellar. The others followed her, and Lili went too.

There on the cellar floor sat the woman, swaying and looking round her as though she wondered where she was, and the axe lay beside her. She had not broken anything. Her face worked, and suddenly she was sick, holding her shawl to her mouth. When she took the shawl away there was nothing much on it, just some green slime.

Madam Ulricke went to the larder, and unlocked it, and brought out milk, and gave it to the woman. At the first sup the woman looked astonished, and frowned. She put up her hand as though to take hold of the cup, then she put it down again, folding it in the shawl. Madam Ulricke cut a slice of bread, and put butter on it. It was the good butter, but even so the woman did not seem to notice it. She ate slowly, like an old machine that needed oiling, and as she swallowed, she choked. Suddenly the saliva began to stream from the corners of her mouth, and Helge said what a pig she was, no better than an animal, hay was what she needed, not butter.

"Just about what she's been getting," said Madam Ulricke. "That was grass that she sicked up."

"Pooh! Why should she eat grass? We pay her, don't we?"

"Suppose she had children, though?" Irma's eyes filled with tears. "She would starve to feed them. Any mother would. If my Lili . . ."

"Starving? Fancy! Is she really starving?"

Anna stared at the woman with interest. Madam Ulricke nodded.

"I know starvation when I see it. You girls have never seen it, but I have. After the last war, we starved."

"Ah, the brutes!" exclaimed Helge. "They starved us. Now *they* shall starve, Poles, French, Russians, English, all of them! And we shall eat and guzzle. Give me something to eat now, something good."

Madam Ulricke went to the larder again. They heard her moving dishes, breathing thoughtfully. The woman sat on the ground, panting and dribbling. Madam Ulricke came out with a bowlful of food; there was lard, cheese, coffee, eggs, the carcass of a fowl, and two goose drumsticks stuck out. Helge said she didn't want any of that.

"You won't get it, my girl."

"What? Is that for her? All that?"

"Yes. I went hungry once. Now I feed well, thanks to our Leader. I don't want to turn my luck."

Helge laughed, but the other girls became tender and excited. They ran about collecting more food—chocolate, herrings, dumplings—which they rammed into the bowl. At intervals they turned to the woman, smiled, and made gestures of bestowal. Madam Ulricke hauled her to her feet, put the bowl in her arms, pulled the shawl over it, and pointed to the back door. The woman looked round like a cat and ran off. Her behaviour, so ungrateful and insensitive, was disappointing. She had not finished her work, either.

Yet to Lili it seemed very nice to feed the starving. It was exciting, it made one feel good. Before they came to Poland she had had a little dog, and she always enjoyed feeding it, throwing a biscuit and seeing him dash after it, holding the bone above his head while he begged and rolled his eyes. It occurred to her that she could feed the starving from her summer-house. She would feed children; no one could much object to that, for they would be Polish children only, all the Jews had been put away.

She began to save and purloin. When she had a basketful of scraps she carried it to her summer-house and sat there, waiting for children.

Before long four children appeared, children whom she already knew by sight. As usual, they were dragging a sledge with bits of wood on it. Some of the wood was already charred. It came from the suburb where the bombs had fallen, everyone went there to steal wood.

"Here!"

She leaned forward and emptied the basket. What a pity, she had meant to throw the bits one by one. The biscuits, the dried plums, the shrimp-heads, and the orange scattered on the muddy road, and the orange began to roll downhill. The children let go of the sledge; it, too, began to run down the hill. Just like the little dog, they dashed to and fro, snatching up bits of food. They even barked, or something very like it.

When they had picked up everything they went after the sledge.

"Here! Here I am!"

She called at the top of her voice. They began looking for

more food; at last they looked up and saw her. She held out her hand, as though more were coming. They stared. She had no more, but at least they had seen her.

For hours after she nursed a violent impression of the contrast between them and herself. There she had leant with her smooth plaits swinging, so plump and white-skinned and smiling so graciously; and there they had stood, turning up their wizened sallow faces, and blinking their sore eyes. They all had swelled bellies. It was funny, it made them look greedy and not starving at all. But of course they must be starving, one could see that by their hollow cheeks, their stringy necks, the toes that came out of their torn shoes, toes so thin that they looked like rats' claws.

That afternoon Major von Kraebeck brought a box of chocolates. She sat on his knee and ate them from between his lips, which made them rather sticky.

"Aren't you lucky?" said Irma. "Luckier than the poor little Polish kids."

Lili tweaked out another chocolate.

"They look so funny, the Polish kids! They all have big bellies and yellow faces. They are like little monkey mothers. Boys and girls, they are all like little monkey mothers."

The Major exploded with laughter, and said he must tell that to the mess. Lili tried to think of another clever remark about the Polish children (she was not often so successfully clever), but before she could do so he had set her down and told her to run away.

Though everyone was so good-humoured, something warned her to keep her summer-house game a secret. The fat Captain was always telling Helge stories about typhus, and Helge saying they should be like the brave men in the English story, who shut themselves up during a plague and would have nothing to do with anyone outside their village. As time went on it became rather a bore collecting the scraps. There was always plenty of cigar-ends, of course, and bits of orange-peel, but real food was harder to come by. It was a good hour when the idea came to her of wrapping pebbles in the fancy papers that had wrapped sweets. They looked charming, and most life-like. The sledge children still paused under the summer-house, though now they were not so excited that they let the sledge run away, and once the boy, finding a pebble in his mouth instead of a sweet, spat it out and threw it at her. Then they came no longer. Perhaps they were dead. There were other children, though, all ugly and with swollen bellies, and ready to eat anything, who paused and looked up enquiringly.

It occurred to her that instead of just throwing food down it would be much better sport to lower it on a string. For then she could dangle it, lowering it and drawing it up again; and quite a little food would last out as long as a basketful. This was delightful: so delightful that she became a much better thief, stealing sprats and little cakes, and taking the bones and crusts that Madam Ulricke put by for the char-woman. And naturally the poor children enjoyed their bits much more when they had jumped for them a little, and fought among themselves. Back in Germany Lili had learned in school how what you fight for and take from others is sweetest of all.

But there was one boy who would not jump, who would not beg. There was nothing to make him so proud, he was just a Pole, and as thin as the others, his eyes were inflamed, his belly was swollen, his hands were covered with open chilblains. Only his hair looked rather strong. It was black, and grew straight up off his forehead, like a forest. Twice when the other children had been jumping for crusts he stopped on his way up the hill, and spoke angrily to them. The first time they listened, and walked away. The second time he scolded them they paid him no heed, but jumped on. After that he always walked by with his nose in the air.

He was stuck-up, and a spoil-sport. Cruel, too, for he tried to prevent the poor hungry children from getting their crusts. Lili hated him. She hated him, and she thought of him. She wondered how tall he was—it was difficult to tell from above. She wondered if he was an orphan and if he had ever worn a hat. She wondered if he had gipsy blood. She wondered if he had lice in his hair, and one day, seeing him scratch his neck savagely, she knew that he had, and was delighted. She hated everything about him: his upstanding black hair, the recollection of his sharp voice, the old satchel he carried under his arm. No doubt he thought himself a scholar, a professor. Sometimes she even wondered if he were not a Jew; he might have been hidden when the others were carted off. The only thing about him which she did not hate was his regularity: every afternoon he came up the hill, late, when the river mists were rising. And sometimes she even hated his regularity, he was like some hateful medicine which she had to swallow day after day.

Her regularity began to match his. Every afternoon she waited for him, and kept the best, the most tempting bit to dangle in front of him. If some grown-up person went along the lane at the same time that he did, so that she could not carry out her fishing game, she was furious. Sometimes, hearing him approach, she thought how much she would like to tumble down a stone, a heavy stone, on top of that black head. One day, perhaps, she might. But not until she had hooked him. That must come first. He must eat from her hand, as the others had done, and look up, and be grateful.

Time went on. It grew cold, a damp wind blew away all the leaves from the pear tree and even the topmost pear that no one could reach. Looking at the forest you could almost hear the wolves howl. You could hear the Poles howl quite plainly. The women had rioted, breaking the windows of the fashionable baker's shop to get at the cakes and golden crescents within. Irma and Helge and Anna and Lisl, even Madam Ulricke, had been terrified, and had run about the house hiding away food and wine and their best clothes in case the Polish women should break in. Anna had pulled her shoes and stockings off, and put a shawl over her head, saying that she would pretend to be a peasant; and the others had laughed hysterically, pointing to her white feet and crimson-varnished toe-nails. On the next day the charwoman was dismissed, for the officers said it was not safe to have her about the house, she might let in the others, and as for the house-work and the washing-up, the girls could manage it for them-selves; and Major von Kraebeck sent in a soldier to chop wood and see to the great stove. The girls were angry, they did not like housework, they had not come to Poland to be drudges. The soldier grew very fond of Madam Ulricke, they would stay a long time in the cellar together, making the stove burn up, Madam Ulricke said. When they came out the soldier would lay his head on her bosom and weep, and say how greatly he longed for home. And Madam Ulricke would make him hot milk.

All these things were observed by Lili, for now that the charwoman came no more she was being more useful. But still in the afternoons she went to her summer-house to wait for the boy; for in the afternoons nobody wanted her. And now she had finer and more tempting baits, for being so much in the kitchen she picked up many good things.

The boy still came by at the same time. She often heard his footsteps long before she could see him, for the mists from the river swelled higher and higher, all the lower town was blotted out in fog. He came up out of the mist and was gone, and never once did he look at the bait she dangled before him. And day after day she fretted more, foreseeing that quite soon it would be dark before he came by.

For three days and nights the wind howled and the rain lashed against the windows. On the fourth morning the wind fell, the air was like ice-water, and snow lay on the moun-tains. The people who went along the lane shaded their eyes against the brilliant sunlight, and pulled their clothes closer round them against the motionless cold, and an old man carrying a cello to the pawnshop slipped on the ice and fell, groaning. The cello groaned too as it fell, it skidded down the hill and crashed against a post and was broken, and the old man went after it on all fours, howling like a beast.

The sun, the tingling air, the snow on the mountains, the excitement of wearing for the first time a little fur coat and a pair of fur gloves, all gave Lili a sense of confidence. Today, surely, her luck was in!

"Bake cinnamon buns," she said to Madam Ulricke. "Bake cinnamon buns, and I will wash all the glasses and polish the saucepans too."

"Why do you want cinnamon buns?"

"To eat in my house," she replied boldly.

"Heavens, child! It is far too cold to play there now."

"No, it is lovely! I will sit there and eat my buns with my gloves on, and look at the sunset, and pretend I am grown-up, and engaged to be married to a General, or a Minister."

But to fix the bun on the string she had to pull off her gloves. And the air seemed to bite away her flesh, so warm and plump, as though it would give her rat's-paw hands, like any Polish child. Then she sat down to wait.

Other children came by, and looked up at her, and held out their rat's-paw hands. But she paid no heed to them, she could not be bothered with them now. She waited. And the colours of the roof-tops changed, the river grew pale as lead, the forest seemed to come nearer. The churchbells jangled, the sky became almost green. The bun was quite cold now. She ground her teeth with impatience. But still she felt sure of him.

At last he came with his black head and his satchel. And today, for the first time, he looked for her as he was approaching. She could not discern much, for already dusk was falling, only that his face was white, and that he was looking at her. Then, just as though to tantalize her, he turned away and leaned on the wall, staring at the river and the forest and the mountains—as though he had not seen them every day of his life. She could see by the movement of his narrow shoulders that he was out of breath.

She tried to whistle softly and prettily, as one whistles to a bird. But her lips were stiff with cold; instead of a whistle she could only manage a squawk.

At last he turned away from the mountains and came on up the hill, walking slowly; and slowly she lowered the bun.

She lowered it so cleverly that it bobbed against his face. Then she whisked it up again.

He leaped after it. He almost caught it. It was frightful that anyone could leap like that.

The satchel dropped from under his arm. His head jerked backward, he fell, and lay in the road, quite still. Quite still, she watched him.

Presently she began to count. Fifty, fifty-one. If I reach a hundred, she thought, and he does not move, I shall think he's dead. Seventy-seven, seventy-eight, seventy-nine. . . . She reached the hundred, and went on counting, frozen in an ecstasy of amassing. She had counted up to eight hundred and ninety when a man came along the lane. It was annoying, she did not want anyone to come by, and the rhythm of his footsteps threw her out in her count. Seeing the boy he stopped, and then knelt down beside him. To her it was obvious that the boy was dead, and at last the man was convinced of it too. He got up, and dusted the frost off his knees. Then, as though an idea had struck him, he stooped again, and pulled the boy straight, crossing his hands on his breast and smoothing the strong hair. Then he took a handkerchief from round his neck, and began to spread it over the boy's face, but changed his mind, and put on the handkerchief again, and knotted it carefully. Then he went away.

So it was true, really true. The boy was dead. He had died of cold and hunger before her eyes, just as they said. Dozens of them were dying so; but hearsay is one thing, seeing with one's own eyes another.

Poor boy! He should not have been so proud, so unpleasant. If he had taken her gifts earlier he might still be alive. It was not her fault that he had died so horribly of starvation. It must be really terrible to die like that, really terrible to be dead.

There was the poor bun, still dangling.

Hastily she pulled it up, and ate it.

RAINBOW VILLA

"SO I have decided to come back."

Her face was flushed, for she had spoken at length, and with vehemence. Now, realizing that it was not usual to pour out such confidences, and so energetically, to the house-agent, she added with sharper decision and a grander manner:

"Quite decided. I am positive it is what my dear brother would have wished. And I have ordered the furniture to come from the repository next week."

At the mention of the dead the house-agent's face took on an easier posture. The expression with which one acknowledges a dead client is formalized, familiar, calling for no difficult adjustments.

"Ah! One does not see many people like Mr. Ensor nowadays."

"I dare say not."

The flush had died away, leaving her face pale with the dirty pallor of age. The vehemence had died away too. She was thinking that Francis would not have approved this promiscuous washing of family dirty linen. There had been no need to tell Mr. Genge that living with Florence had turned out badly, and certainly no need to describe how silly Florence had been about bacon and air-raids. It should have been sufficient to say that she had decided to come back to Rainbow Villa, where she had lived for so long with Francis, where now she would live alone. On the desk between them a ledger lay open. The house-agent looked again at the clean page, so elegantly written, so singularly free from erasures and additions that it resembled a tombstone.

But he looked at it as though it were so importantly full as to be almost undecipherable.

"November 1938. Nine-teen-thir-ty-eight. Practically three years ago."

"Two years and eight months."

"The war," said Mr. Genge. "The war. It seems to emphasize the lapse of time, does it not?"

"Do you find it so? I can't say that I notice much difference. Time seems to go about as fast as usual. Of course, I can remember several wars," said the old lady.

"Seeing so many changes," said the house-agent, "being, so to speak, on the spot, and seeing them personally, makes pre-war days seem quite distant days. War brings changes. That is inevitable. We must bow to it."

He looked so bowed, all of a sudden, that Miss Ensor said:

"I hope you have not had any bereavements."

"No. No, not actually. Actually not. But one sees so many changes. Especially, perhaps, in my profession. Changes of ownership. Changes of tenancy. Changes . . ."

His tone indicated that the changes were mostly for the worse.

"No doubt," said she. "However, I don't expect to find Rainbow Villa much changed. It is really providential that you couldn't find me a tenant for it."

No failure on his part, but the exorbitant rent she insisted on demanding for that small and unattractive house was the reason. But the representative of Messrs. Angel, Genge and Chilmaid replied, sadly and meekly:

"No, we failed over the tenant. But of course one must bear in mind that the house has not been wholly unoccupied."

"Oh, that billeting business. Poor fellows, I was very glad to think of them there, with a sound roof over their heads."

Mr. Genge gazed into his book.

"December thirty-nine to March forty. Twelve weeks. Thirty-five men."

"Shocking!" said Miss Ensor. "Such overcrowding. But better than tents."

"Oh, undoubtedly. The only possible, the only patriotic view to take. Better than tents. Yes. Particularly as the season was so severe. Yes, indeed! Which reminds me, I fear you may find a few little dilapidations. A little damage to the interior wood-work. Some of the palings missing."

"Why?"

"The weather, you know. Such unusually low temperatures. In fact, I think they may have helped themselves to a little firewood. Very natural. A way they have in the army, you know."

"H'm."

"Of course," Mr. Genge continued, "we submitted our claim to the War Office. The forms went through some time ago. To the appropriate department."

"Well, haven't they paid yet?"

"I think not. No. Actually, not quite yet. But, of course they will. It is merely a question of a little patience."

"They should have done it long ago," she said. "What else was damaged?"

"Oh, very little, considering. A pane or two of glass. Various small fixtures. I think the schedule is downstairs. I could have it brought up to you if you wish."

His hand hovered over the desk telephone.

"Don't trouble. I can see for myself, for I'm going there now. I am catching the midday bus."

"No, no!" exclaimed Mr. Genge. "That we cannot permit. Our junior partner, Mr. Brown, will drive you in his car."

His tone of voice had become suddenly warm, free, bestowing.

"Oh, very well. That will be very kind of him."

There was no answering warmth and reception. With the

flippancy of old age she seemed to regard Mr. Brown and the bus as pretty well equivalent. And while Mr. Genge was implying down his telephone that Miss Ensor was the most precious, the most highly valued, of all the firm's clients—as Mr. Brown would, of course, be aware—she was unconcernedly reading the notices of fat stock and farm implements for sale by auction.

To Mr. Brown, who had not seen her before, Miss Ensor seemed unbelievably old: so old that if she had fallen to pieces under the strong midday sun of July, beating down on the street, it would have been a quite natural confirmation of words he had heard once or twice from Mr. Genge on the subject of Rainbow Villa . . . *She'll* never need the house again!

But instead of falling to pieces Miss Ensor climbed into the car as nimbly as a spider.

A jolt, he thought, might finish her yet. But though his agitated misery made him drive abominably, jolts did nothing to Miss Ensor beyond swinging her hat a little farther over one eye.

For Mr. Brown was a compassionate young man, and so much disliked the thought of any unpleasantness, any sight of suffering, that he had prepared himself to be a conscientious objector, not knowing that the state of his aorta would reserve him for civilian sufferings only. Miss Ensor however turned to him briskly and said:

"Why aren't you in the army, young man?"

"My heart," murmured Mr. Brown; and thinking that she was probably a rather nasty old lady, rude and overbearing, became even more afflicted: for it is doubly painful to be sorry for people you can't like.

"H'm."

They drove in silence for some miles. He thought of mentioning the country, the prospects of a good harvest, the changes . . . no, no, good God! Not changes! Not with that wrecked building awaiting them, the mammocked billet of thirty-five freezing soldiers, that Aunt Sally of evacuee children, that doss-house of tramps, that habitation of stray cats and foxes. Suppose that at the moment they arrived a tramp . . . ?

Before he knew what the words would be he had asked: "Why Rainbow? Why was it called Rainbow Villa?"

"My brother named it."

They took the right-hand fork. The road swung between fat hedges, everything in sight looked arrogantly green, arrogantly thriving. If only the house had creepers on it, ivy, ampelopsis, anything to muffle the first impact, make the truth less raw . . . ! But it hadn't. And again his thoughts returned to the question, Why Rainbow?—of all names the silliest for a bare square box of drab roughcast, standing like a sentry-box at the side of the road staring at the landscape with blank rectangular eyes, three above and two below.

"I'm afraid it may be rather a shock . . ."

But the words had been got out too late, for already the car had rounded the bend and the shock had been received. He drew up. After a minute she began to scrabble at the window-lever, saying:

"How does this thing work? I want to get out."

In his hand the keys of the house flashed. At Angel, Genge, and Chilmaid all keys were polished regularly, such small details make a good impression. But there was no need of them, for the door was off its hinges. Instead, he lifted aside the porch of flimsy wire trellis, which had collapsed across the threshold.

A stab of light fell on the sitting-room floor, coming through the hole in the roof and the great gap in the flooring of the room above. It shone on a piece of crumpled paper, on which was printed: *To Let. Apply Messrs. Angel, Genge, and Chilmaid, House Agents, Estate Agents, and Auctioneers, Market-place, Durnford.* It shone, too, on splinters of broken glass and on excrements. They crossed the passage to the corresponding room. Here, too, was broken glass; but it had been swept into a corner, and the centre of the room was occupied by a bed of withering bracken-fronds. On the hearth were some toe-rags, and the scattered ashes of a fire, and a rusty kettle and two beer bottles stood near by.

Looking upward, Mr. Brown said in a voice of dreamy misery:

"The ceiling of this one seems pretty sound."

Silent, she walked out. He followed her to the foot of the stairs. Steps and banisters had been hacked away.

"I don't know if it's worth while going up. I will, if you like."

Still silent, she turned and went into the kitchen, and on from there to the scullery. There was a scuffling noise, and a cat leaped out of the copper.

"Poor thing! Poor pussy!"

Her voice reminded him of a doll his sister had had, a doll which when you pulled its strings said: *Papa! Mamma!*

Standing behind her, ravaged with embarrassment and incompetent pity, he actually began to wring his hands. After a while she moved over to the copper, and looked inside.

"No kittens."

Had she gone mad, an octogenarian Ophelia, or was she revenging herself by playing on his feelings? When he heard a car approach and halt outside, he was so desperate that he really believed that Mr. Genge, repenting, had followed in order to take on himself the burden of this ghastly situation. But the car door did not open; and presently two voices, ladylikely loud, were heard.

"Isn't it frightful? A direct hit. We've had quite a lot of them around here, you know."

"Looks more like blast to me."

"Oh, do you think so? I wonder where the crater is. Did

I tell you about Penelope's land-mine? Of all the amazing strokes of luck . . . !"

Fortunately the old lady was rather deaf. But the visiting voices were loud, and their diction was clear, and agonized by the thought that Miss Ensor might at any moment hear her property (suffering, so Mr. Genge said, from the inevitable dilapidations of a house left empty in war-time) mistaken for a bombed house, Mr. Brown raised his own voice.

"It's chiefly the woodwork, you know. It was so fearfully cold that winter, and some little delay, I understand, about coal. We have sent in a claim for that and for the windows. Though to do the men justice, some of the windows have gone since. There are so many children about now . . . rather wild children. I often wonder if it's seeing all the wreckage in blitzed towns that makes them so destructive when they are sent down here. Psychological, you know. Of course, the roof. . . . But both winters were very severe, and probably the frost cracked the cement, and slates are so easily dislodged. It's not so bad in here. That's the advantage of a bricked floor. I'm afraid Mr. Genge did not quite prepare you for it. The truth is, he has been so extremely busy, and labour and materials are so hard to get just now, and . . ."

Perfectly inattentive, Miss Ensor burst into tears, uttering the loud crowing sobs of second childhood. Snorting and sobbing, she swept past Mr. Brown and his clean handkerchief and his red compassionate face, and went weeping through her ruined house, and out into the glaring sunlight.

"Look! Oh, the *poor* old thing!"

Both ladies leaped from the car and hurried to Miss Ensor.

"No wonder you're upset. It's the shock, isn't it? So frightful, seeing one's home devastated, everything gone in a minute. I do feel for you so frightfully. We both do. I suppose you've lived here quite a long time? That makes it worse, doesn't it?"

Now, while the first lady was patting Miss Ensor, the second lady looked up into the blue sky and exclaimed:

"Brutes! Inhuman brutes!"

"My God, yes! Still, I suppose it's some comfort to think we are doing it to them now. But that won't put your poor house back, will it? We are so sorry for you, you know. It's ghastly, just ghastly! But I'm sure you mustn't cry like this. Can't we take you somewhere and give you a nice cup of tea? That's what you want. Something to pull you together. You'll feel better then. Really, you will. Do come with us, we can all get introduced on the way to tea. After all, there's no room for all that nonsense in war-time, is there? That's one comfort, it has brought us all together in such a rational way."

"Another comfort," said the second lady, "is that it only got the house, not you. That sort of comfort grows on one, I assure you. I *do* know, because my own poor little flat was torn to ribbons; and if I'd been able to get a taxi I'd have been back in it, and in ribbons, too. After all, life means a lot, doesn't it?"

"Oh, it certainly does," rejoined the first lady. "And every one's being so marvellously brave. Think of all those poor souls in the East End, how splendid they all were. And I'm sure you're going to be just like them after you've had that cup of tea. And then you can tell us all about it. Was it a night raid or a daylight?"

This time they paused, and Miss Ensor could speak.

"It wasn't either. It was thirty-five billeted soldiers. And two hard winters. And some evacuated children. So I understand. And a vilely incompetent and dishonest house-agent. There he is. You'd better ask him."

The two ladies looked incuriously at Mr. Brown, and looked away again.

"Oh, I say. What rotten luck! Really, it looks just as if a bomb had got it."

After her furious speech Miss Ensor was again in tears.

"Poor old soul!"

"Of course, billeting can be the very devil. Did I tell you about Badger's billiard-room?"

"He did. Still, one gets compensation, doesn't one?"

"Oh, yes. All that's seen to. A bit slow, of course, but wizard when it comes."

"Well, you can't expect the poor old War Office to turn themselves into walruses and carpenters, can you? After all, they've got to win the war. But they always pay up in the end."

"Oh, yes, they pay all right. Ultimately. There's nothing to worry about."

Raising her voice, she repeated the words, and added:

"You're sure you won't come and have some tea? But I dare say you want to have a heart-to-heart with your house-agent, so we won't take up any more of your time. But do cheer up, won't you? I'm sure everything will turn out much better than you think. It's only a question of time."

The second lady added her plea that Miss Ensor should cheer up and remember that it might have been a bomb. And acknowledging Mr. Brown's rigid glare with rigid in-attention both ladies stepped into the car and drove away.

After a while Miss Ensor began to weep less violently, and presently to sob only, and then only to hiccough. In a rather hen-like way she began to tweak up groundsel from a vaguely-distinguishable circular flower-bed. Mr. Brown, sigh-ing heavily, began to pull up groundsel too. But seeing her pause, and look at him with fury, he said:

"I'm afraid we ought to be getting back. That is, if you have been here long enough, and don't mind."

THE LANGUAGE OF
FLOWERS

The Office of Works has sent flowers from Kensington Palace garden to be planted on the grave of Queen Victoria's governess, Baroness Lehzen, at Bueckeburg.—*The Countryman,* April 1938.

Miss Linda Hopgood, Principal of St. Scholastica's College, to Robert Greene, Ministry of Education. June 25, 1937.

DEAR ROBERT,

Can you tell me, as between friends, what chance of favour there is for this proposal? Many people in my profession are impressed by what the Spanish Government is doing for education, and would like to show their admiration in a practical way. Great quantities of teaching material in Spain —from laboratory fittings down to blackboards—have been destroyed. We would like to remedy this shortage and would be responsible for raising the money and buying the things needed. But, as you know, to send them may be difficult unless we can rely upon some sort of official countenance. Is there any chance that this could be arranged through the good offices of the Ministry of Education?

It is proposed to offer the things as a tribute to Francisco Giner. Giner was an admirer of English methods, his work has placed all teachers in his debt, and it seems appropriate that English educationalists should show their obligation in this practical way.

Robert Greene, Ministry of Education, to Miss Linda Hopgood. June 28, 1937.

Dear Linda,

I am sorry to throw cold water, but I must tell you that there is no possibility of official sympathy for your scheme. And as between ourselves I advise you to drop the whole thing.

If you feel you must go on with it, then let me beg you to leave out any mention of Giner. For one thing, I do not believe that more than a dozen people in this country have ever heard of him, and those who have incline to think him a crank; for another, it would be most inadvisable at this juncture to suggest that cultural association with the Spain of the last century can lead to any sort of partisanship in the present deplorable upset. If you will be guided by me, you will abandon the whole idea.

Mrs. Tringle Willoughby to a friend. July 18, 1937.

I am thinking quite seriously of removing Pamela from St. Scholastica's. I happened to discover that that Miss Hopgood was actually attempting to send *chemicals* to the Spanish Reds, passing them off as coloured inks and mathematical instruments for schools (as if people of that sort cared twopence for education!) and it was all being got up as a tribute, save the mark! to some Bolshevist schoolmaster. I wrote her a furious letter saying that Pamela went there to be *educated*, not to hear about politics. Anyhow, I shall be glad to have Pamela back. Nowadays one can scarcely call one's children one's own.

Pamela Tringle Willoughby to a friend. August 20, 1937.

. . . but my idiot parents seem quite fixed. Home is an awful thing when you're planted there. I can't imagine how I ever looked forward to holidays. Mother still chats on about Hopgood sending explosive inks to Madrid. She started in to tell the Horrid Tale to Dame Primrose Henley, who was here unveiling a drinking fountain. I thought it would

do Dame P. no harm to hear the truth for once, so I gave
her a full account. She listened most attentively. She is really
quite intelligent for a Conservative, she even appeared to
know who Giner was.

*Dame Primrose Henley, D.B.E., to Lady Violet Robinson.
August 22, 1937.*

. . . and the whole scheme was fortunately scotched. But
I mention it to you, partly because I think you should know
that this sort of thing is being exploited, and partly because
the idea itself, rightly applied by the right hands, might be
quite useful.

*Lady Violet Robinson to Sir Mervyn Scallop, C.B.E., M.C.,
M.P. Sept. 1, 1937.*

. . . and you know how important a man he is in Berlin at
this moment. He feels all such moves are a great step forward
towards a better understanding. In particular, he emphasized the value of more *gemütlich* approaches. It would be
so good, he said, especially for publicity purposes both in
Germany and here in England, if we were to make some quite
simple, peaceful gesture, recalling how much the two nations
have in common, and how closely linked they have been in
the past, and, if possible, attaching to some beloved non-
political figure. Of course they must have been dead for
some time. He himself suggested the Prince Consort. I had
to explain that the Prince Consort would *definitely not quite
do*. Whom do you suggest? In many ways Bluecher would be
ideal, but the French might be tiresome. Baron Liebig?
Stockmar? Or what about Baroness Lehzen? There are certain advantages about having *a woman*. Please let me know
what is thought about this.

*Sir Mervyn Scallop, C.B.E., MC., M.P., to Lady Violet
Robinson. Telegram. 9/2/'37.*

Suggest Mendelssohn composed Elijah popular with masses.

Lady Violet Robinson to Sir Mervyn Scallop, C.B.E., M.C., M.P. Telegram. 9/3/'37.

Regret Mendelssohn racially ineligible.

The Right Hon. Egbert Simpkin, P.C., C.B., K.C.V.O., M.P., to Sir Mervyn Scallop, C.B.E., M.C., M.P. Sept. 6, 1937.

Lady Robinson's suggestion seems to me a very useful one. I consider that we might well commence with the Baroness Lehzen, and I opine that there could be no possible objection to dispatching some flowers, of course with a suitable association, to be planted on her grave. May I leave the arrangement to you? Meanwhile, please give my regards to Lady Robinson and thank her warmly for her very valuable assistance in this as in other matters.

Sir Mervyn Scallop, C.B.E., M.C., M.P., to Miss Rose Jones, private secretary. Memorandum. Sept. 8, 1937.

Kindly supply data re Baroness Lehzen.

Miss Rose Jones to Sir Mervyn Scallop, C.B.E., M.C., M.P. Memorandum. Sept. 9, 1937.

Miss Lehzen, daughter of a pastor in Coburg, was governess to Queen Victoria. Afterwards created Baroness Lehzen by George IV. Had great influence in a backstairs way, made mischief between the Princess V. and the Duchess of Kent.. A demure, high-minded, unpleasant character, reactionary, ate caraway seeds with roast beef. Remained after Coronation and Marriage, finally got rid of by Prince Consort, 1842. Retired to Hanover. Died unmarried and *sine prole*. See Queen Victoria, Girlhood of, Journals, etc. Also Lytton Strachey.

Sir Mervyn Scallop, C.B.E., M.C., M.P., to Sir Justin Mani-
fold, K.C.V.O., Office of Works. Sept. 10, 1937.

DEAR SIR JUSTIN,

I shall be much obliged if you will request someone in
the Royal Parks and Gardens Department to see to the following:

Sufficient flowering plants, preferably snowdrops, to cover
a space of approximately six foot by three foot, to be carefully
uprooted from the garden of Kensington Palace and packed
securely for transport to the Continent.

I have been asked by Egbert Simpkin to transmit this request to the Office of Works.

Sir Justin Manifold, K.C.V.O., to Mr. Anthony Jago, Secre-
tary, Royal Parks and Gardens. Sept. 13, 1937.

DEAR JAGO,

Please see to this:

Sufficient flowering plants, preferably snowdrops, to cover
a space of approximately six foot by three foot, to be carefully
uprooted from the garden of Kensington Palace and packed
securely for transport to the Continent.

Mr. Anthony Jago to Sir Justin Manifold, K.C.V.O. Sept. 15,
1937.

DEAR SIR JUSTIN,

Mr. Dodd, our head gardener, tells me that this is not a
suitable time of year to uproot snowdrops. He also points out
that to uproot sufficient snowdrops to cover a space of six
foot by three foot would leave no snowdrops in the garden
of Kensington Palace. Mr. Dodd suggests hybrid asters.

Sir Justin Manifold, K.C.V.O., to Sir Mervyn Scallop,
C.B.E., M.C., M.P. Sept. 17, 1937.

DEAR SIR MERVYN,

Our Mr. Dodd, head gardener at Kensington Palace, tells
me that snowdrops will not survive transplanting at this time

of year. It would be a pity to send eighteen square feet of dead snowdrops to the Continent. Would you consider hybrid asters?

Sir Mervyn Scallop, C.B.E., M.C., M.P., to Miss Rose Jones. Memorandum. Sept. 19, 1937.

Kindly supply data re asters.

Miss Rose Jones to Sir Mervyn Scallop, C.B.E., M.C., M.P. Sept. 20, 1937.

Aster (Michaelmas Daisy). Hardy Herbaceous Perennial. Various shades of purple, mauve, blue, pink. Also white. Cultivation: Sow in early spring in a hotbed, transplant to pots or open ground; or sow outdoors May to July, winter under glass, and plant out following May. Showy and floriferous, much improved recently, many varieties reaching a height of five foot. Especially popular: Blue Boy, Purity, Pink Lady.

Sir Mervyn Scallop, C.B.E., M.C., M.P., to Sir Justin Manifold, K.C.V.O. Sept. 21, 1937.

Dear Sir Justin,

I fear that asters would be totally unsuitable for the purpose in hand. It is essential that the flowers should be under eighteen inches in height and should bloom all the year round. By the way, I omitted in my first letter to go into the question of hue. Mauve shades would be admirable, white also, or a not too bright blue. A pale pink would be permissible, but nothing touching on red.

I must confess that I am surprised by this peculiarity of the snowdrop. It is most unfortunate, as snowdrops would be, in every other respect, ideal.

Sir Justin Manifold, K.C.V.O., to Mr. Anthony Jago, Sept. 22, 1937.

DEAR JAGO,

I think we shall have to be content with an assortment of flowers that will transplant well, but since Scallop is still importunate for the snowdrop, I would suggest that a suitable quantity of these be bought from some respectable firm and added to our plants. If they look too new, they might be planted out for a day or two. Please ask Dodd to go ahead on this basis.

Sir Justin Manifold, K.C.V.O., to Sir Mervyn Scallop, C.B.E., M.C., M.P. Telegram. 9/27/'37.

The flowers are now ready to be dispatched. Please send me full details of how and where they are to be addressed.

Sir Mervyn Scallop, C.B.E., M.C., M.P., to Miss Rose Jones. Sept. 28, 1937.

DEAR MISS JONES,

I am indeed sorry to trouble you during your well-earned leave of absence, but I find I must ask you to ascertain for me the burial place of the Baroness Lehzen. Your previous memorandum on this subject does not go into this. I hope you will be able to do me this service without much inconvenience to yourself, as you always have everything at your finger-tips. I trust you will speedily be restored to health.

Miss Margery Jones to Sir Mervyn Scallop, C.B.E., M.C., M.P. Oct. 4, 1937.

DEAR SIR,

My sister asks me to tell you that the Baroness Lehzen is buried at Bueckeburg, near Hanover.

Mr. Anthony Jago to Sir Justin Manifold, K.C.V.O. Oct. 8, 1937.

Mr. Dodd says that as the flowers were packed nearly a fortnight ago many of them are likely to be dead, and none of them in a creditable condition. Are they to be dispatched to the address given by Sir Mervyn Scallop, or do you authorize me to tell Mr. Dodd to prepare a second lot?

Sir Justin Manifold, K.C.V.O., to Mr. Anthony Jago. Telegram. 10/10/'37.

Please ask Mr. Dodd, with proper apologies, to do it all over again.

Mr. Andrew Dodd to Mr. Anthony Jago. Oct. 13, 1937.

Mr. Jago. Sir:

Regarding the assortment of flowers now being prepared for sending to Bueckeburg, I am sorry to tell you that we cannot spare any more heliotropes. So respectfully suggest filling out with forget-me-nots, Azure Gem, as these are always a favorite.

Lady Violet Robinson to Sir Mervyn Scallop, C.B.E., M.C., M.P. Nov. 10, 1937.

. . . so pleased about the flowers. He asks me to give you a special word of thanks for falling in so readily with the idea. I myself am delighted also, it is so timely a gesture and one bound to make a big appeal. Of course it is only a little thing really, but it is a little thing in the right way, and that means so much. In fact, I am sure that we shall see a real result in time.

I hope you are not too terribly tired, and that the news seems to you on the whole good. I myself am *very* hopeful.

Ever your most loving,

AUNTIE VI.

PLUTARCO ROO

THE world is full of stories of artists who would not prostitute their talents and so died hungry. The world is almost equally full of stories of artists who did prostitute their talents and so died regretful. This is the story of an artist who preserved his ideals and found a steady market for them. It is true that as an artist he was not of much account, but as a human phenomenon he was a rare specimen. The world is singularly bare of stories which have both a happy and a moral ending.

Plutarco Roo was a Mexican, born in the second half of the last century. Being of extremely mixed race, he doubtless carried in him the strands of many national cultures—Spanish, Aztec, Mixtec, Totonac, Zapotec, and possibly Chihuahuan—but these elements were more of a fertilizing than a formative influence; they composed, as it were, an anonymous humus from which flowered an art essentially empirical and of the nineteenth century.

His mother was a hard-working woman of the town. When she died, Plutarco was taken by some good nuns who kept an orphanage. There he was considered satisfactorily pious and adequately industrious, but his creative gifts went unperceived and uncultivated. Plutarco's favorite nun was Mother Remedios, who made the cakes which are sold for All Souls' Day. These cakes are made of sugar in the shape of skulls. The name of a dear dead person is scrolled on to the skull by means of a forcing-pipe, together with some ornaments of tears, lilies, etc. They are bought for picnics in the cemetery, and at the close of the picnics the affectionate relatives eat them.

Under the teaching of Mother Remedios, Plutarco Roo became adept at tears and lilies. He could also put very expressive eyeballs into the sockets, though not every client approved of this variant, considering eyeballs too naturalistic. When the time came for Plutarco to make his living in the world, he was apprenticed to a pastry-cook.

Plutarco Roo's talent was definitely for colour and arabesque. The sculptural element in confectionery made no appeal to him; his buns were uncouth, his crescents unsymmetrical. But his decorative impulse, unfolding with the profusion of a tropical spring, heaped ornament on ornament and ran riot in cochineal and saffron. The pastry-cook accused him of stealing inordinate quantities of sugared rose petals, violet petals, angelica, and small silvered balls in order to eat them. It is true that he stole. But it was not to devour. He kept his thefts in small paper bags under his mattress, and at the hour of siesta, when the pastry-cook and his family were asleep, Plutarco would re-knead a very old and grimy piece of dough (which he also kept under his mattress) and emboss it with various experimental mosaics and floral designs.

He had been reared piously. Now his piety took on a fervent quality. His eyes opened to the delights of religious art, to the hues, surpassing any cochineal or sap green, of nineteenth-century stained glass, to the more than meringue-like suavity of saintly draperies and saintly complexions. He took to wandering from church to church during his working hours. This placed the pastry-cook in a difficult position. It is one thing to track down an idle apprentice to the wine-shop or the market place, whence he can be haled back with a kick and harsh words. It is quite another matter to hale him from the sanctuary where he is kneeling in devout contemplation before an image of St. Mary Magdalene.

For some years Plutarco Roo and the pastry-cook continued in this uneasy relationship. As time went on Plutarco's feeling for religious art so outpaced his earlier passion for pure arabesque that he left off stealing rose petals. The pastry-cook indulged a hope that after all he had not been sold such a bad pennyworth by the good nuns and that there was some prospect that the young man might sober down into a useful tradesman, the more so since he was now of an age when he might reasonably be expected to abate some of his religious fervour and begin to attend to the things of this world.

It was with the design of luring Plutarco's attention to the things of this world that the pastry-cook delegated to him the icing of a cake ordered by Don Isidro Barca. This cake, it had been intimated, must be of a grand and festive appearance, an appearance, indeed, semi-nuptial, since it was intended to celebrate the fifth anniversary of Don Isidro's successful introduction to Doña Mercedes Valles-Bosch, the most admired soprano of the town opera company. "Make it as lively as possible," said the pastry-cook. "Take all the doves. A lyre or two also would look well and be appropriate."

Plutarco was working on the cake till the last possible moment; that, maybe, was why the pastry-cook did not go into all the details as closely as he might have done. It seemed very ornate, very sumptuous, in fact very much what it should be, only rather too sticky. And when, on the morrow of its delivery, Don Isidro Barca came stormily into the shop and slammed it down on the counter, stickiness was the pastry-cook's first thought. "Such a cake," he said excusingly, "takes a long time, takes much thought."

"Such a cake," exclaimed Don Isidro, "takes deliberate malice. But it doesn't take long, or need great perspicacity, to decipher the venomous intention of such insinuations. Look at this! Is that a Cupid? And at this! Is that meagre visionary a nymph? And what do all these harps mean, and all these doves and lilies? I asked for a cake, not for a shrine of the Immaculate Conception. Have I been a Liberal, and a freethinker, and a man of the world for fifty years to be offered a monument of reactionary Gothic? So much for your cake!" And with his cane he whacked the edifice.

Enough unbroken icing remained for it to be quite clear that Plutarco had allowed admiration for religious art to outrun the scope of his material. And as Don Isidro was a man of influence and a good customer, the pastry-cook dismissed Plutarco there and then.

Plutarco did not hesitate over what to do next. He went to a house of Carmelites and asked to enter the religious life. Love of God, he explained, was his motive. Love of art would be his dower. He promised to paint for them such pictures of paradise and of the saints as would make their establishment renowned throughout Mexico and visited by Americans of the North. The Superior seemed unconvinced. For some time Plutarco spoke of art and of vocation, but made little headway. Many young men., said the Superior, felt like this, especially when they had just lost a job. Not many young men, retorted Plutarco, lost their jobs so honourably as he, and he told of the cynical behaviour of Don Isidro Barca and of the treachery of the pastry-cook.

"Persecuted by a Liberal," murmured the Superior thoughtfully. "Have you witnesses for this?"

"Ask him yourself," replied Plutarco. "Ask the pastry-cook. Ask, above all, to see the cake. That will show you what sort of artist I am."

Plutarco was accepted for a novitiate. A novitiate is a very active experience. Plutarco had no time for practising art, and not much time even for thinking about it. He grew despondent; but just then a small earthquake took place, which caused a great deal of dust. It became imperative to spring-clean the chapel. A local firm of ecclesiastical decorators was called in. Statues were scrubbed with soda and wire brushes, altar-pieces were cleaned with slices of raw potato, artificial flowers were renewed, the chapel became almost unrecognizably clean and spruce. At the close of these doings the Superior walked round with the firm's proprietor, and during their conversation the proprietor remarked: "You've got some fine old masters here. Several undoubted Correggios and three Murillos at least. All they need is a little renovation." The Superior said that renovations were costly.

"On the contrary. Such expenses repay themselves in a month. A little paragraph in the newspapers: 'Valuable Murillos in a state equal to new. Connoisseurs admitted every Monday and Thursday between four and five p.m.' You would never regret it."

"It would be costly," repeated the Superior.

The proprietor mentioned a price. The Superior shook his head. In a burst of geniality, the proprietor exclaimed: "See now! I will fix just one of them, that fine St. Joseph yonder, for instance, and charge only for the materials. Then, if you are satisfied, we will agree about the others."

The Superior said that such devotion found its true reward in heavenly appreciation. "But as some slight return for such a favour, we will supply you with an assistant. For doubtless you will need a boy to clean the brushes and so forth."

To watch and not to perform, to clean brushes and not to wield them, to mix paints and not to lay them on was almost more than Plutarco could endure. However, he did endure, observing every stroke and asking a great many questions. As the Novice Master had pointed out, this was a wonderful opportunity for him. A little later, the Novice Master told him that if he were modest and careful and did not waste paint or become vainglorious, he might renovate the remaining old masters. "But only the backgrounds," he said, "and such details as cherubs and feet. For these are all very valuable Murillos. We cannot endanger them. They are works of art and exceedingly antique."

The use of a forcing-pipe imparts a very steady and accurate hand. Plutarco renovated the backgrounds without infringing by a hair's breadth on the main figures. The new backgrounds were bright and glossy, and wherever possible he introduced lilies, having learned a well-credentialled type of lily from Mother Remedios. By using a great deal of turpentine, which at once made brushwork easier and kept down the cost of the paints, and by avoiding any appearance of vainglory, he won golden opinions. He was allowed to proceed with cherubs and feet. Here, too, he acquitted himself to every one's satisfaction. Cherubs and feet alike were pink and dimpled, and his renovation of St. Margaret's dragon (classed as a cherub) was so striking that he was told to go ahead with the Saint herself. She was not so grateful as her dragon; her nose, in particular, gave him agonies. But when she was completed, there could be no doubt of it: the unrenovated saints made a poor, dowdy appearance in comparison with her.

Plutarco was given a free brush. Month by month the chapel became more bright and bowery. Month by month Plutarco felt his powers expanding, felt himself more enfranchised from dependence upon the original outlines and the old, faded colourings. Now not only did he make blues much bluer, he sometimes made them pink. Countenances that had been austere became smiling and youthful, and his virgin martyrs developed an *embonpoint* at once stately and alluring, as though they were so many celestial circus riders. Every one was delighted, and the connoisseurs who were admitted, for a small fee, to admire the old masters, now restored to their prime condition, realized as never before the possibilities of heaven, the beauty of holiness.

And then, just as his maturing talents were in full swing, Plutarco Roo was told that there was nothing more that he need paint, unless he cared to give a lick of renovation to the collecting boxes. No more painting? With incredulity he pointed to the expanses of blank wall. There and there he could portray, in fresco, a St. Agnes with a far curlier lamb, a St. James with infinitely finer legs, a more majestic St. Teresa, and a more appealing St. Anthony.

"No, my son," replied the Novice Master," that would not do at all. They would not be renovations, you see."

That night, in a tempest of indignation, Plutarco Roo left the Carmelites, taking with him the paint brushes, all the remaining paints, and a considerable quantity of gold leaf.

It was the act of an artist, impulsive and unpractical. He had no particular intention of theft, but the possession of so much gold leaf was undoubtedly invidious. There was nothing for it: he must leave the town and cast himself, a wandering artist or a wandering pastry-cook, upon the mercies of the countryside.

These mercies proved very slender. Though he found innumerable churches possessing old masters, he could never win a solid commission for renovations, at best, he could contrive an order to brighten up a halo or two with some of the gold leaf. He turned to secular art, offering to paint decorations for shop fronts and taverns. But his style, so intensively nourished upon ecclesiastical subjects, did not lend itself to such commissions. Just as Don Isidro had resented his cake, vintners and saloon-keepers turned up their noses at his beauties and bullfighters. His young ladies, however plump, retained the majestiy of virgin martyrs, his toreadors recalled nothing but the Archangel Michael. Client after client said to him: "It is too idealistic. Such portraits would not sell a glass of lemonade."

Equally, there was no demand for pastry-cooks in rural districts. Yet because of the gold leaf he did not like to go to a town.

At last, more to get out of Mexico than with any definite hope of doing better elsewhere, he worked a passage to Havana. The voyage made him horribly seasick. Cold and shivering, he sat down in a café near the waterfront and thought to himself that whether he throve or starved on the island, on the island he must remain, for he could never endure another journey by sea. The waiter said to him: "What you need is a Pernod."

The waiter was right. The glass was scarcely emptied before Plutarco Roo felt his vitality returning, began to think of his past as a series of interesting adventures, realized himself as the vehicle of an authentic talent maintained with spirit in a rough-and-tumble world, and started to look around on his new environment. At the next table sat two men, both well dressed and handsome, deep in conversation. He studied them with an artist's eye, debating whether they should be put into turbans and become Doctors Disputing in the Temple or whether it would be better to coif them with simple haloes as SS. Sebastian and Roch.

"Herbert Spencer," said one of them, "an English philosopher. It would be a splendid name for the brand. It would sell it among the English. And they are the kind of cigars that the English are glad to smoke. But the trouble is, there should be a portrait of him inside the lid. And how can one have a portrait if one does not know what the man looks like?"

"I suppose you could get a photograph," said the other.

The first man shrugged his shoulders. "And how is one to get a photograph of an English philosopher? It would mean inquiries and research. You know how it is with such affairs. One begins them, but one never ends them."

"True," replied his friend. "One cannot deny it. Perhaps it might be an imaginative portrait?"

"Then the English would know. And these are cigars very definitely for the English market."

"Yes, they would know. The English are like that."

After a pause the friend suggested: "Why not some other English philosopher?"

"I do not know of one. It would mean more inquiries, more research. Besides, I have already printed the bands."

"Too bad," said the friend.

Plutarco Roo stepped forward. "Pardon me," he said. "But this is a matter of no difficulty. I am an artist. And I happen to be well acquainted with the features of Herbert Spencer."

"How foolish one is to worry," said the first speaker. "One has only to sit in a café and wait. Will you have a cognac?" he said to Plutarco.

"A Pernod, if you please. I find my best inspiration in Pernod."

A religious artist, accustomed to rely upon his sense of the befitting for likeness of saints and martyrs, was not liable to be much troubled in inventing the likeness of a contemporary philosopher. By combining the blandness of St. Joseph with the learning of St. Jerome, by sweeping the flowing white beard sufficiently to one side to display a Gladstone collar, a blue necktie, and a scarfpin representing a fox's head, and by inserting a monocle, Plutarco Roo provided an excellent likeness of Herbert Spencer. A few palms, a distant volcano, and two emblematical ladies, one holding a telescope and the other leading a lion, supplied the background, and the cigar manufacturer accepted the design with enthusiasm and commissioned others. From that day, Plutarco Roo functioned in his new *métier* as smoothly as a cylinder in its sleeve, alternating commission and invention, production and payment, in an easy rhythm.

His works were numerous. Many of them can be identified by the initials P. R.

THE SONG OF SONGS

MR. PITFIELD was a tenor.

Of all professions that of music is the most uncertain, and perhaps Mr. Pitfield was the only tenor in London who made a steady livelihood by being a tenor. This was not because he had a fine voice, or sang well. Mr. Pitfield's voice was rich and slimy, like soft soap, and he had no music in his soul. But he was reliable. He never missed an appointment. He was never out of voice. He never quarrelled with the other performers. He never came in a bar too early or a bar too late, when crochets were dotted he always dotted them, in evening dress he looked like a gentleman and in a surplice he looked like a Christian.

Four times a Sunday he raised his voice in sacred strains, beginning with Sung Eucharist at St. Mungo's, Bayswater, going on to High Mass and to Benediction at Our Lady of Carmel, Fulham, and ending the day with a hearty Evening Worship at the Holloway Tabernacle. On Wednesdays he kept an appointment with the Ethical Church, on Thursdays he travelled to Ealing for a Wesleyan Weekday Service for Men Only.

Mr. Pitfield would have preferred to dedicate his talents to the church—or rather, to the churches. For one thing, chancels are less draughty than concert platforms, for another, church music contains more semi-breves. A nice adagio semi-breve—that gave a singer scope. And when he saw one ahead his eye would lighten; and when he reached it he would seize on it reverently, and make the most of it—as though it were a jujube.

But though church engagements are regular and gratifying, they are not highly paid. So Mr. Pitfield mixed his sacred strains with secular. Calm as a carpet-sweeper he would proceed from Palestrina's *Stabat Mater* to the Stock Exchange Musical Society's performance of *Hiawatha,* and finish off with a five-shilling engagement at the Ancient Buffaloes' Musical Evening at a public-house, careful only to keep his feet dry and his nasal passages clear.

When Miss Serena Leoni said to him, "How would you feel about being Solomon for the Hampstead Amateur Ladies' Choral?" Mr. Pitfield did not ask whether the sacred or the secular side of Solomon's character would be uppermost. He pulled out a notebook and a fountain pen, and said: "When? How much?"

"It's rather short notice," said Mr. Pitfield. "Still, I suppose I'm agreeable."

"The truth is," said Miss Leoni, "that the chap who was doing Solomon couldn't make it. So he chucked it. So I said to Mrs. Bathover—she runs them—'Oh, Mrs. Bathover, why don't you try for Mr. Pitfield? *He* won't let you down.'"

"Who's the bass?"

"There isn't a bass. Just you and I. I'm the Beloved. And the Amateur Ladies, of course, mostly humming with their mouths shut. It's one of these modern things."

"I don't mind that," said Mr. Pitfield. "Once you've got absolute pitch, a note's a note."

At Miss Leoni's suggestion Mr. Pitfield went round to her place just to run through it.

"It isn't what you'd call graceful music," said Miss Leoni.

"I should call it scraggy, myself," said Solomon. "Still, that duet where I keep on saying *Arise* has scope. Tell her I'm agreeable."

He went off with his part. When he reached home he went through it attentively, noting the places where there was scope. Then, as was his method, he learned the notes. Then he learned the expression marks.

Owing to the fullness of Mr. Pitfield's engagement book it was not possible for him to rehearse with the Amateur Ladies. This did not matter, Miss Leoni explained to Mrs. Bathover. Mr. Pitfield was so reliable, there was never any need for him to rehearse. So while Miss Leoni warbled and the Amateur Ladies hummed, Mr. Pitfield was represented by the pianist's thumb; and on the morning of the performance Solomon and the Beloved would go to Mrs. Bathover's place for a final run through.

Mrs. Bathover's place looked so dilapidated that Mr. Pitfield began to feel pensive about his guineas. But the instant he smelled Mrs. Bathover (and he smelled her immediately) he was reassured. Only a woman with money to throw away could look so like winter and smell so vernal.

"And now," said she, "I've got a wonderful surprise for you both. I've got Mr. de Lazlo."

As Mr. Pitfield had omitted to notice the name of the composer he just continued to look reliable.

"So now we shall be told exactly how the music should go."

Mr. Pitfield laid down his hat, his gloves, his overcoat, his muffler, and his umbrella. He knew these composers, he had had to put up with composers before. That was another thing in the favour of sacred music. The composers of sacred music were invariably dead. He shook hands with Mr. de Lazlo and expressed pleasure at meeting him.

On learning that Mr. de Lazlo would play the piano for them he felt happier. Composers who accompany are less obstructive than composers who just sit by in order to criticize. He took up his music, raised his eyebrows, and prepared for song.

"*The voice of my Beloved,*" declaimed Miss Leoni in an animated manner. "*Behold, he cometh leaping upon the mountains, skipping upon the hills.*"

Mr. Pitfield stood like a rock, counting the useless bars that must pass by before he had anything to do with it.

"My Beloved is like a roe," sang Miss Leoni, *"or a young hart."*

Mr. Pitfield expanded his chest, and advanced one foot.

"My Beloved spake . . ."

Mr. Pitfield cleared his throat

". . . and said unto me . . ."

"Arise!" boomed Mr. Pitfield, coming in as usual dead on the note and dead on time.

It was the passage to which the defaulting tenor had objected, remarking that Solomon may have gone round intoning *Old Clo'es,* but that he wouldn't. To Mr. Pitfield, on the other hand, this passage had seemed to offer scope. So while Miss Leoni discoursed with runs and skips about vines and foxes, figs and turtles, he continued to exclaim *Arise* at due intervals, *amorosamente e sempre animando.*

"There will I give thee my loves," concluded Miss Leoni.

One of Mr. Pitfield's maxims was that a singer should attend to his own part and not worry about what the others were doing. Now that the music ceased, however, he realized that the duet had been a trio; and that the third voice was still going on.

It was an astonishingly loud voice, loud and sinister: a baritone, with remarkable nasal resonance.

"Mra-ow-oo! Mra-ow-oo!"

"Oh dear, it's Sennacherib!" said Mrs. Bathover. "I hoped we shouldn't hear him if he was shut in the kitchen."

"That," said Mr. de Lazlo, swinging round, addressing Mr. Pitfield, *"that* is how you must sing. Exactly so. Like Mrs. Bathover's Siamese cat you must sing."

Miss Leoni gave a tactful little giggle. Mr. de Lazlo smote the keyboard, and Miss Leoni was once more the Beloved.

"Arise," sang Mr. Pitfield, exactly as before.

"No, no! That is not as the cat sings. See! You will model

yourself on him. No words, the words are nothing. It is the *timbre* that matters. Just sing Mra-ow-oo."

"Me-oo," sang Mr. Pitfield.

"MRA-OW-OO!" exclaimed the cat, surpassing itself.

"What production!" said Mr. de Lazlo.

Mr. Pitfield was interested in production. He admitted that the cat's production was very forward. But not musical, he said.

"It's what I want," said the composer.

The room was hot, Mrs. Bathover's scent was cumulative, the piano was extremely loud, the cat even louder. Like one in a fever-dream Mr. Pitfield felt himself giving way, heard himself emitting most unwonted sounds, heard, which was even more unnerving, these sounds warmly approved. Meanwhile Miss Leoni trilled on about foxes and turtles, or compared him to the hart and the roe.

"It's quite a menagerie," he said, during an interval while Mrs. Bathover refreshed him with egg-nog.

After the egg-nog they went on to the second duet. By now Mr. Pitfield's sense of the usual was so maltreated that he was able to compare Miss Leoni's navel to a round goblet and her nose to the tower of Lebanon that looketh towards Damascus without any particular sense that these endearments went rather too far for the concert platform. Whatever the words, however recondite or biblical, they were an improvement on Mra-ow-oo-ing. Then, when Mr. Pitfield and Miss Leoni and the Siamese cat had simultaneously declared that many waters cannot quench love nor the floods drown it, they went back to the first duet: just to make sure, Mr. de Lazlo said, that Mr. Pitfield had got it.

This time all agreed that he had got it.

Mr. Pitfield, on the other hand, felt that it had got him.

The cat was still yowling as he left the house, its cries were still audible as he turned the corner, and rung on in his head long after he was out of earshot. Or was it his own cries, those reiterated love-notes, *amorosamente e sempre animando,* that echoed in the memory?—for during the last repetition only a key signature and a time signature had distinguished Solomon from Sennacherib. Suppose I've got into the way of it?—he asked himself. Such things did happen to singers. They were called mannerisms. It was one of the dangers, like damp feet and the blocking of nasal passages, to which the artist's temperament is exposed. Some tenors developed the *coup de glotte*; others the tremolo. And in opera you might hope to pass it off, as expression; but not in the chancel: in no chancel, however broad its outlook, is there a place for Siamese cats. Meanwhile the voice of memory continued to exclaim *Mra-ow-oo,* and under cover of the voice of the bus Mr. Pitfield tried a *sotto-voce* "Arise." There was not a pin to choose between them. He could no longer call his *bel canto* his own.

He broke into a sweat of terror. If he could not keep the cat out of a *sotto-voce* what hope for him in full cry? He could not keep it a hushed secret, this very evening he was pledged to stand forth in public, wearing evening dress as Solomon, and making a noise like a Siamese cat. Not that he felt the pledge any obligation, he would have broken it with the best will in the world, an experienced artist knows better than any composer what sort of interpretation is needed; but it did not seem to him that he would be able to break it. A changeling was entangled in his vocal cords. He tried another *sotto-voce* exorcism. The bus stopped. His neighbour looked at him inquiringly, and Mr. Pitfield left the bus.

The cool English air struck on his forehead, and simultaneously he remembered that at 2:30 he had an engagement for a funeral.

Thank heaven for that! A funeral might pull him together. He consulted the notebook, just to make sure of it. Yes, there was the funeral; and in the margin was pencilled H.A.G.— Hymn at Graveside. That meant two pairs of socks. Like one treading a quagmire who for a moment feels solid ground beneath his feet Mr. Pitfield was able to recall, quite rationally, quite securely, the sensation of wearing two pairs of socks.

Death—in this case the death of Mrs. Annie Tomlinson—came as a friend to Mr. Pitfield. Of all church services he liked funerals the best: they are so well conducted, and so well paid. With quiet thoughts about mortality: of how easily churchyard clay leads to cold feet, cold feet to a chill, a chill to pneumonia, and pneumonia to churchyard clay; with thankful thoughts about the merits of wool; with speculations on the cost of the coffin, with admiration of the flowers, with tranquil contempt for the clergyman's voice production and anticipations of a nice cup of tea afterwards, Mr. Pitfield held the Siamese cat at bay. It got its head out once or twice during the psalm, but he squeezed it back again. The hymn at the graveside, presenting more scope, presented also great dangers, and during the earlier verses he walked circumspectly. But in the final verse his *bel canto* trolled forth a Christian confidence, and by the end of the ceremony the cat was securely buried with Mrs. Tomlinson, and the wreaths lay over them both. Meanwhile the necessity of wearing two pairs of socks had prompted him with a blameless yet unassailable defence against any last-moment nonsense from Mr. de Lazlo. Nothing is more sacred than a tenor's larynx. To make assurance doubly sure he asked Mrs. Bathover to make a preliminary announcement, and took a couple of lozenges during the prelude. And when his press-cutting agency sent him the notice of the concert from the *North London Herald and Highgate Mercury*, having pasted the cutting into his book he drew beside it, in an *ex-voto* spirit, a neat hand pointing to the words:

Though suffering from a slight cold, the role of Solomon was sustained by Mr. Devereux Pitfield in his usual able manner.

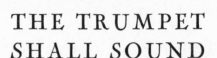

THE TRUMPET
SHALL SOUND

NO DOUBT, thought Mrs. Mullen, looking at her niece, no doubt at all, everything was made uncommonly easy for these young ones, not like it was in her time. *Then* you didn't have a death in the house without knowing it.

Rightly speaking, you couldn't call this a death in the house; for poor old Dick, falling over a bicycle in the black-out, had been taken to the hospital, and in the hospital he had died; and from the hospital, no better than a parcel, he had been taken to the undertaker's place to await, no better than a parcel, the day of the funeral.

Flowers c/o Messrs. Kedge, Ring St., Lower Town.

That is why the house felt so queer. No corpse in it, no black weight at its centre to keep it steady. No reason to step softly, no door with silence behind it. Not even the blinds drawn.

The spring sunshine shone full into the front room. There was a fire burning too, the room was very warm. But Cathie kept on shivering and pulling up the collar of her coat. Not tired enough, thought Mrs. Mullen. If Dick had been brought home to die, the nursing and the running about and the sitting up and one thing and another would have knocked the nerves and the shivers out of her, left her in the right frame of mind to appreciate the repose of a funeral. These young women who thought they were making things so much easier for themselves, small families, bakers' bread, nowadays not even the whites boiled, were making a great mistake. If you'd got to be a woman it was better to be an old-fashioned woman, with plenty of work to keep your mind off it.

68

Cathie sat on the sofa, and beside her sat Gwennie, Dick's sister-in-law, and Gwennie's girl, Ramona. Ramona yawned incessantly. She was working in munitions, and this week was a night turn.

Soon we shall all be yawning, thought Mrs. Mullen. She glanced at the clock. There was still some time to run before the car came for them.

By the window sat Freda, Mrs. Mullen's unmarried sister, and Reg, Cathie's husband. He had got leave for his father-in-law's funeral. He sat on a small chair, leaning forward, with his hands dangling between his knees. Beside him stood the boy Alan, staring at his shoulder-badge and corporal's stripes, and slowly drawing them on the air with his forefinger.

"There would have been time for a cup of tea," said Cathie.

"There's time now," said Reg. "I'll go and put on the kettle."

"Don't trouble for me," said Freda.

"Nor me, either. Six cups. That wouldn't leave much of Cathie's ration. Ah, you'll miss your poor old dad's ration, won't you, Cath? It'll make a difference."

"I had a nice cup of tea on my way here," said Freda. "Between the buses."

"How long did it take you to come?"

"Matter of three hours. They've taken off the Kitley bus, so now you have to go round by Swopham. And who do you think I met on the bus, Lottie? Old Mr. Tanner, who used to keep the fish-shop. You've never seen a man so changed."

"Well, he must be getting on, mustn't he?"

"Sixty-seven. You remember how rheumatic he was, and how he always wore a hat because of his face-ache? There he was, strolling into the bus bare-headed, with a potted flower under his arm. Why, Mr. Tanner, I said, this war seems to be agreeing with you. And he told me he hasn't had a twinge for the last ten years, and all because of wearing iodine socks. He was right sorry when I told him about poor Dick."

"Iodine socks? Yes, you do hear of them. All I know is, they never did anything for Florence Gander, Florence Toogood that was. Still, *she's* constitutional. You remember Florence, don't you, Gwennie? One time it looked as though she were going to marry poor old Dick."

"Didn't she sing, or something?"

"Sing or something?" Mrs. Mullen's voice expressed reproachful surprise. "Why, she played on the violin, and passed examinations for it up in London. That's how Dick took up with your sister. For in the last war Florence went round with a concert-party, all in a bus together, called The Five Lucky Beans, or something, and Dick, he was in the army, of course, and the first time he came back on leave, 'What's become of Florence,' he said, and mother said, 'Why, haven't the girls told you about her engagement?' meaning the concert-party. But just then the maroons went off and there was that awful Zeppelin, and so Florence went clean out of our heads, and Dick thought she'd taken up with some other boy, and when he came back next he got engaged to your Jessie, and Florence married Nat Gander. Just a misunderstanding, you see. Five children she had, one after another, and not a note of music among them. It's funny how things turn out."

"Mum," said the child. "I think I'll just feed my rabbits."

"I'll go with him," said Reg, rising with alacrity.

Cathie looked as though she were about to speak, but said nothing. The three aunts exchanged glances, and then settled down more easily.

"Do you remember Buster, Lottie? And the day he took round the collecting bag at chapel in that blue suit of his?

Lord, what a look he gave me as he went up the aisle!
Impudent? He was worse than the seven monkeys."

"And all the time he'd got two wives, one in Chelmsford
and the other somewhere in Wales. Well, I don't mind
admitting it now, the day that news came out I cried my
eyes sore."

"Yes, and you weren't the only one, either. And it wasn't
only us girls that took on about it. Mrs. Blandamer, George
Blandamer's wife, who got up the whist-drives and socials—
well, Julia Kinnear told me that she swallowed half a bottle
of disinfectant, and only didn't die of it because they'd happened to eat some bad fish the evening before, and the fish
and the disinfectant all came back together."

"Yes, I heard something about that, too. Well, they do
say, Lucky at cards, unlucky in love. What about George,
though?"

"Oh, all *he* ever knew of it was the fish."

Ramona had shut her eyes and begun to breathe heavily.
Now she slumped forward. Cathie put an arm about her, and
settled the sleeping head on her shoulder. Her face lost
its look of nervous strain as the sleeping girl's warmth in-
vaded her.

"I should like a bit of tinned salmon, though. I haven't
seen a tin for months," said Freda.

"Ah, you should have bought it and put it by," said Lottie
Mullen. "Hoarding or no hoarding, a person's got to keep
even with the future. I don't mind telling you, if Lord
Woolton were to come along and look under my old double-
bed he'd see more than the chamber."

"In reason, I grant you." Gwennie eased her scantily-cut
black skirt over her knees. "But the way some people behave, it's a scandal. You know Mrs. Mortus, whose Irene
works along with our Ramona? Well, last Thursday week I
saw her get half a pound of biscuits in a queue, and then go

back to the tail of the queue, and take off her glasses, and work her way up and get another half-pound. Well, I said to myself, now I suppose you'll go back again and take out your teeth. Oh, it makes my blood boil!"

"Yes, it makes one want to say something, doesn't it? But talking of bare-faced cheating, what about . . ."

"Mum! Mum!"

The child ran in, flourishing his cap.

"The car's outside, Mum. It's waiting for us."

"Good Lord! And we were so happy talking over old times, we never heard it. Dear, dear! Poor Dick. Not even brought back for as much as to come in and go out again. It doesn't seem quite reverent, does it, to go out of a house for a funeral with no corpse going before. Where's my gloves?"

The undertaker's car was old and stately, so roomy that it held them all. Reg and the boy sat in front, where Reg and the driver conversed in undertones about double declutching. Cathie and Ramona still clung to each other, and the aunts, ennobled by the deep springing and all the little amber knobs, sat silent and upright, glancing at the shabby streets as though a Jug and Bottle Entrance meant nothing to them.

Outside Mr. Kedge's establishment the hearse was waiting, the four mutes standing beside it. As they neared, the mutes scrambled up and it moved off. Another car which had been waiting swung out to follow theirs.

"Well, my goodness, whoever's that? Cathie! Who's in that other car?"

"I didn't see."

"Well, surely, you ought to know. People don't follow a body uninvited. Here, Gwennie, you're the limberest among us. You watch out of this back window and see who it is."

"It's the Blackbones. Fred and Mary and old Dodger Blackbones."

"*The Blackbones?* Well!"

"The Blackbones?"

"Gwennie! Look again. It can't be the Blackbones."

"Yes, it is. And in mourning, too, as far as one can see."

"I've never heard of such a thing. After the way Mrs. Dodger walked off with our Aunt Mabel's furniture, and Dick never getting as much as a teaspoon, and all of us knowing he was her favourite nephew. Cathie! What are those Blackbones doing at your father's funeral?"

"Well, I suppose they are coming too, Aunt Lot."

"My word! And is that all you can do about it?"

"Well, what can I do?"

"Did you know they were coming?"

Ramona came stare-eyed and assertive out of her doze.

"Why shouldn't they come, Mrs. Mullen? It's Uncle Dick's funeral, I suppose."

"Hush, Ramona dear."

"Uncle Dick's funeral? That's just what I'm complaining of. If Dodger wants to go to a funeral, I should think he could pick out some other funeral where he'd be more in keeping. Or wait for his own. Why, it would make Dick turn in his grave."

Cathie preserved an unassenting silence. Ramona yawned with deliberation. Gwennie, her face mottled with blushes, looked steadily out of the window.

"Well, wouldn't it? After the way Dodger treated your Dad?"

"Dad and Cousin Randall got on all right, Aunt Lot."

"D'you mean to say . . . ?"

"They used to meet at the Buffaloes, and Cousin Randall was very fond of Dad."

The car drew up before the church. The coffin was lifted out, the clergyman came from the porch to meet it.

"I am the Resurrection . . ."

When he began to speak it was obvious that his teeth were

false and didn't fit. On every sibilant he sounded a shrill whistle.

"Who on earth's this awful old parson?" whispered Mrs. Mullen, as she and Freda, Cathie, Reg, and the boy, came up from their knees in the front pew. "Why haven't you got Mr. Dacre?"

"He's gone to be an army chaplain, Aunt Lot."

A little farther down on the opposite side of the aisle sat the Blackbones. Freda, who had no dignity, kept twisting herself to look at them. Mrs. Mullen continued to look steadfastly before her, where the coffin, mounted on trestles, seemed irreconcilably large and dominating for anything representing Dick. In the pew just behind Gwennie was freely and comfortably weeping.

Well, perhaps the coffin was in the right of it. Perhaps her impression of Dick was a false one, after all. For one can't be sure, even about one's own brother. Dick had been reconciled with Dodger. For years he had been meeting Dodger at the Buffaloes, going round to the pub with him afterwards, talking to him of carrier pigeons and tomato blight. Her own brother—and she had never so much as suspected it.

Staring at the coffin, so aloof and so imminent, Mrs. Mullen was penetrated by a realization of the vanity of this world. What's the use, she thought to herself, what's the use of sticking up for one's principles, what's the use of getting up into one's best corsets to attend a funeral, why pay burial insurance, why have wars? There, across the aisle, was Dodger, grown old in wickedness, and here was she, worn out with keeping respectable. And to that whistling clergyman there, not a pin to choose between them. Just two elderly persons who would soon be funerals, and the only odds, which happened to come first.

A lot of good horse-sense would be buried with her. And Dodger, he'd take more knowledge of the world than he was born with down into the grave with him. But nobody would dig for it, nobody wanted the wisdom of the old, any more than they wanted those big mahogany sideboards. That sideboard of Aunt Mabel's, and the dumb waiter, and the eight chairs, so solid you could hardly lift them: Dodger had got them, and Mrs. Dodger had dusted them; but young Mrs. Fred would sell them as soon as Dodger had hopped it.

"For the trumpet shwee!—all shwee!—ound . . ."

But had Saint Paul, thought the Reverend Mr. Amwood, foreseen these funeral countenances, blankly unconvinced, glumly polite, amid this funeral incense of dying flowers and mothballs? And with which mourners had Mr. Kedge, thriftily complying with the petrol restrictions, ordained that he should ride to the cemetery? Saint Paul, *in watchings often, in fastings often, in stripes above measure, in prisons more frequent, in deaths oft,* had not been required to take over, in his old age, the duty of an industrial parish, under a most energetic and uncongenial Bishop, and on a heavy clay soil.

"Therefore, my beloved brethren, be ye steadfast, unmovable, always abounding in the work of the Lord, forasmuch as ye know that your labour is not in vain in the Lord."

The coffin was lifted and carried from the church. Mr. Kedge approached the clergyman.

"Well!" exclaimed Freda. "If those Blackbones aren't taking the parson with them! What next? I've a good mind to fetch him out again."

"Do let be, Freda," said Mrs. Mullen. "And try to remember that this is a funeral, not a remnant sale."

"Always did fight like cats, those two," whispered Gwennie to her daughter.

It was a long way to the cemetery, and they drove in silence, except once, when Lottie Mullen, driven to speak her thought aloud, said heavily: "What's the use?" Then they looked at her inquiringly; but as each left it to the other to take up the question, no one answered.

The cemetery lay on the outskirts of the town, rising above the sad slow river, the countless identical ridges of slate-roofed artisan dwellings, the factories and warehouses. It was a newish cemetery, the farther half of it lay unused, the trees planted by the Town Council still had a youthful tender look. So many of the graves had bunches of daffodils on them that the cemetery appeared to be twinkling with daffodils and responding with yellow flashes to the April sunlight. Two other funerals were taking place. They seemed very small and unimportant among the expanse of completed graves.

Shining, too, in the April sunlight the coffin on its six black legs proceeded like some queer quadruped, turning first right, then left, as though unerringly nosing out its lair. The newly-dug clay, heaped up, was yellow and shiny like the coffin, the walls of the grave had an ochreous glister. The grave-digger was standing a little aloofly behind a neighbouring headstone.

Up shuffled Dodger, his boots creaking. His face was pinched, his few locks of grey hair lifted in the wind. Not long for this world, thought Mrs. Mullen. No wonder he's having a good look. Raising his eyes from the open grave Dodger's glance met hers. Still vibrating to thoughts of mortality she tried to convey by her expression that the past was being overlooked. Dodger blinked once or twice, and turned away.

Up here above the town the wind was blowing quite briskly. White clouds raced over the blue, the daffodils wagged, the clergyman's surplice rustled as he stood waiting while the bearers lifted the wreaths from the coffin, and the mourners took their places. Freda was having trouble with her hat. Once it almost blew off, and Mr. Kedge sprang forward, noiseless as a shadow, to retrieve it.

How tiresome Freda was, always a fidget, always coming to bits just like her own parcels. And there was that girl Ramona, looking at her so sarcastically, and Mary Blackbone ostentatiously not noticing. Why must such unpleasantness mar the funeral, just at the most solemn moment, too? But the outdoor part of a funeral usually went wrong, at Hilda's funeral George had had a fit, at George's funeral the wasps were something chronic. If only that clergyman would begin!

He began. Under the heavy rhythm of the burial sentences everything subsided into order and a dreamy majesty, except his own surplice, in which the wind now made a most extraordinary drumming, and fluster. Suddenly the grave-digger jumped out from behind his headstone, waving his arms, and shouting:

"Look up there! Look out!"

His voice ripped through the ceremony. They looked. He was pointing to the sky. There, just coming out of a cloud, was something like an enormous pale bird with beating wings. Dangling from it, as the mouse dangles from the claws of the white owl, was a dark object. Now that they looked the noise of the beating parachute, the drumming and flustering, seemed overwhelmingly loud. The noise grew louder, the thing came lower.

Reg seized Alan, and dropped him into the grave. Then he grabbed Cathie, and dropped her in beside the child.

"Jump in, jump in! It's a land-mine coming down."

One after another the mourners got into the grave. The mutes came to the edge, hesitated, seemed inclined to follow. Mr. Kedge, with a recalling gesture, pointed them to some bushes. Remembering their position they retired there, and lay down. The clergyman still remained standing. Mr. Kedge touched his elbow, pointed to the grave. The clergyman, on such an occasion, would rank as one of the family. But Mr. Amwood shook his head. The parachute came lower, reeling and billowing. It seemed to fill the whole sky. Pursing his lips, Mr. Kedge lay down also.

There seemed to be no end to the waiting. Away in the town an engine blew off steam, and one could hear the birds singing. Meanwhile Mr. Amwood had knelt down at the graveside and was whistling through the commendatory prayer for the dying. Dodger, pressed close and bony to Lottie Mullen, commented in her ear:

"Bit previous, isn't he, giving us all up for lost like that?"

His pale wrinkled face was lit with an expression of indomitable craft and assurance.

"Amen," said Mr. Amwood rapidly, snatched out his teeth, and cast himself down face forward.

There was a crash that swelled into a long roar. The mourners in the grave were thrown pell-mell against each other. The breath of life seemed to be dragged out of them, they gasped and choked. The air became darkened by a cloud of dust, in which dead leaves, pebbles, twigs, daffodils, clods of earth, shreds of stuff and paper, fragments of wood and stone and metal, were suspended. Glancing into the spattered darkness Mrs. Mullen saw two funeral wreaths, her own and Gwennie's, rise up, hang twirling, and fall dishevelled into the grave.

At last, into this darkened air, they saw Mr. Amwood erect himself, tall and ghostly-white, saying:

"You may come out now."

Aided by shoves from Fred and Reg they scrambled out, and looked around. The coffin was lying on its side. Near it was a large fragment of marble, lettered *Also Emma*, and Mr. Kedge was holding a bloodstained handkerchief to his ear, and saying it was a near go. Everything was covered with dust and rubble. At the western end of the cemetery a column of dust was still boiling up, and beneath it some small figures were scurrying to and fro.

The funeral proceeded. The coffin was lowered into the grave, earth was scattered on it, and the last prayers were said. Walking rather unsteadily the party turned away. It was then that Dodger went up to Mrs. Mullen, remarking affably:

"Hullo, Lot. Looked as though we might be spending the night here, didn't it?"

She gave him an unmoving full-face glare, and walked on.

"Well," said Gwennie, walking beside her. "I'll tell you this. I'll be more than thankful to sit down. I never heard any aeroplane, did you?"

Providential, Mrs. Mullen was thinking. Providential. If it hadn't been for that landmine, like as not I'd still be forgiving Dodger. And leaving him my best tea-set, I dare say, to show bygones were bygones. And all just because of coming over so soft in church, giving way to the funeral, and thinking *Poor old Dodger!* That's what funerals do, if one's not on one's guard. And Dodger as ready to get round me as a terrier round a rat.

"I heard one thing," she said, "and that's what Dodger Blackbone said to me in the grave. All those Blackbones tumbling in without so much as a by-your-leave, and Mr. Kedge and that poor old parson left to perish on the brink. Trust Dodger! Trust him to find a safe place to start blaspheming in! Dodger by name, and Dodger by nature."

"What did Dodger say?"

"I could no more bring myself to forgive it," said Lottie Mullen, "than I could bring myself to repeat it. Not if it was my dying hour."

She strode on firmly towards the cemetery gates.

WHEN SWEET VOICES DIE

WHERE the hell shall I go today? thought Isabel Rabjohn, standing conspicuously inconspicuous in her London clothes at the junction of Market Street and Honiton Road. Every summer when she came home to visit her parents in Smurden she found her native place more boring, and her native diet more stodgy. It was the diet that drove her to go for so many walks. She was a shop-girl, and her figure was her fortune.

Suddenly she remembered Angel Street, where as a child she had been forbidden to go because it was rough. She would walk along Angel Street. Quite an adventure.

Angel Street ran between the factory and the river. It was a slum, and retained some fragmentary airs of good breeding: a handsome stone-built mill, made over into warehouses, and a walnut tree growing in a butcher's yard. But ten minutes brought her to the end of what to her childish mind had seemed an endless vista of danger and wickedness. Angel Street petered out into Chapel Prospect, a semi-circle of small narrow houses, where almost every parlour window had a dirty pasteboard announcing Rooms to Let, where peeling stucco and dirty tight-closed windows announced a shabby-genteel, devitalized poverty more alarming to Isabel Rabjohn than any slum.

A street door opened, and a man smelling of sweat and straw came out backward, carrying one end of an upright piano.

"To you!" grunted a voice still within the passage. The piano shot forward, the second man came out. The piano was plumped down on the pavement. A harsh echoing sigh came from its entrails.

It was a very old piano. Its backing of faded cloth was moth-eaten and mouse-eaten, its woodwork a mournful black. There was a good deal of tarnished brass trimming on it, and it had two candle-arms, one of which was dangling upside down. Between them was a fretwork panel, and behind the fretwork was a square of fluted silk, dry with age and dust.

The cover was down over the keyboard, but Isabel Rabjohn knew perfectly that the bottom D, at any rate, had lost its ivory. For it was Mrs. Morgan's piano, on which, as a child, she had played *Studies* by Heller, and *To a Wild Rose*, by MacDowell. It was the original Old Piano, poor old thing! And now the two men picked it up again, and hoisted it on to a cart, and drove away. For a moment she paused, looking at the house it had been brought out from, a house that, like the others, acknowledged Rooms to Let. Then she walked on, saying to herself:

"Smurden to the life."

Smurden was not much of a place for music. It was a small hard-headed West of England town that made cheese. Few of its citizens were more than a generation removed from rustics, and still retained a tough earthy indifference to anything beyond square meals and stuffed suites.

So when Dr. Morgan died and his widow proposed to eke out her money by giving piano lessons people were able to say with considerable certainty how many pupils—or rather, how few—she would get. There would be the grocer's daughter, and the Baptist minister's daughter (piano lessons would come in quite useful for her, for what's the difference between a piano and an organ?), and Lena and Delia Small, and Isabel Rabjohn. And so it turned out to be; but the half-dozen was made up by Charlie Prowse, whose mother always gave in to him so foolishly, though what a boy needed with piano lessons Smurden was unable to see.

Little more than a year had gone by, and no new pupils had come in, when Mrs. Morgan perplexed Smurden by the further statement that once a week there would be an Appreciation Class.

"What be there to appreciate?" asked Mr. Prowse. "Music's notes, bain't it—some black and some white? Appreciation, arrh! She'll be putting of it up to auction next."

"I can't understand it at all," said Mrs. Rabjohn to Mrs. Dominy. "And I don't know that I want to. I'm sure we were very pleased to have Isabel learn, and she's getting on nicely. It's really pretty to see the way she crosses one hand over the other. But last Saturday she came back talking of nothing but love."

"Gracious goodness!" replied the minister's wife. "What a thing to tell young girls about! What sort of love? Our Blanche never let on a word about this."

"Some music-teacher who fell in love with some young Countess. Shoo . . . Shoo . . . something to do with shoes. Foreigners, you know."

"So I should hope. And all Blanche said to me was that Mrs. Morgan played a piece with a lot of bumps in it. Well, well! How very extraordinary. It's not very nice, though, is it?"

But as the Appreciation Class was gratis, and as next week Mrs. Morgan was reported to have told her pupils to imagine meadows with little lambs in them, alarm died down and Appreciation continued.

To Charlie Prowse, feeling only the born executant's desire to be doing it himself, the Appreciation Class was a lot of silly talk about flowers and dead folks. But the little girls rejoiced in it, at first as a novelty, and therefore indescribably comic, later as a weekly repast of steady enjoyment, enjoyment sublimated beyond giggles. For the Appreciation Class allowed one to take a good look at Mrs. Morgan's surprising parlour, which, when seated at the piano with Mrs. Morgan at one's left, one could only skim with occasional right-eye glances. No other parlour in Smurden was like it, no other parlour had so many things in it, and so many of them unparlourly. For besides the Japanese fans and the pictures of mountains and other pictures of sad-faced ladies, some holy and some not, but all sad-faced, two warming-pans and several skillets hung on the wall, and a great china pipe hanging by a tasselled cord; and below the richness of a silk scarf embroidered all over with sequins and beetle-wings there was a common dairy crock with common bulrushes in it. And on the mantelshelf, where one would look for the clock and the ornaments, were three old broken teapots and a quantity of plaster busts, gentlemen who had been music composers.

Then one could study Mrs. Morgan, and wonder why she was so thin, and if those long earrings didn't hurt, and if it was true that she never really had enough to eat, and even went out after dandelions which she ate raw. And if it was also true that she had hundreds of grand relations and bottles and bottles of wine.

When tired of looking, one could listen. For all the while Mrs. Morgan was either playing or talking, or both. Sometimes picking out a bit with one finger, and asking if it were not just like an autumn wind. Sometimes rushing ahead, and crying out from amidst the music as though from a merry-go-round in full swing: "Listen! Here come the knights on their galloping horses!" or "There's the gondola," or: "Now we are floating in the blue, blue sky!"

Appreciation was much nicer than music. Appreciation meant that everything was a story. The sun was shining, the roses bloomed round the ancient castle, a young girl opened her window and a dove came flying in. Or the clouds whirled over the moon and the ravens were croaking, and deep in the forest the monks were singing a funeral hymn. A note in the bass was a bell at midnight or the stealthy tread of a bandit, an arpeggio rocked a ship or unloosed an avalanche, and heartbroken sobs and cuckoos could be recognized with the greatest ease.

Raising her hands from the last chord, Mrs. Morgan would lean back as though exhausted. And presently she would rise in a sleepwalking manner, and wander towards the mantel-shelf, and pluck from it one of the plaster busts, and gaze at it as though at a dear friend. Still clasping the composer in her thin hands she would tell the Appreciation Class of Beethoven's troubled mind, of the untimely deaths of Chopin and Weber, or recount the ideal love-life of Robert and Clara Schumann.

By the end of the Class every one (except Charlie Prowse) was in a beautiful frame of mind. Herself, too, in a beautiful frame of mind, Mrs. Morgan would exclaim: "One kiss all round!" (only as she lisped, what she actually said was *One kith*); and then she would press her projecting teeth against the hot young cheeks of her listeners.

It was the sensation of Mrs. Morgan's teeth that had revealed to Isabel the affinity between Mrs. Morgan and Mrs. Morgan's piano. Mrs. Morgan's long narrow teeth were like the yellowed keys; and the pleated silk over her flat bosom was like the rusty flutes behind the fretwork panel, and her hair was like black wood that had lost its polish, and her long golden earrings resembled the brass trimmings on the piano, and clattered, just as the candle-arms did, in the vehement passages. Naturally, having made this discovery Isabel imparted it to her fellow pupils; and soon every child in Smurden and most of the elder people too called Mrs. Morgan *The Old Piano*.

And now all this, good Lord! was twenty years ago. Lena and Delia were married, and Blanche Dominy ran a dancing saloon, and Charlie Prowse, more sullen and violent than ever, was in the Air Force. And Mrs. Morgan, presumably, was in her coffin.

But suppose she was still alive?

I ought to have gone straight in and asked, thought Isabel. Yes, suppose she was still alive? And Isabel began to imagine a train of circumstances, all natural enough, poverty, and age, and sickness, and the fact that no one now wanted any music beyond what they could get from the radio, which would conduct Mrs. Morgan to a room to let in Chapel Prospect, and to a plight when she would be obliged to sell the old piano. Of course she might have grown too rheumatic to play on it any longer. But such a thin woman would be more likely to develop tubercle. Well, she would feel quite at home, dying of such a musical malady.

Isabel fancied herself paying that visit which now she certainly would never pay, climbing the grubby lodging-house stairs, striking her foot against the slop-pail which had been left in a dark corner of the landing, entering a room at the back of the house, a bed-sitting-room, where a lighter oblong on the dirty wallpaper showed whence the piano had been taken away. There on the mantelshelf (for no one would give a penny for them) would stand the plaster busts of the composers. And *The Old Piano*, thinner than ever, with wild bright eyes and scarlet cheekbones, would wave her bony hand towards the bust of Frédéric Chopin, and gasp proudly:

"*His* disease!"

Yes, it seemed without a doubt most life-like and probable. But whether it was true she would never know. For never would she be able to bring herself to pay that visit, and now she could not even ask what had become of *The Old Piano*, lest the news that *The Old Piano* was still alive might fasten on her conscience, and drive her to it.

THE WATER AND
THE WINE

BECAUSE of the fall of the Channel ports, Mrs. Hawley at a meeting of the Knitted Comforts for Seamen Circle found herself winding wool off the hands of a stranger, an elderly lady, short, with a jowl, removed from the Isle of Thanet to Hertfordshire. Presently Mrs. Hawley found too that the stranger knew the beauties of the neighbourhood better than she did. It turned out that she used to live at Amble.

"Why, I live at Amble!" said Mrs. Hawley. "Such a dear little town, so untouched! You wouldn't find it in the least changed. And we have such a charming house—historic, really. Sylvester Gauntlett once lived in it."

"So did I," said the lady. "He was my father."

"What! Are you Sylvester Gauntlett's daughter? Oh, you must come and have tea and see the house. It's quite simple. The Amble bus——"

"I am old enough to bicycle," said Miss Gauntlett. "Let us disregard the bus."

Mrs. Hawley's pleasure was qualified by a sensation that Sylvester Gauntlett's daughter was not worthy of Sylvester Gauntlett, a writer so polished and whimsical that critics often referred to him as "that lesser Lamb." There was nothing whimsical about Miss Gauntlett except her knitting, and that was not polished. But during the course of the week-end Mrs. Hawley rearranged the impressions first formed at the meeting of the Knitted Comforts for Seamen Circle, and by the day Miss Gauntlett was due she was expected with the compassion proper towards a dear old lady revisiting the house of her girlhood—"almost like a ghost," Mrs. Hawley remarked to her daughter.

On arrival, Miss Gauntlett proved less like a ghost than like a verger, a verger implacably resolved on showing tourists round a temporarily obliterated cathedral. Her grip on the past was only equalled by her indifference to the present. She put out any possibilities of a fire on the Hawleys' open hearth by the way she said "Should be a stove" and abolished a whole vista of rambling roses by one glance from a window and the words "Weren't there."

Having converted the drawing-room to a dining-room, she made over the dining-room into a parlour. "A Turkey carpet," she stated, tramping over the parquet. "Books here. More books there. A sash window. None of those exposed beams. Green wallpaper—a deep leaf green. Green was my father's favourite colour. And the gas brackets"—the roar of a passing plane overcame her, but when the noise had evaporated, she was ready to go on—"had very pretty opalescent shades imitating whelk shells. Tiresome, rowdy creatures, one can't get away from them! I might as well have stayed on at Broadstairs."

"Green," said Mrs. Hawley. "How interesting! I can't tell you, Miss Gauntlett, how enthralling it is to be able to picture it all as it was in your father's day. We have so often wondered. Haven't we, Pamela?"

Behind the mother stood the daughter, staring coldly at the chatty old hag whose youth had been illumined by gas, whose father had been yet another of those far too numerous English men of letters.

"Now we shall be able to imagine it all," Mrs. Hawley said. "The green walls, the books, your father at his desk."

"My father always wrote in his dressing——"

Another plane flew over. Dressing-room, dressing-gown? Gown sounded more literary. Mrs. Hawley waited with an understanding smile, a smile touched with humour and tender indulgence for the whims of genius, till the plane allowed her to say: "So much more comfortable!"

"Quieter, at any rate," Miss Gauntlett allowed. "Being on the first floor, and at the back."

A troubled expression crossed Mrs. Hawley's countenance. She seemed to be calculating how many floors her house had and, indeed, how many backs.

"I'll show you," Miss Gauntlett said.

Briskly she walked upstairs and along the landing. Familiarly, as though it were nothing to her to open a door on the shade of a minor master, she opened the door of the bathroom.

"Oh!"

"Did your father write in his bath?" asked the daughter.

"*Darling!*" Mrs. Hawley's voice was attuned to a much younger daughter. "It wasn't a bathroom *then*."

It was not the recollected figure of Sylvester Gauntlett, stocky and arrogant, with plump hands stained by nicotine and the large head turning with the bull-like regard of its little, twinkling eyes, or the remembered smell of Latakia tobacco, that immobilized his daughter on the threshold of Mrs. Hawley's bathroom. She saw, as distinctly as if it had actually been there, a tin saucer bath, and beside it a brown hot-water can whose paint, rather scabby with reiterated scaldings, was beginning to peel off; and the smell in her mind's nose was a mingled smell of Old Brown Windsor soap and heated enamel. In the bath, steaming gently, was a shallow lake, perhaps a couple of inches deep. Rising from the lake were legs—the legs of statesmen and warriors and men of letters; the legs of scientists whose opinions cracked the foundations of society and of judges whose verdicts cemented the cracks again; the legs of bishops and the legs of agnostics; aristocratic legs that had been buckled round with the Order of the Garter; and fine, rose-tinted legs that had lain in a royal bed. And among all these were the legs of Sylvester Gauntlett and Sylvester Gauntlett's daughter. Round about the knee all the legs disappeared, lost in the tendrils of steam rising from the two-inch lake.

No one nowadays, thought Miss Gauntlett, has any conception of the comfort, the luxury, the privacy, of a saucer bath in one's dressing-room. Turning her eyes from the legs of a past generation to the faces of Mrs. and Miss Hawley, she knew that this was exactly the trouble. Such a conception had never occurred to them. They just thought it a rather dirty way of bathing. Not that a bathroom was any novelty to Miss Gauntlett. The Edith Hotel, Residential, for Ladies, where she had lived for the last twenty years, had two bathrooms on each floor, each bathroom supplied with constant hot water and every convenient accessory, including a tin of cleanser and a mop with which each residing lady was expected to leave the bath as she would wish to find it. No comfort, no luxury, no privacy—and no one a whit cleaner, either. But in Mrs. Hawley's silly countenance and in the girl's swimming pop-eyes, Miss Gauntlett read plainly enough their conviction that no amount of saucer baths could remove the dirt of England's golden age.

The crowning unfairness of it all was that no shade of dirt would rest on the memory of Sylvester Gauntlett. Unquestionably clean, he would arise from the saucer bath and shine; and so would they all, the statesmen and the warriors, those who wore the Garter and those whose garters were unloosed at a royal command. But Miss Gauntlett, relict of a bathless order, must inherit all their opprobrium, be badged with all their scum and sullied with all their rinsings, and exist in the eyes of these mere Hawleys as a funny old lady who never took a bath, as a grubby antique.

She pulled herself together. With her small eyes darting furious glances over the white paint and the chromium, she described the dressing-room, with its walls of a darker shade of green, its brown paint, its curtains of deep olive-coloured serge. She made it all as dark, as poky, as possible.

Mrs. Hawley said that it sounded so cosy.

Downstairs there was tea, white curtains fluttering from open windows, sandwiches that were gone in an instant, the girl fidgeting and eyeing the radio. Presently, Mrs. Hawley began to fidget too. She was sorry for the poor revisiting ghost who ate so much, whose false teeth served her badly, who must be feeling so distressed at the changes in her old home, and who would not go. Of course, in the Victorian age visits went on for hours. There was so much leisure then.

"Don't you feel, Miss Gauntlett, that there is much less leisure now than there used to be? One of the things that I feel so specially drawn to in your father's essays is the feeling of leisure. I can't imagine him hurrying over a single sentence."

"He took more than half an hour to shave."

"Well, of course, that was a work of time then, wasn't it? No electric razors, no hot water," Mrs. Hawley said. And then she thought: Heavens, I shouldn't have said that! "What *did* we do before electric kettles?" she asked brightly.

"Used spirit lamps," replied Miss Gauntlett.

No wonder the poor old thing was upset, Mrs. Hawley thought. How awkward it had been about the bathroom— Pamela so tactless, poor child, Miss Gauntlett so angry— though perhaps it was only Gauntlett's daughter resenting the conversion of such a father's dressing-room.

"But a garden is always so peaceful, don't you think, so restful? You must let me show you the garden before you go."

The house was built on a slope, and to reach the garden one had to go downstairs and out through the basement. All the way down the stairs (lemon-coloured distemper, a light matting, clear glass in the place of the old clouded pane▪

darkened by bars and blurred by ivy), Miss Gauntlett was saying to herself: "Unclean, unclean!"

"Here's one innovation I must show you. We're really quite proud of it, though I'm afraid your father would have thought it almost barbarous." Mrs. Hawley opened a door, switched on a light. It showed a small, windowless room with walls newly painted, furnished with some light chairs, a bridge table, tea-things, a first-aid box, a pack of cards. "Our air-raid shelter," she said.

Miss Gauntlett looked in. As she looked, her face assumed an expression of extraordinary blandness. Her wrinkles smoothed out, her small, angry eyes became clear and serene. "Ah, yes. The wine cellar."

Her pointing hand moved from wall to wall. The gesture was no longer that of any mere verger. No, this was the cathedral's bishop himself, graciously displaying the treasures of the episcopal strong-room.

"Claret there. Burgundy below. Champagne there, and brandy. My father never cared for any other kind of spirits. Hock and Moselle. White wines, especially a Hermitage and a Montrachet *aîné*. And there, just by your little red buckets, Imperial Tokay." With a commanding hand, she switched off the light, closed the treasure house. "Times have changed, haven't they?" she said.

As Miss Gauntlett bicycled home to her lodgings, she thought how Sylvester Gauntlett, that lesser Lamb, would have capped the situation by some delicate quip about wine being changed into water. But she felt no regret that the epigram was unspoken. She was contented with things as they were.

MY SHIRT IS IN MEXICO

AS SOON as the train left London, we went along to the buffet car for a drink. The train was crammed, a wartime train loaded with soldiers and with parties of women and children travelling inland to get away from air-raids. It was difficult to move along the corridor; one had to edge one's way past soldiers sitting on their packs, heaps of hand luggage, train-sick children being held out of the window, people queued up sheepishly outside the toilets. But the buffet car was almost empty and looked like something belonging to a different world, with its clean, light-painted walls and red leather upholstery.

We sat down at a little table, and presently the attendant came along with the tariff card. He was a middle-aged man with a good face, innocent and humane like a rabbit's. When I said I'd like a cup of black coffee with rum in it, he made no difficulties, though it was not down on the list.

Coming back with our drinks, he looked at us as though we were already friends of his. The rum was in a measuring glass, and as he poured it into my coffee he said: "Excuse me mentioning it, madam, but I see from your bag you've been in Mexico."

His voice was full of confidence and excitement. For a moment I wondered if I shouldn't take a chance on it, but I was feeling tired and unsure of my powers, so I said, honestly: "No such luck. The bag has, but it's only a loan."

Now we all looked at the label, which was printed with a gay view of flowers and white-clothed tourists riding on festooned mules. And thinking how hard it must be for a man who apparently wanted to go to Mexico to spend his life

travelling in a buffet car from Plymouth to London and back
again, I said that the friend who owned the bag had liked
Mexico very much.

"Oh, yes, it must be a wonderful country," he said. "All
those hothouse flowers growing wild, and the volcanoes, and
the Mexicans making such wonderful artistic things. And
everything so old, and yet, in a manner of speaking, only
just beginning. Building roads, and learning to read, and
getting vaccinated."

"Sensible beginnings," said Valentine.

"Yes, that's right. Oh, I'd like to go to Mexico. It must
be beautiful. . . . I've got a shirt in Mexico," he said.

"How did that happen?" I asked. "You're one up on me.
I haven't got anything in Mexico."

"It's an uncommon thing to say, isn't it? Oil shares, now,
or a cousin—that's to be expected. But not a shirt. It all
happened before the war, because of a German gentleman, a
refugee. I noticed him the moment he came in—he sat down
at that table over there—and I thought to myself: Now, he's
somebody. A bald man, and thin as a lath, and most remarkably clean. Bald but not elderly, you understand. Presently he ordered a large coffee and a slice of cake. Well, that
didn't tell me much, except a nice manner and a German
accent. But when I brought along his order, he'd opened his
wallet, and there were his papers spread out—a single to
Plymouth and a third-class steamer passage."

"To Mexico?"

"No, to New York. Well, he didn't say anything I could
take hold of. But I'd still got a card up my sleeve—there was
the ashtray needed emptying. When I went to change it, he
said he didn't smoke. Now, I don't smoke either, so that was
a beginning. And once you've got a beginning, it's easy, isn't
it? From smoking we got round to seasickness, and then I
could ask him if he had crossed the Atlantic. 'No,' said he,
'but now I shall.' Living in Plymouth, naturally I know a lot

about New York, so I could tell him things he'd find useful. Puddings being called desserts, and luggage baggage, and how you can check it through. He laughed, and said he'd be able to carry all his."

I could see my way to the shirt now.

"Yes, just a suitcase and what he stood up in. What you'd take away for a week-end—and he was going to America for good and all. But not worried in the least. What's more, he seemed so pleased with what he *had* got. Made me feel his suit to see what good wool it was and told me all about a wonderful pair of silk pyjamas he'd been given. And you could tell from the way he spoke he was the sort of gentleman who knows about clothes—quite a dandy, in fact. He said straight out his shoes were a disappointment to him—they were a gift, too. And he was quite right; they were very poor articles. Then all of a sudden it flashed on me he could have my shirt. It was a very nice shirt. Providential, really— I'd bought it that very morning and was carrying it down with me. I always like to buy my shirts in London. You get a better style. Well, he wasn't the sort of man you can have pretences with, so I told him straight out I'd like him to take my shirt. Wasn't I lucky to have it with me, though?"

"You were," said Valentine. "I can't wish anyone better luck than that."

"Yes, and he accepted it so pleasantly. But what I liked best was the way he opened the parcel and looked at the shirt most carefully—how the buttons were fastened on and all. Examined it all over, he did. If he had just taken the parcel, that wouldn't have been the same thing, would it?"

"And now he's in Mexico?"

"Oh, no. He's in New York. It's the shirt that's in Mexico. With a friend of his. Look, this is the letter he wrote me from New York."

Often read, always carefully refolded, the thin sheet of

paper already had the air of something beginning to be historic:

MARCH 11TH, 1939.

DEAR FRIEND:

I have to tell you how I have made good journey and am settled here in New York City. And I have meet other friends here also, and I find some work shortly. And the beautiful shirt you gave me, it is not ungratefully that I bestow it to a comrade going to Mexico when he has greater need than I. I do not forget the kindness. I hope you are well and make always new friends. I thank you again.

Cordially,
RENATUS LEUTNER.

P.S. New York is very fine.

"You must feel happy about that shirt," I said.

"I do," he replied. "It was a blue one, just right for a sunny climate. I've always wanted to go to Mexico."

NOAH'S ARK

"POOR little things," said Mrs. Purefoy. "I'm afraid they'll find it a bit strange."

"Nonsense!" replied Mrs. Temple briskly. "They'll be *perfectly* happy. All town children are happier in the country. Think of the Fresh Air Fund. Think of that orphanage that came down for the day from Birmingham. They'll be *quite* happy. It isn't as though their mother were coming, too, to unsettle them."

"I'll do my best, I'm sure. Though nothing can take a mother's place."

"You must send them out of doors, Mrs. Purefoy. Send them into the fields (of course you'll explain about shutting gates and not walking over crops or chasing cows or tearing up plants by the roots). Why, it will be a new world to them! They can pick wild flowers and look at the birds and the lambs. I dare say they've never even seen a lamb."

These were the first evacuated children to be received on the Temple estate. Mrs. Purefoy felt that children from a bombed town would arrive, if not in blankets, at least in rags. She pictured them yellow and thin and bare, like young birds; and, like young birds, with enormous eyes and incessant appetites. But when Malcolm and Venice arrived their clothes were tidy and their hair was shiny, and they ate so moderately they might almost be gentry children.

Mrs. Temple deposited them. And after a few words about happiness and gratitude and pale cheeks she left them.

It was tea-time. Scarcely had the first cups been poured out when the children began to talk about air-raids. But that, Mrs. Temple had said, must not be encouraged. It

would make them morbid. So Mrs. Purefoy repressed her
longing to hear more when Malcolm spoke of how the corpses
were heaped up where the old coffee-stall used to be, and
snatched the cover off the canary, whose songs soon put an
end to unsuitable conversation. After tea they were shown
round: the bedroom under the thatch, the back-kitchen, the
pump, the garden, the privy at the end of the garden, the
lane—all mud and celandines—that would take them to
school.

The leafless orchard (where later on, Mrs. Purefoy explained, there would be apples) was filled with birdsong and
carpeted with young nettles.

"Do you eat them?" Venice inquired.

"Eat nettles, my dear?"

"Teacher said people in the country ate nettles. And
scraped the burned crusts into the teapot. And boiled dande-
lion roots. Because they were so poor, Teacher said."

"Goodness gracious me, no! Why, we eat nice cabbage."

"Teacher said, 'Men of England, wherefore plough for
the lords who lay ye low?'"

"You'll see them ploughing to-morrow, maybe. And the
little lambs," said Mrs. Purefoy. Everything was swaying in
an urgent spring wind and both children looked cold, so
they went indoors.

Because of an epidemic of measles the school was closed.
So on the next morning Mrs. Purefoy sent the children out
for a walk, giving them careful directions about gates and
arable and not having anything to do with the little Dominys.
Gravely they set out, gravely they returned, and offered their
bunch of primroses to their hostess politely.

The primroses were tied up with an old bootlace which
they had found in a hedge.

"And did you see the little lambs?"

"Yes, Mrs. Purefoy. We saw quite a lot of lambs."

"And didn't you think the lambs very pretty?"

"Very pretty. But they aren't white, not all of them. Some of them were grey and spotty-looking."

"Yes, dears. That's the kind of lambs they are."

"Oh! Well, they were very nice all the same. Have you ever seen a tiger?"

"No, I can't say that I have."

"We know several tigers. Especially a tigress called Queenie. She's nine years old, and when she licks you can hear her tongue. She's very sweet-tempered really, and underneath she's a lovely lemon-colour. But when she gets in a temper you should just see her. She yowls and shakes the bars of her cage, and her hair stands out, and as for her claws . . ."

"What dread hands," murmured Venice. "And what dread feet?"

"Yes, my dear, their claws must be dreadful. Let alone their teeth."

"And when she thinks her dinner's coming she goes weaving round like a dance, and purrs."

"But the polar bear," Venice broke in, "is much more dangerous, though he looks kind. His little head comes up out of the water, and he looks round with his little teeny-weeny eyes. And if you were on the rock he'd give you one biff with his paw. And you'd be dead. But most likely he wouldn't trouble to eat you. He'd just roll you over with his paw, and snuff at you."

"I think he'd eat her," said Malcolm; and frowned at his sister for her lack of courtesy. Unheeding, Venice went on to tell Mrs. Purefoy about panthers, jaguars, and a fight she had seen between two crocodiles. She described the scene so vividly that Mrs. Purefoy dreamed of crocodiles all night.

The next day it rained heavily. Mrs. Temple had not indicated what course should be followed with children when they can't be sent out of doors, but Mrs. Purefoy, with a

feeling she had hit on the right thing, went off to a neighbour
and borrowed a Noah's Ark. It was only a qualified success;
after a little while they went back to the horsehair sofa and
sat talking in low voices. Presently, to Mrs. Purefoy peeling
potatoes, it emerged that they were discussing someone called
Flora, who was dear to them.

"Who's Flora, my pretty? A relation of yours?"

"No. At least, she wasn't. But she's dead."

"Deary me, how sad! And do you miss her a great deal?"

"Oh, yes! No end. Oh, she was so lovely! She had big
blue eyes, and because her mother died Mr. Butcher brought
her up himself with a bottle. And she knew us quite well,
she really did recognize us."

"What a sweet little thing! What did she die of, then?"
There, I shouldn't have asked that, she said to herself. *It
doesn't do to ask about deaths, nowadays.*

"Some fool gave her a kipper, Mr. Butcher said. Poor
darling Flora! Now there's only Jimmy, he's handsome, but
terribly wild. Have you ever seen a caracal, Mrs. Purefoy?
It's like a very big cat, but it has tassels on its ears. As big as
a dog. Bigger than most dogs. Flora was a gentle one, but
mostly you can't go near them."

They were back on their wild animals again.

That night Mrs. Purefoy was chased by baboons, and
found herself trying to feed an ant-eater from a hot-water-
bottle.

Mr. Purefoy, however, enjoyed the wild animals a great
deal. As he was the shepherd, this showed magnanimity.
He might have been expected to resent the implied slur on
the charms of his lambs. Actually, being a shepherd, Mr.
Purefoy had exhausted those charms, and found lions a
pleasant change. He bought the children a drawing-book
and some coloured chalks, and commissioned works of art,
such as Tigers pulling down an Elephant, or A Boa Con-
strictor climbing a palm-tree after a Bear; and when neigh-

bours dropped in he would display the pictures and call on the artists to tell more.

They complied most willingly. Questioned on any other subject, they retreated into a cautious melancholy reserve, but once launched upon their circle of friends in their home-town Zoo they talked with passionate animation, and with the 'superb social calm of those who describe dukes and duchesses in their native habitats. And for hours after they would look pink and proud, and at ease in their new sur-roundings. As Mrs. Purefoy said, regretfully admitting what she could not approve and could not deny, it was as though wild beasts were meat and drink, home and mother, to those poor dear children.

The red and yellow chalks gave out first; then came a spell of bears, camels, and walruses; crocodiles and trees ex-hausted the green chalk, and the blue was expended on baboons, the heavens, and a few rather grudging birds. When only the purple chalk was left Mr. Purefoy sought to commission a rhinoceros. The children shook their heads. They had no purple friends.

"But here be a green monkey."

"He was green," explained Malcolm.

"Not quite *so* green. But a greeny colour," added Venice.

Mr. Purefoy said:

"Well, think of that!"

For Mr. Purefoy was able to think with calm pleasure of green monkeys. Mrs. Purefoy was not so happily constituted, even a modest brown or grey monkey, entirely unrelieved by brighter tints, was enough to get into her dreams and worry her; and a word used by Mrs. Temple returned to her thoughts, and strengthened her in a conviction that it would do the children no good to be always talking of their menagerie. *Morbid.* That was the word. Surely it was morbid to be for ever dwelling on tigers and serpents, and evoking

frightful unsurmised aspects of creation called Binturongs
and Peccaries and Kinkajous. It was as morbid as talking
about corpses heaped up where the old coffee-stall used to
be; and having denied herself the corpses which she would
have taken a natural pleasure in, it seemed hard to Mrs.
Purefoy that she must endure tigers and kinkajous.

So presently she was able to convince herself in good faith
that it was very sad for the poor children to have so many
wild animals imprinted on their memories; that just as other
evacuated children one heard of had lice in their heads, the
heads of Malcolm and Venice were infested with carnivores.
It was no fault of theirs, poor little things, just a token of
what town children are exposed to; and with all the zeal
of self-delusion she endeavoured to distract them from their
painful recollections and secret fears. Since the local fauna
interested them only as remembrancers of wild beasts, she
thought they might be weaned away into the vegetable king-
dom, and gave them each a small plot in the garden, and a
trowel, and some packets of radish and turnip seed. They
dug; and dug up worms; and the worms recalled snakes, and
in a moment the garden was, so Mrs. Purefoy felt, crepitating
with cobras and rattlesnakes.

But the crisis of Mrs. Purefoy's compassion was not
reached till the afternoon when Venice began talking about
wolves.

It was the worse for beginning with a misunderstanding
—Venice's account of playing with wolf-cubs being taken by
her hostess as referring to play with members of the Junior
Branch of the Boy Scouts. Mrs. Temple approved of the
Scout movement. It was the antithesis of being morbid. And
Mrs. Purefoy, feeling that here at last might be the answer
to prayer, said encouragingly:

"You know, there are several cubs here."

"Oh! Are there? Where are they? When can I see them?"

"Whenever you like, I dare say. Perhaps they could come to tea."

"Malcolm! Did you hear? Mrs. Purefoy says there are some wolf-cubs here, and that we could have them to tea. How I'd love to play with wolf-cubs again, and rub my nose in them, and snuff up their funny smell!"

"Why not be a Brownie?" said Mrs. Purefoy discriminatingly. "That's for little girls, you know."

"But what could we feed them on, Mrs. Purefoy? They don't really like anything but meat. And meat's rationed. Perhaps you could get them some *old* meat. Or some horse-flesh."

"Venice, dear!"

"Who keeps their mother, Mrs. Purefoy? Is she a big one?"

"*Malcolm!* Don't be rude! I can't ask any little boys to tea if you are going to talk like that."

Malcolm turned pale, and began to expostulate. But his words were obliterated by Venice, who was swinging round and round with her eyes shut, and chanting:

> "When the wolf that nightly prowls
> Bays the moon with hideous howls.
> Wa-oo! Wa-oo! Hideous howls!"

"Hush, child, for heaven's sake. Whatever's come over you?"

"Venice loves wolves," her brother explained.

"Hideous howls! We're going to play with wolves. We're going to smell of wolf. Not even with scented soap you can't wash the smell off. Oh, Mrs. Purefoy, why didn't you tell us before there are wolves here?"

Shuddering, Mrs. Purefoy said:

"I never told you any such thing. I was talking about nice little children, not savage beasts."

Venice stopped in her dance. Her hair, still whirling, swept across her eyes. Malcolm put his arm around her.

"Oh well, it can't be helped. Come on, Venice. You couldn't really expect wolves in the country, you know."

But Mrs. Purefoy had never felt quite so sure. Lions, tigers, rattlesnakes, they belonged to foreign parts. Wolves were nearer the bone. There had been wolves in England, and might be again. The neighbourhood of a shepherd's cottage was just where they might be expected, and if anything would fetch them that child's bloodcurdling screeches would. She sat down heavily, and began to tremble, and was still trembling when her husband came in.

"If this dwelling on wild animals goes on, George, I shall have to say something to Mrs. Temple."

Only desperation, he realized, could speak thus. For himself, he would have preferred any amount of wild animals, dwelled on or dwelled with, to an intervention by the lady of the manor. He set himself to reason with his wife, at first admitting artfully that all this menagering would get on any one's nerves, but developing the great truth that if it isn't one thing it's another, and that if Malcolm and Venice were not so set on their fancy animals they might turn to real ones, trying to milk cows, falling into pigsties, or bringing home—he had heard of such things—snakes, lizards, and hedgehogs. Then he worked on her softer nature, and finally on her chivalry, declaring it was bad enough for children to be bombed without having Mrs. Temple after them into the bargain. And when Mrs. Purefoy had passed from interruptions to sobs, and from sobs to smoothing her apron, he judged it safe to conclude:

"What's more, I won't have it. You leave them be!"

Upstairs, Malcolm was saying:

"After all, it wouldn't be much good even if there were wolves here. They'd milk them, or kill them like their own silly animals."

No wife gives way unreservedly. Mrs. Purefoy now took to sighing at the names of outlandish animals as though such names were blasphemies. But Mr. Purefoy bought another set of coloured chalks, and commissioned more scenes of natural history, expressing a particular passion for ocelots, gnus, Tasmanian Devils and pandas; and Mrs. Purefoy relapsed into her earlier stronghold: that it was dreadful for the poor little things to be so obsessed by all those awful creatures they had been driven to take up with because town life has no natural pleasures for children, and that she only prayed it wouldn't come out in their dreams. Indeed, at the last it was with an almost genuine benevolence that she handed a copy of the paper across the table.

"Here's something you'll be interested in, my dears."

Beside a small paragraph her thumbnail had made a deep indentation. *Owing to the continuance of blitz bombing the authorities of the Plymouth Zoo have caused all the dangerous animals to be destroyed.*

The girl stared in front of her and the boy, with desperate solicitude, stared at the girl. *O God*, he prayed, *O God, don't let her cry!* She did not cry.

Their Ark, so brightly painted, so gloriously companied, had foundered under them. They swam on the waste of waters, and for a little it seemed that a few small harmless beasts swam with them; but presently these disappeared, and nothing broke the surface except a distant unpeopled Ararat. As Mrs. Purefoy remarked, you could see with one eye what a weight had been lifted off their minds. By the time the school re-opened they were drawing bombers and stoning water-rats like any other children about the place.

AN UNIMPORTANT CASE

IT WAS a January afternoon, still and sunless. The sky was covered with a web of grey cloud, the fields showed either the whitey brown of the chalk soil where the plough had bared it or the grizzled tint of winter grass. One had only to look at the telegraph poles along the high-road to know that one was in an unimportant part of England, and that the road was of no great importance either.

Along this road a man and a girl were walking. The man was bareheaded, he carried a suitcase. The suitcase was battered, and his raincoat was shabby, though he had belted it in round the waist, and this gave it a certain air of swagger. He walked with a slow upspringing stride, the gait of some-one who walks as a matter of course and without any in-terest in the act of walking. He was small and lightly built, but he carried the suitcase easily enough. He was young, but the crown of his bare head was already going a little bald.

The girl was plump. Her coat had cuffs and collar made of rabbit imitating some more expensive fur. She seemed to be walking with much more energy than the man, taking rapid decisive steps and swinging her arms. But it was obvious that her town-bred gait would flag long before his.

It was a silent day, and they walked in silence. When a car went by the girl fell behind, drawing close to the road-side, and then hurried forward to walk by the man's side again. Now, at a turn of the road, she spoke.

"Look at those trees, Alan. Whatever are they?"

"Some sort of willow."

Where the road dipped down to a small stream a group

of sallows rose out of the pinched grey landscape. The leafless boughs were a brilliant astonishing tint of flame-colour.

"Don't they look like a fire?"

"They go that colour at this time of year," he answered.

"They *do* look lovely. Just like a beautiful big fire that someone's lit up out of doors."

Presently he asked her if she was feeling cold. She shook her head, staring at the trees.

A car approached, and again she hurried to the side of the road. But this time she remained behind, loitering, staring at the trees as though she would fill her eyes with them.

"Alan! Stop a minute, do! I *do* believe . . . Yes, there is! Look, there's a house there, in among them. And it's empty!"

It was a bungalow, small and new. But the windows were broken and the track leading off from the road was overgrown with brambles.

"It's empty," she repeated. "Alan, let's have a look."

Already she had turned down the disused track, her heels twisting in the ruts. He glanced this way and that along the road. There was no one in sight, and he followed her.

All round the house were the willows, screening it from the road. He lifted the broken gate, and they passed into the little enclosure, that must have been meant for a garden though now only the sagging wire-net fence distinguished the grass within from the grass without. He took her arm and kissed her.

"Shall we live here, Ivy?"

"Oh, Alan!"

Her voice expressed such profound feeling that he dropped her arm, and stood holding the suitcase and looking at her with an expression almost of enmity. But in a moment she was gay once more, and exclaiming:

"What a love of a little green water-butt!"

She went up to the broken window and looked in.

"What's it like inside?"

There was no answer. Only when he was beside her, staring in at the dusky room, did she whisper:

"It smells as though they'd had a fire in here."

"Just what they have had. It's been burned out."

Still pungent, the smell of burning dwelt in the empty room, and the gay paper on the walls was blackened with smoke.

They walked round to the back of the house. Here the stale smell of burning was stronger, and the charred woodwork and broken roof showed where the fire had burned its worst. A plank had been wedged against the door to secure it, but he knocked it aside and together they entered. Neither spoke, and it was as though they had walked into a church, for their demeanour was awed and constrained, and their feet knocked loudly on the echoing floors. Only one room was tolerably intact, with a ceiling, and the colour of the paint and the pattern of the wall-paper still discernible.

"Hadn't they done it up pretty, too?" said Ivy compassionately.

They stood looking out of the broken window at the willows burning under the grey sky.

"Do you know what I'd like to do? Light a fire, and have a cup of tea."

With a grave face he opened the door, and called into the desolation of the back of the house.

"Parker! Bring in the afternoon tea. And don't forget to polish the silver tea-pot."

"No, but I mean it, Alan. I *would* like a cup of tea. Here, give me that suitcase."

She rummaged in it, and presently fetched out a little spirit lamp and a kettle, a tea-infuser, tea screwed up in one piece of paper and sugar in another, and a bakelite mug.

"There! All we want's a drop of water from the water-butt. You can drink rain-water if you boil it."

"Good Lord, Ivy, fancy you bringing all that along."

She blushed.

"I thought it might come in useful, us being on the road. I thought we might want a picnic, sometime. And anyhow, I had to bring along my spirit lamp because of curling my hair."

"Gipsy Ivy," he said. "You'd look pretty with gold earrings and one of those gipsy hats with ostrich feathers. You look pretty anyhow, my darling."

"Get busy with that kettle," she replied.

Left to herself, she dusted a piece of the floor and arranged the lamp and the mug and the infuser, her eyes darkened with brooding pleasure. This was romance, this was what she had foreseen when she ran away to go with Alan. She sat back on her heels, and sighed with contentment. A soft rustle from the corner of the room answered her sigh. It came from a heap of willow-leaves, which had blown in at the broken window and lay drifted in a corner of the room. The rising wind that wagged the bare stems outside stirred them where they lay. They were thick, they were heaped up like a bed.

"Pardon the absence of milk," she said grandly. They sat down on the suitcase and shared the strong sweet tea from the bakelite mug.

"Alan. I've got another idea now. Suppose we stay the night here? We could get some sticks, and light a proper fire to warm ourselves."

He shook his head.

"Someone might see the smoke, and then we'd be copped for trespassing."

"Never mind. We'll just go to bed early, then."

"Bed?"

"Look at that lovely great heap of leaves. Soft as a feather-bed."

"You wouldn't like it, Ivy darling. You've never slept on a floor, you don't know how hard it is, and how cold. Better push on."

"I *would* like it, I would. I'd like it better than sleeping in places where they look at us so paltry and suspicious. And if we slept here, there'd be nothing to pay."

"There wasn't much to pay last night."

She was silent. That morning they had gone from their lodging without paying the bill. It was her first taste of dishonesty, and though she laughed at the time, and told Alan about the time when she went to the cinema in her mistress's stockings, she was uneasy at heart. He saw her face cloud, and knew why.

"She was a horrible woman, anyway," he said.

It was seven years since he had been regularly employed. Looking for work had turned imperceptibly into tramping the roads; mates had been friendly and girls kind, and after a shallow fashion he had been contented with his lot. Then, amid the dreariness of a holiday resort in winter, Ivy had come to the door holding out a clumsy sandwich, and suddenly her round bright eyes had filled with tears of pity and she had slammed the door in his face to stand waiting behind it—he had heard her through the door, and her steadfast fibbing replies to her employer's cross-questionings about young men and cold meat. Since that day the road had no purpose except as leading to a job; and now he had Ivy with him, and the job was still to seek. But to her the road was romance, and to be footsore with walking through a winter's day a proud adventure after being footsore with trudging all day up and down the stairs of a provincial villa. Let her have her thrill while it lasted, he thought, his Gipsy Ivy.

After dusk he went out and collected fallen willow-leaves in his raincoat. Each time that he came in with a fresh load it was as though he brought a sighing summer with him. They had half a loaf and a couple of saveloys, these made their supper; and with his raincoat beneath them and her coat above them they fell asleep in the rustling willow-leaf bed.

In the morning she began to pack the suitcase.

"Even when we have a little place of our own, Alan, I will always remember this house and how happy we were."

"Would you like to stop on for a bit?"

She looked up, astonished. The willow leaves drifted around her, for now a strong wind was blowing, and they swirled about the room in the eddying draught.

"Stop on?"

"I'm thinking we might as well. The wind's gone round to the north, we shall have snow if I'm not much mistaken. Might as well stay where we are for a bit."

"And be snowed up?" Her voice was delighted. "Oh, Alan! Would you really like to?"

"As a matter of fact, I shouldn't be sorry. I'm not feeling too grand, this morning."

He had heart-burn, and felt dizzy, he said. She brewed him some more tea. After a while he asked her to walk back to the village to buy a loaf, and some cold meat, and some more tea.

"Go now, before the wind gets worse, there's a good girl." As she was leaving the house he called after her, "Remember that tea."

When she returned he was lying under the willows at the back of the house with his face to the ground, writhing, and clutching at the grasses.

"Is that you, Ivy girl? Go along in. I'll come in a minute. But I've got to be sick."

She fell on her knees beside him, spilling the parcels. He raised up a face livid with agony, and said in a loud in-attentive voice:

"Don't you hear what I say? Get along in, I'll come presently."

She went indoors and began to arrange her provisions along the window-sill, staring at the bright twisting flames of the willows outside. After a while she saw that something was volleying through the broken panes, and spotting the loaf and the parcel of cold meat. It was snow. The food would be ruined if she left it there. As though the pound loaf and the four ounces of ham were leaden weights she moved them out of the way. The willow leaves whirled about the floor. She tried to heap them up into a bed again, for Alan would want to lie down when he came back.

Alan was lying in the snow, being sick. With a sob of panic she fled out of the house.

At first, amid the whirling snowflakes, she could not find him. He had crawled farther under the trees; he lay quite still, his face was pinched and grey.

"O Lord, I've had such a doing."

"A cup of tea will do you good. Are you better now, Alan?"

"Such cramps!"

"A cup of tea's what you want. Come in, my darling."

He got up, groaning, and was immediately bent double with pain. Somehow she hauled him into the house and he lay on the leaves, sipping tea and shuddering.

"Don't you suppose you're going to cover me with that coat of yours," he said after a while. "No, I won't have it. O Ivy, I don't like to play you up like this."

"Try to get off to sleep now," she said.

She sat watching him. Cars went by along the road, going so fast that no one in them would guess there was a house among the willows. She wondered what time it was. The whirling snow seemed to obliterate time. At intervals Alan got up, groaning, and went out to be sick, and came back shaking and shivering. After the fourth bout he did not protest when she spread her coat over him as well as his own. Sometimes she made him tea. There was a moment when she realized that she herself was famishingly hungry, and she ate the loaf, almost without knowing it. Fewer cars went by now. She looked out of the window and saw one pass with its headlights on, sallow in the haggard dusk of snow. Night was coming.

"Alan! Alan!"

He stirred, but did not open his eyes.

"I am going to the shop. I shall be back in half an hour."

He nodded drowsily. He doesn't understand, she thought.

Out of the far world where he was lying he murmured: "Be careful with those cars."

The snow clogged her steps, it was difficult to run. She met a woman who said that the doctor lived at Enley.

"Where's Enley?"

"About two miles along the road."

She ran on. The woman hurried after her.

"You're going the wrong way for Enley, my girl. Enley's back-along."

She turned about, and the wind met her. Enley, and the doctor, must be beyond the bungalow, then. She began to wonder if she should stop and have a look at Alan before she went on. Better not. It might torment him to see her, and then to see her go out again. But she would look through the window, there was still daylight enough for that.

Where the track turned off there was still daylight enough for her to see deep footmarks in the snow, large and new beside the scuffling print of her own tread. A man's track. Suppose some tramp, some awful tramp, had gone into the bungalow for shelter. Suppose he had attacked Alan, killed him? . . .

After the glimmering white dusk the darkness of the house was like a blow. The blow of darkness was followed by a stab of light. The beam from an electric torch turned from Alan to her, and a voice said:

"Is this your young man?"

Though he spoke kindly, he was a policeman. So instantly she began to lie, explaining that Alan had been taken ill on the road, that they had come into the bungalow for shelter, that they had only been there for a few hours. The beam of light from his torch dwelt for a moment on her, then flicked onward to the suitcase, to the loaf, to the kettle, to Alan lying huddled under the coats with his feet sticking out. He was lying so still that if it had not been for his heavy snoring breaths she would have thought he was dead.

"He can't stay here, you know. I'll get on my bike and telephone. It'll have to be the ambulance."

"O God, is he as bad as that?"

He was going. She called out;

"You'll come back, won't you?"

For now it seemed to her that she could not bear to be left alone in this desolate house that was so icy cold and smelled of stale burning, hearing the willow-leaves drifting about the floor and the wind rumbling in the chimney. She knelt down by Alan, rearranging the coats, patting him, and trying to read his face in the bleak dusk that echoed the pallid snow-covered landscape outside. He is asleep, she thought. I must not wake him. And a moment after her anxiety became too strong for her, and she tried to rouse him. He did not answer. She touched his cheek. And at the contact with her cold hand he flinched, and burrowed his face into the leaves with a complaining moan. Appalled at having hurt him she started back. But presently her body's need mastered her, and whimpering and suppliant with cold she squirmed herself under the coverings and lay beside him. He did not stir.

The policeman came back. So substantial and well clothed, he seemed to warm the room by entering it. Ivy had never supposed that she could be glad to see a policeman, but now in her relief she began to chatter, to apologize that there was nothing for him to sit on, to offer a cigarette.

"Thank you, but I don't smoke," he said. His voice sounded gloomy and constrained. Presently he said:

"You'd better start packing your traps."

While she packed he stood by the window fidgeting with a note-book, and every now and then he drew a slow considering breath, and held it, as though he were about to speak, and then puffed it out again.

"Your name, please?"

"Ivy Carter."

"And is this man called Alan Young?"

"Yes, sir."

"And did you both spend Tuesday night at Mrs. Hamble's, 7, Pond Street, Gillinghurst?"

"Yes. We're together," she answered defiantly.

"Well, I'm sorry to tell you that your young man's wanted on a charge of fraud. And you will be wanted as a witness. And it's my duty to take you both in charge."

She was mute, and his first sensation was one of relief that she should take it so quietly. But after a while he began to wish for any lamentation that might break the silence, for it was as though he had spoken among shadows.

It had been a neat piece of work on his part, or rather, since he was not thinking of them, for it seemed likely that by now the pair would be a day's journey hence, it had been a good piece of observation. No. To be quite honest, it had been an accident. It had been the colour of those trees, burning sombrely amid the snow, that had caught his eye. He had looked at them, thinking of the bright fire that awaited him at home, and of how glad he would be to get into slippers, and light a pipe, and exchange the wide bleak landscape for the curtained room, small and bright as a jewel. And then he had noticed the foot-prints along the track, and would have supposed them to be the track of some village child, for they were small, if it had not been for the separate indentation that betokened a woman's shoes with high heels. That's what it is to have quick eyes, and training.

The man called out in a high frightened voice:

"Ivy, Ivy! Where are you?"

"It's all right, darling, it's all right. I'm here."

"Oh, Ivy, I think it's coming on again. Ivy, don't go."

"Of course I won't go."

He tossed among the rustling leaves, and under cover of the sound the policeman moved gently into a dark corner. Training. That was it, training. He began to rehearse the evidence he would speak. "On Thursday the 27th of January, shortly after 5 p.m. I was proceeding" . . . A voice from the Bench struck into his imagined words. "Speak up, can't you?" A difficult gentleman, Mr. Courthope, and likely to be none too merciful with this pair, for of all things he most resented the unemployed, and for the last ten years his wrath against them had been growing. He must remember to speak up, to speak as one is trained to do. Training. That was it. Duty.

"Ivy, I thought you'd gone. You won't go, will you?"

"Never, my darling. Nothing shan't part us."

Headlights reared up above the hill. They neared, they slowed to a standstill. The willow boughs stood out, black as charcoal, they cast the pattern of a net on the snow. With a sigh, with a feeling of profound embarrassment, the policeman stepped forward.

THE MOTHERS

THE children of England get their primary schooling either in national schools or church schools. Only a blind man could remain unaware that the school at Long Twizzel was a church school—and he, if he got inside it, would have known by the smell, which was vaulted, mouldy, and gothic. It was a very small building with an inordinately high-pitched roof. Over the peaked porch was engraved in curly figures 1859. Inside, high above the chimney-piece and the rusty stove-chimney, was a faded water-colour portrait of a young man in Hussar's uniform, and under the portrait was painted in letters equally curly: D. C. H. 1833-1855. *Christi in pauperibus suis.*

For years the water-colour Hussar had been no more than a variant of the school walls, like the lancet windows, and the map of the world with British possessions coloured pink. The windows were cobwebbed, the map was fly-blown, the young man was faded. They were all educational, all of a piece. But in September 1939 Mrs. Pitcher began to tell the class how the young man, full of virtue and gallantry, had died for his country fighting the Russians, that he was young Mr. Dewhurst Charles Hunter, and that the sorrowing Hunter family had built the school in his memory. This revived his colours. Every child in the village knew Sir Charles and Lady Hunter, who came to Long Twizzel every autumn and shot partridges—though with no perceptible sorrow for a soldier son.

Mrs. Pitcher herself was another demonstration that the school was a church school. She was a middle-aged woman with an anxious contentious face and a bilious complexion.

Every line of her body, every note in her voice, registered superiority and how painfully superiority is attained and preserved. She had a crippled husband, who cleaned the church. It was also rumoured that he cleaned for Mrs. Pitcher, and cooked their midday dinner—a fact, if true, equally disgraceful to himself and to his wife.

To be so superior, to have so many sick headaches and a husband who cooked for her, added to Mrs. Pitcher's statutory unpopularity as village school-mistress. Mrs. Mutley, Mrs. Bing, Mrs. Alsop, and Mrs. Bert Hawkins—whose maternity provided a steady quota of the Long Twizzel school attendance—were always on the look-out for further reasons to dislike Mrs. Pitcher. Now, to her affectedly small consumption of beef sausages, her stuck-up airs at Holy Communion, her nonsense about birds'-nesting, and her old rainproof, the war added a series of rousing new grievances. War was no sooner declared than Mrs. Pitcher started putting ideas into the children's heads. She told them about the bombing of Warsaw, and the shooting of Polish civilians. She told them of hospitals burning and children starving. She told them about submarines and food supplies, and made them wear their gas-masks for half an hour every Monday. When she started to tell them about German concentration camps and the persecution of the Jews it was felt that these outrages had gone far enough. A deputation of mothers, sullenly mumbling, called upon Canon Dimple, and Canon Dimple called upon Mrs. Pitcher.

"One must remember, Mrs. Pitcher, that these are simple country children. They are not likely to come in contact with these horrors."

"That is why I thought they ought to hear about them. If we are in the war, they should know it."

"Surely, surely! Of course we must all take our part in the struggle. For instance, there are the special prayers. You use them, do you not?"

"Every morning."

"Excellent, excellent! Then I have been thinking that it would be good to set up a School National Savings effort. *That* is a campaign in which we can all share."

"Several of the children are buying savings stamps already. But do you think that's enough?"

"Well, every little helps. And later on, no doubt, there will be other openings for service. The farmers, for instance, will certainly need occasional labour. And for the rest I venture to suggest that it will be wisest to concentrate on the British effort. After all, Mrs. Pitcher, we are British first and foremost. Well, I suppose we must soon be thinking about Christmas decorations. *Good*-afternoon, Mrs. Pitcher."

Concentrating on the British effort, Mrs. Pitcher soon afforded the village mothers another reason for dislike. She had two sons in the army, and both were non-commissioned officers.

"My son here and my son there, and sticking up bits from picture papers all over the place," said Mrs. Mutley. "I suppose she thinks she owns the war."

Pictures of Libya, pictures of India. In the autumn of 1941 the pictures of India were supplemented by pictures of Singapore. In January 1942 the pictures of Singapore had to be removed and their place filled by pictures of the United States—for, as Canon Dimple remarked, we are English-speaking first and foremost. The shadow of death is always a reconciler, and for some weeks after the fall of Singapore every mother in Long Twizzel, overlooking the past, was sedulous to inquire of Mrs. Pitcher if she had heard anything about Sergeant Pitcher yet, if she expected to hear soon, if the strain was not terrible, and if it was not too awful to think of any one being taken prisoner by those torturing little Japs; and in return Mrs. Pitcher, more than ever ghastly with superiority and sick headaches, would speak with a rigid elegance about patriotism, sacrifice, and a willing endurance.

By the spring, of course, she was as briskly loathed as ever. Indeed, Mrs. Pitcher was always particularly unpopular in spring because of Nature Study.

In spring it is the duty of every village school-mistress to foster a love of nature and kindness to animals. While encouraging the children to gather wild flowers for the Easter church decorations she must remind them not to uproot primroses and violets, or tear up bluebells, or break off boughs from fruit trees, or trespass into the Manor woods after daffodils. In spring too she must avail herself of young lambs and birds' nests as the ideal means of approach to a reverent understanding of biological processes, and also prevent the children from stealing birds' eggs, cutting the wings off fledglings, and throwing stones at valuable pedigree calves. For years Mrs. Pitcher had hated spring. In spring her headaches were at their worst. In spring her chilblains broke. In spring the cuckoo came, and sang on and on, shouting her down as she led the school prayers and the recitations of the multiplication tables and the "The Lake Isle of Innisfree." In spring the children were nothing but little nuisances; and the lambs and the birds were nothing but nuisances either—always provoking to sin, and not able to look after themselves.

In the spring of 1942 Mrs. Pitcher realized with horror that a pair of swallows had chosen to build in the peaked porch.

"Shoo, shoo!" she exclaimed, waving her umbrella. "Don't you build here, you silly creature!"

The mother swallow flashed past her, no more to be turned aside than a bullet.

There was nothing for it. On the morrow Mrs. Pitcher gave the children a lesson on the swallow. The swallow, she said, is a migrant. Every spring swallows come to England in order to have their little ones, flying all the way from Africa, led by the most wonderful instinct (*and more fools they*). All through the summer we can see them catching flies, horrid little stinging flies, in order to feed their babies. And in autumn, warned by an instinct equally wonderful that there would be no more flies, they gather their young ones and fly back to Africa (*if they have survived to do it*).

"Africa's where the fighting is," said Mona Mutley. "I expects lots of swallows get killed there now, don't they, teacher?"

The swallow, with young ones to feed, catches more than twice its own weight of flies in a day, continued Mrs. Pitcher. Every one loves the swallow, so clever, so harmless, and so useful, catching the flies that would otherwise become such a nuisance. Such wonderful little birds have had many beautiful poems written about them.

"Your other son's in Africa, isn't he, teacher?" said Ruby Bing.

On no account was the swallows' nest in the porch to be touched. Any child climbing up to finger it, or daring to steal one of the eggs, would get the cane. For they must all be proud that a mother swallow had chosen to build on the school, actually inside the porch. Next year the swallows, if not molested, would come again. And perhaps by then, said Mrs. Pitcher, they will have seen a great British victory in Libya, and we shall be at peace.

The swallows' nest became an obsession with Mrs. Pitcher. If the birds had been building in her stomach she could not have been more painfully aware of them. Above the yawns and the giggles and the scuffling feet and the droning voices of the class she heard the whirr of the swallows' flight and their twittered conversations. Steadfastly glaring at Bobbie Mutley or Irene Alsop she still saw their shadows flash past the window, momentarily flicking aside the steady beat of the sun. The plastered nest, the beam splashed with their droppings, the fragments of down that stuck to it—she knew it as well as her own parlour. And hearing the first squawks of the fledglings she began to sweat and tremble. Still the nest was untouched. She could not make out why. She had not noticed that the children realized—better than she, maybe—how jealously she watched over the nest in the porch, and so found it more convenient to go birds'-nesting along the hedges.

One wet Saturday she said to her husband that she reckoned the young swallows would be flying by midsummer. He looked up from his own preoccupation, and said:

"Looks like Tobruk will have fallen before midsummer, too. Why don't you think about your own flesh and blood for a change, instead of those bloody birds?"

His expression was so haggard and furious that she turned away and began to busy herself with the window geraniums. Suddenly, with a sort of bark she rushed out of the room.

In the school-porch was Kenneth Fearon. Why him? she thought; he had always seemed a negligible creature, pale and dull and born to be bullied. He had thrown a rope over the beam and noosed it, and now was swarming up the rope. She caught him by the collar and swung him down.

"Now what are you up to? Are you after those swallows?"

He was silent, staring at the ground.

"Are you after those swallows, I say?"

He drooped before her. With the tip of a pale tongue he moistened his pale lips.

"Why can't you leave them alone? Don't you know it's wrong to take birds from the nest? Why, it's cruel! Think of the poor mother!"

Still he was silent.

"Do you hear what I say?"

He wriggled, and wrenched himself free. Scrabbling up handfuls of pebbles he began to stone the nest.

"I hate them! I hate them! I wish I had a gun, I'd shoot

the lot. No, I wouldn't! I'd catch them and wring their heads off."

The porch was full of his screams, his stampings, the noise of pebbles spattering against the beam. Suddenly the swallow flew in. Straight as a bullet she aimed herself at the nest, folded her wings, disappeared. A moment later the doorway was darkened by the shape of Mrs. Fearon, panting violently.

"What are you doing to my Ken? I could hear him half across the village?"

"I shall have more to do to Kenneth," replied Mrs. Pitcher. "He is a very naughty boy."

"If you dare lay a finger on him . . . Look at his clean collar, all pulled about. Never you mind *her*, Ken. Come along with me, and shut up, do!"

"I hate you all!" he exclaimed; and escaping between them ran down the street.

The swallow flew out again, to hunt more food. The two women, their anger dashed by embarrassment and a kind of dismay, stood watching its flight, each glad to have an excuse not to look at each other. Smoothing back her wet red hair Mrs. Fearon mumbled:

"Upsetting a child like that . . . Now he'll be sick, like as not."

"You had better put him to bed," said the schoolmistress coldly. She began to walk across to her house. Mrs. Fearon unnoosed the rope, and followed her, looking like a frustrated hangman.

"Good-afternoon, Mrs. Pitcher. Good-afternoon, Mrs. Fearon. *What* a dreadful day!"

Composing themselves they turned and greeted Mrs. Dimple.

"Still, I dare say the gardens need it. The Canon was saying that if it weren't for the hay he'd really have to pray for rain! I've just seen Kenneth, Mrs. Fearon. So wet, poor child!"

"Oh!"

"Any more airgraph letters from your boy in Libya, Mrs. Pitcher?"

"No."

"Ah, well! Of course he's busy just now, isn't he? How lucky I am to meet you both! I'm just going round to explain to the members that our next Mothers' Union meeting will be on the twenty-first. The Canon is going to talk to us on Motherhood. Of course, you'll both come, won't you?"

WITH THE NATIONALISTS

NOT since the war (which he had enjoyed extremely) had Mr. Semple known livelier satisfaction than he now felt, entering the lounge of the Hotel Aurora, in Salamanca.

Though Mr. Semple had been a rich man all his life, his social convictions compelled him to live modestly. No one seeing Mr. Semple at home, going to his office by tram, returning to a homely supper and a quiet respectful Mrs. Semple, and going to bed at ten sharp, would have surmised that Mr. Semple owned a very tidy little shipping business. But at a time of national emergency Mr. Semple could match himself to the greatness of the hour, ride in a Daimler, dine at the Ritz, make himself agreeable to a hostess at a night club with anybody, since in times of national emergency Mr. Semple's importance made him a charge upon the public funds. Even when summoned to London to attend an inquiry upon some ships of his which had happened to sink in the Bay of Biscay, under circumstances which could never be ascertained since the ships were not fitted with wireless and all hands were lost, Mr. Semple preserved his custom of being paid for, his host on this occasion being Mr. Ignatius Wumphrey, senior partner in the firm of Wumphrey, Tabb, and Maligo, dealers in church and table wines, and an old business friend.

When Mr. Semple visited London a few months later in order to give evidence that a cargo of Wumphrey's celebrated Fino Puro had paid all port and customs duties, it was Mr. Wylde-Biggs, totally unconnected with the wine trade, who had the pleasure of paying for Mr. Semple. But when the next national emergency arrived, causing Mr. Semple to travel to Spain, it was Ignatius Wumphrey who sketched his route and supplied him with introductions.

It would, of course, have been a simple matter for Mr. Semple, a business man upon a business errand, to procure a visa for Nationalist Spain through the Foreign Office, but Mr. Wumphrey strongly recommended an alternative mode of travel through Portugal, which had, he said, many advantages. So Mr. Semple travelled through Portugal, enjoying a few days' repose and sightseeing with one of the British Non-Intervention Observers, and hearing much that was interesting and admirable about the Government of Senhor Salazar. In the Observer's car, a Mercedes-Benz, he reached the frontier; and after a little pause, and a drink with Senhor Silveira (who had been the third passenger in the Mercedes-Benz) he went on to Salamanca in a Frazer-Nash with Herr Beinlein, who had been doing a little business with Senhor Silveira.

At intervals Herr Beinlein pointed out some deplorable aspects of the Spanish landscape, its aridity and brutish lack of charm; and deplored the absence of forests; but otherwise the conversation was non-political. Herr Beinlein exposed his project for opening, quite soon, an automobile works in Spain, expatiating on the advantages of Spanish metal and the Spanish labour-market; and though Mr. Semple did not go so far as to offer Herr Beinlein a donation towards this project, he thought about doing so; for as a patriot he could not be unaware of storm-clouds on Britain's horizon, and it seemed to him there was much to be said for placing a little nest-egg abroad.

"You will like to wash-up," said Herr Beinlein, in the tone of one knowing the English through and through. "Well, at the Aurora Hotel the sanitation is admirable. It was installed by a German firm."

Left to himself, Mr. Semple turned a number of white

porcelain taps, but no water came from any of them. It was vehemently hot, and the air rang with klaxons and loud-speakers. Mr. Semple stepped on to his balcony. He looked down on a street thronged with cars, on a wide pavement thronged with strollers, on a café thronged with bald heads and newspapers. Every one was behaving in a very character-istic manner. The military characters were walking with military precision, the religious characters seemed borne along without feet on a favouring gale of suavity, the ladies in the cars bowed and smiled and waved their fans with feminine grace, only the waiters in the cafés went on be-having like waiters anywhere else.

"What a sight, eh? What animation, what dignity! The old Spain, romantic as ever, but brought up to date. Permit me to introduce myself. Charlie de Lobo. Are you newly arrived?"

Mr. Semple bowed from his balcony to his balconied neighbour.

"My name's Semple. Oh, thank you. I generally smoke my own, but I'll take one. I say, there seems to be something wrong with the taps in my room."

"Of course, of course!" exclaimed the serpentine young man. "Dear old Spain! You must ring and ask for a jug."

Mr. Semple hesitated.

"They all talk English here, you know."

Mr. Semple said: "As a matter of fact, I have rung."

"Spain, Spain!" fluted the young man. And disappeared from his balcony.

But the quality of the whisky more than atoned for the quantity of the water, and Mr. Semple had scarcely seated himself in the lounge before Mr. de Lobo's friend, Mr. Washington Kelly (also a journalist) had ordered him a double. The next round was paid for by a Mr. Beetle, who did so, he said, as a representative of his dear old friend

Iggy Wumphrey, from whom he had heard of Mr. Semple's impending visit to Salamanca; and Mr. Beetle paid also for Herr Beinlein, Dr. Siegfried Muff, Major Kurt Fleischer, and Major Attila von Pugstahl. The two military gentlemen spoke English fluently, but were more austere in manner than Herr Beinlein. This, Mr. Semple felt, was quite natural. Dr. Muff, an expert in chemistry, stood the next round of drinks, insisting that it should be brandy. Charlie de Lobo protested that it was rash to mix grain and grape.

"As it is," he said frankly, "I have had terrible diarrhoea for a fortnight. It is quite a problem," he continued, turning to Mr. Semple, "acclimatizing northern stomachs. I don't know if it's the food or the heat, but really it has been quite truly a problem."

"A soldier-stomach knows no problems," said Major von Pugstahl.

"I don't know if those poor Wops have tummy-ache too," mused Charlie. "Of course it is not so much of a jolt for them."

Looks of disdainful indifference settled on the military countenances. Mr. Beetle and Dr. Muff started in to abuse the Italian forces, presently every one was abusing the Italians, though Charlie de Lobo, who had left his brandy and ordered himself a Pernod, put in a mitigating word. "I can't help it, it's my little weakness. But I *do* find the Latins rather appealing."

"Milksop swine," said Dr. Muff firmly. ". . . If you are not drinking that brandy . . ."

Abuse of the Italians became so loud and free that Mr. Semple, always a man of discretion, began to look around at the other guests.

"Fear not," said Herr Beinlein. "They don't get in here."

"This hotel," added Mr. Kelly, "is kept for the white races."

"Unless some journalist gets in," remarked Major von Pugstahl."

At that moment Mr. Semple saw a sudden look of constraint cross Mr. Beetle's countenance, and realized that for some time a courteous paw had been tapping his shoulder.

"Mr. Semple, I think," said the courteous paw's bland voice. "I heard of your coming from Ignatius Wumphrey. In fact, he asked me to keep an eye on you, you know. My name's Tancred Wormegay. And here, come especially to greet you, are two of the most distinguished men in Salamanca. General Fusco and General Bottesini."

Tancred Wormegay had that air of being a hybrid between an angel and a clothes-horse which enabled Mr. Semple to recognize him instantly as belonging to one of those old English families which are at once almost innumerable and very distinguished. The two Generals were short and swarthy. They held themselves extremely upright and streamed with sweat.

Mr. Semple was pleased to see some Spaniards at last—he did not count the waiters. Moreover, Ignatius Wumphrey had told him that Tancred Wormegay, for all he looked such a nincompoop, was the very man to put through that little piece of business which Mr. Semple had at heart. So he smiled upon the Generals, and, knowing no Spanish, addressed them in French.

"*Comment portez-vous la Générale Franco?*"

The swarthy visage did not light up. Mr. Semple turned to the other General.

"*La Générale Queipo, est-il bien?*"

"*No!*" exclaimed the second General, in a tone so round and decisive that it did not seem, somehow, applicable to anyone's state of ill-health. Mr. Semple glanced round for Mr. Wormegay, but Mr. Wormegay was occupied in ordering drinks. Relieved to find that the second General spoke English, Mr. Semple continued:

"You're Spanish. Good! Shake hands. Tell your friend that . . ."

But the hand of friendship was ignored, and the Generals began to pour out a torrent of angry foreign words. Mr. Wormegay turned round in a hurry, snapping his dry fingers. Both the Generals addressed him with indignant bellows, and as they bellowed they pointed at Mr. Semple. Mr. Beetle, Mr. Kelly, and Charlie de Lobo joined in. Only the Germans remained aloof and impassive.

"I'm sorry, Semple, but you've made a bad break. General Fusco and General Bottesini are Italian. The Italians—er—don't like being mistaken for Spaniards. It's—er—quite understandable. Er—one wouldn't, would one? But I think you had better authorize me to apologize to these two gentlemen on your behalf."

The apologies were made, and umbrageously accepted. More drinks—since some glasses had been overturned, and others unaccountably emptied during the misunderstanding —were ordered. Peace was restored. But now the two Generals would do nothing except glare at the two Majors, and the two Majors did nothing except glare back. Feeling that something must be done to restore harmony, Mr. Semple said,

"Well, what about the Señoritas? When am I going to see them?"

But his confidence had been broken, his voice was not so loud as usual; and the inquiry passed unheard, for at the same moment Mr. Wormegay and his Generals rose.

"My friends must be going. Their duties, as you will understand, do not allow them much spare time."

(The two Majors stamped to their feet.)

"And I, I'm afraid, must be getting along too. But I shall call for you to-morrow morning, Mr. Semple. You have arrived just in time for to-morrow's ceremony, you will see Salamanca *en fête*. A parade of the Moorish troops. And the Archbishop . . ."

Mr. Wormegay's voice took on a thrilling note of tenderness, sank to a reverent hush:

". . . is going to present them *all* with medals of the Sacred Heart," concluded Charlie de Lobo.

TO COOL THE AIR

POUNDS melt away in dollars, and when I was living in New York in the summer of 1939 I thankfully frequented a cheap department store in West 14th Street where, as the season advanced, the wares seemed ever more lavish, garish, and fugitive—like flowers from a penny packet.

I was there, gathering a few random poppies, so to speak, when I came on Miss Filleul. It was a long time since I had seen her and I had no idea that she was in America, and at first I did not know who she was. Inevitably we recognized each other as compatriots by our hats, so realistic and so English. We were engaged in the English custom of not noticing when suddenly I realized that it was Miss Filleul. We advanced to a meeting through the counters of beach wear and play suits and Mexican hats, and vast garden lounges, and presently we were saying that we should have known each other anywhere.

"Oh, quite ten years ago, I should think," said Miss Filleul airily. "Where was it, dear? At Selfridge's?"

Middle-aged then, Miss Filleul was middle-aged now. Now, as then, she wore a neat tailor-made suit and untidy beads. Her hair was still braided in shells over her ears, and the short umbrella dangling from her arm swung madly as she made her rapid, pecking gestures, and though she was certainly hotter now than she had been then, her face was exactly the same shade of pink and her neck a deeper shade of pink than her face. Except for a sprinkling of Trylons and Perispheres, Miss Filleul was unchanged; it made the recognition more poignant to find Miss Filleul exactly, so to speak, where I had left her—in a department store during a summer sale.

"Still shopping," said Miss Filleul, reading my thoughts. "Isn't this a wonderful place? As nice as Fifth Avenue, and so much cheaper. I'm sailing on the twenty-fifth. On the *American Merchant.* I'm buying things to take home. Look, this is what I've got for Angel."

She spilled out of a bag a pair of cotton pyjamas, colour-printed with palms and cocktail-shakers.

"No, that's not Angel. That's Edward Cook. He's an archdeacon now, you know. But just as simplehearted as ever. Here's Angel! No, that's poor Clara—or is it Helen Bidworthy? Have you heard, she's taken up psychoanalysis, only she calls it something else, psycho-something-or-other, a word like 'chiropody.' *Therapics!* The effect is just the same, only some sides of it are left out. Clara, I mean, of course. Not Helen Bidworthy. Nothing would tear her from her cockers. This is what I've got for her. Do you see? Dogs' heads all down it. I went to the man's department for that. One's always sure of dogs in a man's department. Personally, I like the St. Bernard best. Ting-ting! There's that funny bell again. It reminds me of the Alpine cow pastures. But where's Angel's? I can't have lost it. I hope I haven't lost it. It's a wonderful shade of—here it is! No, it isn't," she said, looking speculatively at a magenta bathing suit. "I can't have bought this for Angel."

"I think you picked it up by accident when you picked up Archdeacon Cook's pyjamas."

"Good heavens! No doubt I did. I might have stolen it, mightn't I? Now that I look at it, I see that it is not in the least like Angel's cardigan. I do like these New York shops so much. Such astonishing things! It will be almost like returning from the tropics, you know. And what a time I shall have with the customs! I think I shall have to do a little smuggling. Why shouldn't I? It all goes on armaments now, and I've been Peace Pledge Union for years."

"You must be careful," I said. "Smuggling's much more dangerous now that it all goes on armaments."

"Dreadful!" exclaimed Miss Filleul. "No wonder we come to the World's Fair to forget all about it. Isn't this a delightful country, dear? I don't mind the heat at all. Particularly here, where that little bell keeps on ringing, sounding so cool and so much like Switzerland. Do you know, it's my belief they ring it on purpose, to cool the air."

"It does sound pastoral," I said. "But somehow I don't believe it's to cool the air."

"No? Well, then," said Miss Filleul, "I'll tell you what else it may be. I expect it rings every time any one buys anything. To encourage the shop people, you know. These big American shops do so much of that sort of thing."

From behind a canoe a salesman leaned forward and explained that the bell was rung to summon important members of the executive staff to the telephone.

"How ingenious!" she said. "And how clever of them to know it's for them! I don't believe I should ever learn, however hard I listened. But everything's so different here. A different civilization, really. Nicer," she added, in case the salesman should feel slighted. The salesman said that the bell was also used to convey a warning through the departments if a shoplifter were loose in the store.

Miss Filleul, engaged in ramming back my Aunt Angel's cardigan and Archdeacon Cook's pyjamas, did not seem to hear. Her face was flushed with the struggle and the paper bags crackled like a small thunderstorm. The umbrella swung frantically and grazed my nose as I stooped to pick up three pairs of socks—one peacock blue, one canary yellow, one striped. I suppose that these also had been bought in the man's department, and though there were no dogs on them, I asked: "Are these for Helen Bidworthy, too?"

"No, no! They're for Edward. At least, they're for Edward's secretary, such an excellent young man! His mother was a widow and left very badly off, for her husband went away with a fortune-teller, and when he was born he was an albino, and she was in despair, for they were so terribly poor they had to make money somehow, and people do have a prejudice against albinos, you know. But just then Edward became an archdeacon, so he took the poor boy for his secretary and has never regretted it. And she is so devotedly grateful! And he simply adores bright colours. I suppose it is compensatory, don't you think?"

We had moved out of earshot of the salesman, who, still peering round his canoe, looked after us with regret. And when he reappeared a few minutes later it seemed to me that he had tracked Miss Filleul to the perfume counter as poets track nightingales.

"Pardon me," he said, "but did the lady happen to take away an air cushion?"

"Take away an air cushion? No! But I will. It's just what I want for old Mr. Cowls. How fortunate that you should suggest it! Terrible sciatica, poor old soul, ever since the cat set fire to the summer-house. There's that bell again. How innocent we were, dear, to suppose it was just to cool the air!"

We returned to the canoe and bought an air cushion. The salesman seemed somehow troubled, but that may have been because the cat and the summer-house were not further developed. When Miss Filleul extricated her note-case to pay for the air cushion it came out with a shell bracelet dangling from it. And dangling from the shell bracelet was a price tag.

"Are you thinking of Undine?" she said. My face must have looked thoughtful, but I was not thinking of Undine. "*Now,*" said Miss Filleul, "we will go and enjoy ourselves among the Notions."

"I think you should come and have a drink with me," I

suggested. "Doesn't that bell remind you of ice clinking in a tumbler?"

"One minute! Let me run through my list and see if I've got everything." She laid down her parcels on a counter bubbling with cheap gloves and handed me a neatly typed list. "You read, dear, and I'll check."

" 'Clara. Handkerchiefs.' "

"Right."

" 'Angel. Something woolly.' "

"Right."

" 'Edward. Something typical.' "

"Right."

" 'Helen Bidworthy. Bathing suit.' "

"Right."

" 'Mr. Cowls. Air cushion.' " I had read this before I could stop myself. I looked at Miss Filleul with embarrassment.

"Right," said Miss Filleul calmly. She had just finished re-arranging her parcels, and the hands that came out of a brown paper bag and twisted its corners together were now, all of a sudden, encased in light-blue silk gloves. She looked up and caught my eye.

"Gracious goodness! I've just caught sight of myself in that mirror over there, and do you know what I've done? All this time I've been wearing my hat hind-part-before!"

Easy as a squirrel, she removed her hat, reversed it, and put it on again, dabbing it into place with Mary-blue silk paws. "Whatever shall I do next?" she inquired with interest.

A saleswoman from across the aisle came up to offer Miss Filleul the use of a hand mirror.

"Thank you so much, thank you so much! There, it looks better this way, doesn't it? But I'm getting more forgetful every day. And here in New York I'm so excited, I'm really not fit to be out by myself."

"You must be careful crossing the streets," said the saleswoman. "Traffic's faster here than in England, I believe. Hope you like our city."

Swinging her bag, her umbrella, her parcels, Miss Filleul began to express her admiration and to demonstrate the right-hand drive.

"I shall be so confused when I get back that I shall certainly get into trouble with the police again. Did I tell you, dear, how I was actually summoned for reckless driving? I was coming away from Mildred Fanshaw's—it's the house on the left with those marvellous hydrangeas that completely block the view into the road—and as I turned out I suddenly remembered poor old Dr. Lavender and forgot to sound my horn—he's almost stone-deaf now, you know—because I'd promised to fetch him for the village glee competition, and seeing how late it was—Mildred always talks so much there's no getting away from her—I momentarily forgot everything and turned straight into Mr. Goodbody's handcart. He's the new sweep. And being a new-comer, he complained to the policeman, who's a new-comer too, and if it hadn't been for dear Henry Erskine sitting on the bench and explaining everything to Dr. Lavender, I really might have been in Queer Street. I wonder if Mildred would like these gloves."

"Come and have that drink," I said.

"Well, my dear, that's very sweet of you. But mind, I insist on paying my share. And do you think we could go somewhere quieter, somewhere where there isn't a bell? I am beginning to find that bell a little monotonous. I wish the man had not told us about tinging it for shoplifters. One doesn't like to be reminded of such things."

We went to a place where there was no bell. Miss Filleul drank a sturdy whisky-and-soda and continued to charm the listening air with news from Devonshire. All around us I saw faces bewildered and bemused. And when at last we went away, kind helpful hands gathered and held out to us the parcels which had fallen from Miss Filleul's plenteous lap.

Whether Miss Filleul is an absent-minded innocent or a brazen and accomplished thief, I cannot decide. But it really doesn't matter. What matters is that, absent-minded or brazen, Miss Filleul, with all her presents, got home.

I would dearly love to know what Archdeacon Cook thought of the cotton pyjamas, so brightly colour-printed with poems and cocktail-shakers, and whether he wears them in his Morrison Shelter.

OUT OF MY HAPPY PAST

WHEN I was young there were two things that I lived for. One was music and the other was advice. In the matter of music I was fairly eclectic; I liked listening to it, performing it, transcribing it and composing it. In the matter of advice my tastes were purer; I only liked giving it and, to interest me, it had to be uncontaminatedly my own.

If the young are sufficiently single-hearted, they can generally get what they want. By the time I was twenty-four, I had the trustees of the late Mr. Andrew Carnegie paying me one hundred and fifty pounds a year for keeping up my interest in English church music of the sixteenth century, and an attentive circle of young friends calling at my flat in London for advice and guidance. I had a considerable clientele of the middle-aged also, but it was the young I really valued. Though the passage of years had disillusioned me, I was still young at heart.

Of all the young people who came to me for advice, Billy Williams came oftenest, came most urgently, and was most welcome. He had a great deal of temperament and a great deal of intellect; it was gratifying to have such a brilliant creature relying on me, the more so since he could argue the hind leg off a donkey (the only trait, I suppose, he derived from his father, who was a K.C.). I had first met Billy when he was still at school, where he was successful, popular, and unhappy. At home he was merely unhappy. I had not met his parents, for on the two occasions when he took me to his home, they happened to be already in bed, and Billy and I sat in the kitchen looking at a large volume of Hogarth prints, discussing whether there was a place for morality in art.

Billy left school with a scholarship to New College, Oxford. Going to the university is traditionally a weighty step in a young man's life, an advance from tutelage to independence. I shall never forget the evening when Billy Williams came to see me just after his father had given him his first cheque-book and an exhortation on what a young man must know. He came into my flat pale and trembling, appalled by his father's too abrupt introduction to the responsibilities of English manhood, and I sat up with him for hours, soothing him and explaining about the banking system and assuring him that I had had a cheque-book for years and had never suffered from not obeying the advice printed inside the cover about keeping it under lock and key when not in use. At last the colour crept back into his cheeks and the trusting look returned to his eyes, and we made another brew of coffee, and about three in the morning he walked home, quite happy again and leaving his cheque-book behind him.

The action of the trustees of the late Mr. Andrew Carnegie enabled me to see quite a lot of Billy Williams while he was at Oxford, for my work on sixteenth-century church music involved consulting some music manuscripts in the Bodleian, and the Bodleian closes at dusk. This was fortunate, for during the autumn and winter Billy Williams continued to need advice. The teashops and the Botanic Garden, the Cherwell and even the Northam Road heard Billy's fevered questionings and my lucid replies. It was just the same trouble as before. He was successful, popular, and unhappy. His acrobatic dancing was the admiration of all who saw it— even dons granted that he had unusual talents that way; his tutor assured him that he would get a first in Greats if he would only give his mind to it; and various other people of standing were urging him to go in for politics, interior decoration, or the church, only premising that he should give his mind to it.

Meanwhile, his mind was given over to doubts and questionings and to a growing conviction that he should quit this sort of thing and become a simple artisan. The Oxford climate disagreed with him, the quantity of pseudo-Gothic architecture weighed on him like a catarrh, and more and more he found himself morbidly drawn to go and look at the Shelley Memorial, where the poet is made to appear as though he lay drowned in his bath. The root of Billy's malaise, I told him, was æsthetic. No one could live contentedly in his section of college, where there was so much pitch pine and so many cusps. I advised him to move out and find lodgings in the town with a kind landlady and some cheerful photogravures after Marcus Stone, where he would be allowed to keep a cat.

This conversation took place on a dreary winter's afternoon. We had been for a walk to Boar's Hill and had spent some time standing in a sleety rain looking at the outside of Gilbert Murray's house. We said farewell with chattering teeth, and going back to London by train, I knew that I had caught a cold and suspected that my advice had not been so restorative as usual.

It was a few days later, and I was still sneezing, when my doorbell rang. A middle-aged lady stood at the door. She said: "You are Miss Warner, are you not?"

I agreed and asked her to come in.

Seating herself, she looked at me with a resolute but unquiet glance and remarked: "I am Hubert's mother."

I could only recall one Hubert, and he was an orphan.

Looking at me more sternly, she continued: "Hubert Williams."

Then I remembered that Billy Williams was called Billy because he was also called Williams and that he had once confided to me he could not endure to be addressed by his baptismal name, as it gave him the feeling he was in disgrace. So this lady, no doubt, was Billy's mother. Perhaps she too had come for a little advice. With the impression that some kindly gesture must be made as soon as possible, I said: "Do let me take your umbrella."

She gave me the umbrella as though it meant little to her just then. Clearly she had come in search of something, but scarcely advice. People who come for advice do not stare about the room as though they have mislaid something, and those who await wise and soothing words do not have their ears cocked quite so alertly as this lady's. Could it be that she had lost the key with which she locked up her cheque-book and wished to borrow money? I felt that on the whole I would rather lend than counsel. For though to advise two generations of a family simultaneously should theoretically produce ideally harmonious results, I had found in practice that it did not work out that way.

"We are rather anxious about Hubert. I think you saw him not long ago. How was he?"

I said that he seemed to be catching a cold and added that Oxford is a place where one catches colds very easily. Then I sneezed. She turned her examining glance from my desk to my nose. I said I thought it quite likely that my cold was derived from Billy's. My hope that this might make her feel more at home with me was unfounded. She continued to look uncomfortable and displeased and to stare around the room while I went on to say that Cambridge, too, encouraged colds and that the draughts inseparable from Gothic architecture were a clear proof that people in the Age of Faith had little regard for human life and human happiness.

Her face became suddenly red and she exclaimed: "Hubert left Oxford two days ago without telling any one where he was going. It is very worrying for us and quite inexplicable. Why, it's only a few days more to the end of term!"

This last sentence seemed to me very odd, and I might have asked her why she would have felt it less if Billy had waited till the end of the term before disappearing, but she went on: "I'm sure you will forgive me for coming to see you like this. I know you have been so kind to Hubert, and the poor boy has such an admiration for you."

Mother love can do anything. Red in the face, genuinely agitated, and weeping with mortification, she nevertheless conveyed with clarity a conviction that her son was slightly infatuated with a charmless harpy, and probably at this moment in my coal-hole.

It is difficult to dry the tears of a person who doesn't like you. It is difficult, too, to dislodge a respectable English-woman who thinks her son is in your coal-hole. I wished then that I had not taken away her umbrella, for, though without consoling properties, an umbrella is always a reminder that one is due to go away again. I was very sorry for her. I could see that she was a woman with strong passions and an orderly nature, and such a woman would deeply resent mis-laying any one of her children.

"Perhaps he wanted a change of air."

"Why? Did he talk about going away?"

"No. But a bad cold in the head might drive one to any-thing. Had he been borrowing any Bradshaws, do you know?"

"All his friends have been interrogated. Not one of them knows anything."

I said it looked like a sudden decision.

"It has been a terrible disappointment to his father."

I became increasingly sorry for this poor woman. If at last she relinquished her theory that Billy was in my coal-hole, she would very likely turn to a theory that he was drowned in the Thames. And a husband so liable to disap-pointment would be more of a responsibility than a comfort. I began to wonder if I should not advise her to run away too. She could explain the step by saying she was going to look for Billy and, once away from home, she might develop new interests.

"Of course," I said, "if one enjoys travelling—and I know Billy does enjoy travelling—one might feel a sudden impulse to go to some place one has read of. Don't you ever feel such impulses? I think Billy told me you sometimes went to Fiesole. Italy must be wonderful at this time of year. I suppose it is just one mass of anemones and——"

At that moment my bell rang again, and the sleuth look returned to the face of my visitor.

It was a telegram. It said,

"FEELING SO MUCH BETTER PLEASE WRITE SINNER'S ARMS MARRAMACK CORNWALL BILLY."

I betrayed Billy without hesitation, betrayed him for his own convenience. It seemed clear to me that if his parents remained much longer in ignorance of his whereabouts they would be having him searched for by the police and that the police would sooner or later find him, and then he would be fetched home and there would be a great deal of recrimination, reconciliation, loss of dignity, and subsequent references to the expense of tracing one's child through Scotland Yard. Whereas, if they knew his address, they would almost certainly content themselves with writing some reproachful letters of forgiveness, which he need not read unless he wanted to. So smiling, I said: "You needn't worry any longer. Here's a telegram from him."

Having grabbed it and read it, she recovered herself and said musingly: "What an extraordinary address!"

I hadn't paid much attention to the address. I said that Cornwall was full of queer place names—Marazion, for instance, and St. Just-in-Roseland—and that many people found them very attractive.

"The Sinner's Arms," she repeated.

"Some inn, no doubt. Some crested Cornish family called Sinner."

"I have never heard of a Cornish family with that name," she said.

But when she had got over the address, she became strangely melted and forgiving and told me how relieved her husband would be to know that Hubert was safe in Cornwall. She told me, too, about her other children and their difficult temperaments, and I gave her some general recommendations on the best way of dealing with adolescents. She stayed on till after dusk and then invited me to go home and have supper with her.

One hundred and fifty pounds, even when paid regularly by the Carnegie Trust Fund, was a narrow income, and I had made it a rule of life never to refuse a free meal. I don't know why she asked me. It may have been as hush money to her conscience for having misjudged me, it may have been that she thought it would interest her husband to have a look at me, it may even have been that she felt it would be as well to have another woman around while she broke the news to him that his son was safe in Cornwall. If it was hush money, her conscience could not have needed much hushing, for it was a very moderate meal—poached eggs on a tray, Mr. Williams was still out and about being a barrister and snatching a mouthful at his club. When he came in we told him that Hubert was at a quiet little village called Marramack, in Cornwall. My obligingness in getting a telegram from him was mentioned, but I realized that Mr. Williams saw nothing in me—I doubt if he even saw me as a bad influence. And when I made a move, he rose with alacrity to let me out. With his hand on the latch, he said: "What I cannot understand is his failure to appreciate Oxford. He has always pretended to *like* architecture."

I said that the amount of architecture in Oxford was perhaps almost overwhelming. But he shook his head, as though I were paltering with the truth in a witness box.

When Billy Williams came back from the Tinners' Arms (for that was the name of the public house, but the telegraphist could not have known about the Cornish mining industry), I told him of his father's parting words and expressed the opinion that they were rather pathetic. He disagreed, saying that they were not in the least pathetic, they merely showed that his father was a snob. I advised him to cultivate a broader outlook towards his parents; by doing so, I said, he would insure himself against possibilities of irksome and unavailing regrets after they had passed away.

A NIGHT WITH NATURE

THE English summer of 1921 was exceedingly hot. By the end of June the overworked grass in Hyde Park was turning brown, leaves were falling, and Borough Sanitary Inspectors were ordering carbolic powder to be sprinkled around gutter-gratings. It was unusual, it was almost portentous, to see the rosy bloom of carbolic powder in London streets before the end of the season.

As for me, I was doing pretty well, because the Printed Books department of the British Museum was allowing me to work in the North Library. Just to walk through the Reading Room and push open those swing doors gave me a sensation of cool elegance. But on Sundays I felt the heat like any one else.

One Sunday afternoon my friend Billy Williams came to see me. He was wearing a new pair of corduroy trousers, and in consequence smelt very rural. I commented on this, and said he was as refreshing as a day in the country.

"Why don't we go and have a day in the country now?" asked Billy.

I said it was rather late in the day to start.

"Well, a night in the country. Here, listen to me! We'll find some agreeable heath, and sleep out. I'm sure we both need a night with nature. How much money have you got?"

Summer is always an expensive time for me. I buy green peas and roses off barrows. I had one shilling and ninepence and a pearl necklace—but pawnshops are closed on Sundays. Summer was an expensive time for Billy too. The beggars in the street looked so thirsty, poor things, and relays of his cousins came up from the country, needing to be squired around. But by some special providence he had five shillings and fourpence.

We spent some time looking at a map of London and its environs, and debating where we might find a heath that wasn't Hampstead. Passingly, we were strongly drawn towards the Bugsby Marshes; but though the map showed them to be totally uninhabited it indicated the South-Metropolitan Gasworks near by; and where there are gas works there are often railings too, and other obstacles to spending an unfettered night with nature.

At last I made some sandwiches, and we walked down to the end of the street, and studied the destination boards on the buses. The pavement was intolerably hot, and that was probably the reason why we got on a bus that went to Croydon.

Though it was exhilarating to see the Crystal Palace looking so like the Crystal Palace, and to count the public-houses and places of public worship along our route and see which won, it took a long time to reach Croydon, and when we got there we seemed no nearer to nature. However, we found another bus, whose conductor assured us that for the price of twopence we could be carried, as he said, glancing at Billy's trousers, "into the wilds." I said to Billy that I expected he thought we wanted to bury something.

At the end of our tickets he waved us off the bus with an enlarging gesture. Standing in the road and watching the bus dwindle away we certainly felt that we were in the wilds, even if we were not altogether in the country. There is something peculiarly wild about the outskirts of London, they are wild in a lunatic way, as though they had been driven so.

We scrambled up a bank, and found ourselves in a landscape of rough fields broken with old gravel-pits, and prickled with notice-boards advertising Land for Sale. The browned blossoms were showering off the elder-bushes, and there was a strong metallic smell of London. We were hot and hungry, and so in a devil-may-care spirit we sat down and ate the sandwiches. After that we felt better, and walked on more gaily, and presently were rewarded for our trust in nature by finding a deserted laundry.

What made the deserted laundry even more interesting and delightful was that it was no mere antique, but of quite recent construction. Strolling through its empty halls and tapping rusty boilers we speculated why it should have been abandoned in its young prime, and Billy worked it out that almost certainly troops returning from some Eastern campaign of the late war had brought back plague with them, and that the laundry had been built hastily and privily under a government contract to wash the plague-stricken garments; and that with the armistice it had been cast aside like a withered flower. The situation of the laundry, he said, practically proved it. If you had to hide the existence of a laundry from the nation this would be the ideal place for it. To this I replied that I remembered the late war much better than he did, and could assure him that if the War Office had wished to conceal a laundry from the nation it would have built it on the summit of the Wrekin, installed several funicular railways and smothered the whole in periwinkles. It seemed to me much more probable that the laundry had been run up to meet an expected increase of rescued fallen women due to war conditions, but that the increase had not justified expectations, and so the Rescue Society had discarded it in a pet. Just as we were leaving the laundry, talking quietly about the previous generation, Billy stooped down and burrowed under a patch of dandelions and came up with half a crown.

Feeling yet more trust in nature we walked on, looking for a heath where some smoke, *gracefully curling* as in the song about the woodpecker, Billy said, would indicate a cottage that would give us supper. It was cooler now, the sun was setting, and as we walked we sang duets by Purcell. Presently we came to a heath—as much heath as we needed, for there was some heather, and a scrubby little wood, and no notices to tell us to keep off; and near by was the cottage that would give us supper.

From the first I was not sure about that cottage. For one thing, it was really a villa; for another, there was no smoke, graceful or otherwise, curling from its chimneys; for yet another, it was named Osborne—and people dedicating their house to the nastiest known biscuit were unlikely to be hospitable; finally, it had a pasteboard in the window which announced Bed and Breakfast. People called Osborne, I said to Billy, who proclaim Bed and Breakfast mean what they say. To ask such people for supper would be like asking the Moderator of the Church of Scotland for a free pass to Lourdes, if he took my advice he would look around for something more latitudinarian, like a King's Head or a Spotted Cow.

Unfortunately, this was one of the occasions when Billy would not take my advice. The door was opened by a woman with a great deal of vigorous hair under stern control, and a stern clean face. Without a word she shot us into a parlour and looked us up and down, keeping a large table between herself and us.

"We see you have beds and breakfasts," was Billy's ill-judged opening.

She replied:

"It depends."

"So we hope you may have suppers too."

She seemed quite unaffected by our hopes.

"We don't need any beds, we are sleeping out," continued Billy, "But we should love some supper. Eggs and bacon would do perfectly. In fact, it's really breakfast we want, but we want it now. It's merely a question of turning night into day."

"I never serve suppers to strangers," she replied. "Very sorry, but it's a thing I don't do."

"Surely that's very illogical," said Billy, sitting down and taking her cat on his knee. "For strangers are just the people who need suppers. If we lived here we should now be having supper in homes of our own; but being strangers, how can we get supper unless we come to you for it?"

By now the cat was leaning on Billy's bosom; and if he had been alone I don't doubt but that the woman would have seen the light of reason that shown on Billy's brow and illumined his words. Unfortunately she saw me too, and she had taken an iron dislike to me. So Billy and the cat were torn apart, and we went off to look for a Spotted Cow, Billy remarking that such women wove Old England's winding-sheet faster than any harlot's cry.

We could not find a public-house. All we found was a widow who sold minerals. This time I advised Billy to leave it to me; and by explaining to the widow that my brother was an artist suffering from shell-shock and that I was hoping to find him a quiet home in the country I got some bread and ham, and the widow's assurances that he would come all right in the end.

The minerals were warm, and the ham was stringy, but the bread was all right. We smoked to keep off the midges and listened to the fern-owls, and when the midges had left off biting we burrowed ourselves nests in the heather and lay down to sleep.

Heather has to be exceptionally bushy and well grown before it is tolerable as a bed; and this heather was stunted and patchy. I was lying on my back, yawning, and looking at the stars between my yawns, when I heard a slow, rustling approach, which I took to be that of a cow. But it was a woman, carrying a large bag and trailing things behind her. She turned from side to side, she seemed to be looking for something. Billy woke, and sat up, and she hurried towards him. It was us she was looking for.

"Good evening! I do hope I have not disturbed you. I have brought you each a blanket."

We thanked her for this, and begged her to sit down and have a cigarette.

In the half-hearted summer darkness she seemed to be rather cloudlike, with a round pale face like a misty moon. But the spurt of the match displayed a wrinkled and rather missionary countenance, the face of one devoted to high hopes.

"Such a beautiful night, isn't it? Midsummer! And you have come out for a midsummer night's dream. But even so, I expect you'll be glad of blankets. This one's a real horse-blanket, the other's Witney. I often sleep out myself, you know."

We said it was a nice thing to do.

"It's how one *ought* to sleep. You are wise. I think the young are always so wise. Have you come far?"

"From London."

"Ah, yes! London. I've got a husband in London. But we have very little in common. I like to live in harmony with nature, and you can't do that if you're always going to the fishmonger's."

"I suppose your husband is very fond of fish?" I remarked.

"He likes haddock. I don't know if you can call that being fond of fish."

"No," I said, having thought it over.

"Smoked haddock, I suppose?" said Billy.

"Yes, I think so, I believed it was smoked. But I try to put all that sort of thing behind me."

Her tone was slightly rebuking, so we sat in silence, repressing the remarks about haddock that kept bubbling up in us.

Billy, following—as he afterwards explained—the light of reason, inquired if she were a vegetarian. In a pleased voice she said she was.

"So are we. We have been vegetarians for years," Billy exclaimed enthusiastically. "Sylvia's a total vegetarian. Personally, I incline to follow Arbuthnot."

"Arbuthnot?"

"His touchstone is legs. *Nothing that has legs*, that is his first Commandment. Eggs, but not chickens. Tadpoles, but not frogs. Molluscs, but not crustaceans. Fish . . ."

He stopped short. Again we were leading this poor woman back to haddocks. Speaking as a total vegetarian I began to pick holes in Arbuthnot, pointing out that legs are implicit in tadpoles, and that if principle were to count for anything . . .

Musingly she said:

"But pigs have legs."

It seemed that she must have sat down on a rejected piece of ham. Wishing that Billy were not always so anxious to please, a fault nurtured in him by too much family life, I began to meditate how I could explain that some ham had been given us through mistaken kindness, and rejected on principle. She must have very keen sight to see the ham in the darkness, and if she had known it was there just by sitting on it she must be as sensitive as the Princess in Hans Christian Andersen. But perhaps she had nosed it out? Meanwhile Billy was speaking of the guiltless gaiety of pigs, their beautiful characters, still cheerful and trustful after centuries of exploitation. It was rather as though Tolstoi were speaking of the Russian moujik. She listened, but without much concurrence, so presently he moved on to divination. It was strange, wasn't it, that mankind had never attempted to divine the future by the curls in pigs' tails? Did she believe in second-sight?

"But surely I'm not mistaken? You *are* the young couple who called at Osborne and asked for bacon and eggs?"

Billy's laugh rang out, free and untrammelled.

'How ridiculous! Yes, of course we are. It shows how easily these absurd misundertandings arise, how impossible it is to hope to be a historian. We asked for bacon and eggs just to make it easier for her. But we should have given the bacon to the cat. And Sylvia would have given her egg to me, because earlier in the day she ate my share of the lettuce sandwiches as well as her own."

"I see. Yes, that explains it all. At first, when you spoke of being vegetarians, I thought there must be some mistake. You see, I felt sorry for you being turned away like that that I decided to come out and look for you. She's my land-lady. But quite, quite darkened. I shan't stay with her long."

I said that she struck me as darkened.

"So conventional! So dreadfully narrow-minded! It's im-possible to make her realize the joy of life. I'm afraid that's one reason why she wouldn't give you supper. So I thought, The poor young things, I'll take them some tomatoes. Wait a minute!"

While we waited, murmuring about kindness and the pangs of hunger, she was fumbling in her bag.

"Here are some candles to begin with. There! I always think candles look so pretty burning out of doors. I don't suppose they'll set fire to the heather, do you? What's this? Oh, I think that's soap. Here are the health biscuits, I'm afraid they're rather crushed, but health biscuits do crush, don't they? Tomatoes! Here are some peanuts . . . no, those are the malted milk tablets. *These* are the peanuts. And in here, you see"—she removed the lid of a small milk-can—"I keep my cheese and butter."

"Heavenly tomatoes," said Billy, with juice running down his chin.

"Do have another! Take two. Do you know their old English name? *Love-apples!* I always prefer to call them love-apples."

"What a wonderful bag," I said.

"It's my camping-out bag. I often sleep out, too. Or some-times I light a candle and read some beautiful poem. But you won't need poetry, I'm sure. You *are* poetry."

A trifle stiffly Billy said:

"She's church music."

The lady gave me a sharp glance. In it I could discern a clear resemblance to the glances given me by the lady at Osborne. Unwilling to be scorned twice in one night I muttered:

"Sixteenth century."

That seemed to put it right again. She begged me to have some more love-apples, and said she could tell by my hands that I was musical.

When we had finished our tomatoes, and some health biscuits, and all the peanuts we wanted, and had smoked some more cigarettes we began to wait for this kind lady to go away. As Billy had foretold, the air of the heath was much cooler than the air of London. In fact it was by now positively chilly, and I began to wind the Witney blanket around me, leaving the horse-blanket—a wrap with more definitely virile associations—to Billy. When the candles guttered out I sank furtively into the heather and the blanket, and drowsed, while the lady and Billy talked on about ghosts and aunts and Richard Jefferies and vaccination and the Suez Canal. When I next became conscious she had lit some more candles, and Billy was saying we must sing her our Purcell duets. So we sang *Two daughters of this aged stream are we*, and *Let us wander, not unseen*, and finally addressed each other as *My Dearest*, and *My Fairest*, and expressed a mutual compulsion to languish. If there were any poachers or game-keepers about they must have thought it very odd. But the lady sat there, wakeful and approving, her beady eyes bright in her shabby face and fixed on us in hungry attention. It was as though she too were waiting for something, just as we were waiting for her to go. At last some far-off church clock began to strike twelve. She rose with a flutter, and gathered up her traps. Out of her bag fell an alarm-clock.

"Would you like it? No, you don't need it. Happy creatures, the birds will wake you. Well, good night, good night! I shall be sleeping out myself, a little farther on. I shall think of you. Just leave the blankets at Osborne. Good night. Be happy!"

She rose, the candles burning at her feet made her seem tall and vaporous, as though she might lift into air and vanish. Suddenly she exclaimed:

"I never think evil."

Billy gave me a glance of anxious interrogation. I shook my head, and reassured he began to roll himself up in the horse-blanket. I waited till she had trailed away out of ear-shot, then I blew out the candles. They left a warm sweet imprint on the impartial air of night.

THE DOG'S TRAGEDY

IN MITCHELL COUNTY, North Carolina, we had a neighbour, a kind woman who was a Seventh Day Adventist, and the scones she baked were as plump and light as down pillows. She was a big stout woman with eyes like a bull's—small, honest and bewildered. Like a bull she would come charging up through the pasture to our cabin, hurrying to bring us the scones while they were still hot. She was so nice to us that we itched to perform some retaliatory kindness.

Many large women are timid. When she told me that Mr. Macdonnell had to go into Tennessee on business I was not surprised to hear her add that she was feeling nervous at the thought of being alone at night. Here was my chance. I would stay the night with her, I said. She demurred a little, said it would be a shame to fetch me out, said their place would not be so comfortable as ours. But I was firm with her, and had my way. That was how I came to see the picture of "The Dog's Tragedy."

It hung in a corner of the room, and overnight I did not notice it. The morning sun placed it before my eyes, and its story struck full on my tender early-morning consciousness. The bulk of the picture showed a wide and turbulent river, full of cross-currents and boiling eddies. In the foreground was a rock. On the rock was spread out, tidily and thriftily, a toy sailing-boat, a butterfly net, a child's hat, and a child. The child was a little boy, about three years old. He lay so flat that it was obvious he was in a fainting condition. It was also obvious that a minute before he had been in the water, for rivulets, scrupulously painted, were trickling from him. (Even before the most story-telling picture technical considerations will intrude, and though the story of this work of art was harrowing my feelings I had time to think how those rivulets would have rejoiced Ruskin.)

Half in the water, half supported on the rock, was a large black and white dog, a Newfoundland, or perhaps a Labrador, or perhaps just a trusty cross-breed. He was looking at the sailing-boat, the butterfly net, the hat, and the child, and one could see at a glance that he had just rescued all of them from drowning, being one of those dogs to whom water is a natural element, and brave and kindly acts the commonplaces of an existence selflessly devoted to man. All of this could be read in the Dog's countenance; and the way his tongue lolled out showed that it had been no easy matter, even for so strong and watery an animal, to drag those four helpless objects from the flood. But there was more in his face than that: there was a look of disillusionment, of growing uneasiness. Plain as print the Dog's face said: "I've done my duty. *But what's gone wrong?*"

The rest of the picture made that clear. On the river's further bank, solitary amid forest and mountain-side, was a log-cabin; and in front of the cabin, holding up her hands in horror, was a woman. There she stood, gazing across at her half-drowned and inaccessible child. For between her and the rock flowed the wide turbulent river, and just foundering in mid-stream was a canoe.

Very likely it was her shriek, echoing through the mountain solitudes, that had first brought it home to the Dog that something had gone wrong. In a minute or two it would all burst upon him: his fatal error of judgment in laying a delicate, half-drowned child on this comfortless and isolated rock instead of carrying him back to where his mother could get at him. Then in an agony of regret he would say to himself: "Damnation! I've gone and done it again. There's no pleasing that woman." But now the poor darkened devoted intelligence was travailing with the first suspicion that things weren't so good as he'd meant them to be.

Lying in bed I stared at the picture of "The Dog's Tragedy," and tried to pry some mitigating circumstances out of it. Maybe a man would come and do something? But if so the woman would be off fetching him, whereas she stood motionless, the image of despair. No. Either she was a widow, or her husband, like Mr. Macdonnell, had gone into Tennessee on business.

But the dog was a strong dog, and the child, though temporarily so limp and damp, probably had a good deal of stamina. After a while the Dog could tow him back again, and fetch, on subsequent journeys, the hat, the butterfly net, and the sailing-boat. So strong and willing an animal would think nothing of a little extra trouble. I looked at the river. It wasn't the sort of a river to do a child any good, and another trip through it would infallibly ruin the hat. Even if everything passed off better than one dared hope, even if the child suffered nothing worse than a cold in the head and the hat was an old hat anyway, the Dog would never get more than the poor credit of having retrieved an error.

I could bear it no longer. I got up and began to dress. There were several other pictures around the room, and a magazine with an article about the Dies Committee, saying that the Dies Committee was saving the United States from subversive elements. But I found no comfort in them. The pictures were just pictures of babies and prize cows and great-uncles, the material from which tragedies are made. For "The Dog's Tragedy," I said to myself bitterly, is the tragedy of any one of us who tries to do good to others. However courageous we are, however selfless and devoted, and however well we can swim, it's a hundred to one we get it wrong somehow, and land the child on the rocks instead of restoring it to its mother. The Dies Committee themselves, devotedly saving the United States from subversive elements, will find that they have handed over the United States to something worse.

All day my thoughts were coloured by these gloomy reflections, and at dusk, going for a stroll down the dirt road that led to the main road, I was pensive still. Presently I saw Mr. Macdonnell driving home, and he stopped for a neighbourly word. I asked after the business in Tennessee. He said it had gone all right, and I thought: Well, if it's just a business deal, maybe that's so. But not if there's any philanthropy in it. Then I said:

"Mrs. Macdonnell will be pleased to see you back so soon. Last night she felt rather worried at being alone in the house."

His face cracked open in a smile.

"I guessed she might be feeling that way. Marilda has always been wild to sleep up at your place, but till now she's never got around to it. Marilda, she's got quite a passion for sleeping in other folks' houses."

Half in the dirt road, half clinging to an imagined rock, I and the Dog kept each other company.

PERSUASION

IT WAS the First of May. A false premature summer made the asphalt of the pavement flabby underfoot. Colours were too bright, sounds too clear to be wholly comfortable. All along the street the little trees were coming into blossom, their various rose-colours colliding with the red brick of the houses. Each house had a very small front garden, each front garden had a flowering tree. At the end of the street was a spit new church, red and white, like a cake iced in the austerest good taste.

It was the First of May, and in Europe, and America, and Asia, and Australasia, and Africa, people were walking in procession behind red banners. A year ago Mr. Alban had been walking behind a red banner, too. Now he was walking down Esmond Road, N. W.3, carrying four doughnuts in a light cardboard box and a volume of Jane Austen from the Public Library.

Seeing him walk off with *Emma*, the Public Librarian had stifled a cry, as though at some monstrous rape.

Mr. Alban, too, strongly disapproved of his choice. He and Jane Austen had nothing in common. He wished he had never read a word of the woman, he scorned her characters, he scorned her style, and he scorned her. But he had once incautiously lent his ear to the siren, and now he could not keep off her. He would be sober for months on end, then the craving would start up again. On his way to fetch her he would tell himself that he enjoyed reading Jane Austen because she gave such a perfect picture of the bourgeois mentality; and once or twice he mentioned this to Public Librarians.

But the moment he had dragged her into his den and sat down with her upon his knee he had to give up this pretence. He read her because he liked her. Meanwhile, he was man enough never to buy her. She was his light-of-love, he kept her in the Public Libraries.

It is hasty to assume that all Trotskyists wear whiskers. Mr. Alban, for instance, was a clean-shaved man. He had an ominous intellectual look, his clothes were shabbier than they needed to be. He was Foreign Language clerk at the office of Pinn, Harvey, Justin, Pinn, and Colley, stock-brokers. Clients of that firm, catching sight of him through a glass-topped door, were astonished at his revolutionary appearance, some of them even raised their eyebrows at him.

Though Mr. Alban now looked like a man going home to tea, carrying a parcel from the confectioners in one hand and a book he would read at tea in the other (as was indeed the case), he was also closely involved with all those people who were marching behind red flags. They were taking part in a demonstration. Mr. Alban was being a counter-demonstration down Esmond Road.

Last year he had marched in company, demanding an afternoon off, saying in unvarnished tones: "Tomorrow afternoon I shall not be here. I shall be in Hyde Park." And Mr. Colley, wearing a splendid home-grown Polyanthus in his button-hole, had bowed to the will of the people, replying: "By all means, Mr. Alban." For even in the firm of Pinn, Harvey, Justin, Pinn, and Colley, Mr. Alban had never made any concealment of his political views. They knew he was a world revolutionary, that he was only biding his time in the firm till he could overthrow it. Sometimes Mr. Colley would argue with him about the necessity for money-markets, the place of financiers in the universe. Suave and flabby, he was no match for Mr. Alban, and seemed unaware of his peril.

Last year Mr. Alban had marched with the Independent

Labour Party, though his heart had been a roaring raging furnace of doubts and scruples. Hemmed in among Communists and Christian Socialists he had compared himself to a rattlesnake compelled to take part in a circus parade. The rattlesnake is untamable, it will never tune the wild music of its caudal bones to the strains of a United Front, never demean itself to wriggle to the piping of Moscow. Coming into the Park he saw the banners displayed before him, do as he might he could not keep his eyes unspotted from the beaming black-a-vised countenance of Stalin. "Just like a great tomcat," he said to himself. And aloud: "Whoosh!"

The boy marching in front of him turned round, startled. His heels had already been kicked several times, it is the fortune of demonstrations, but this was the first time that the kick had been accompanied by a cry of "Whoosh!"

"That's right, comrade," he replied.

But now the United Front had been formed, and Mr. Alban marched alone. He turned off from Esmond Road and continued his counter-demonstration down Melina Street. Melina Street had no front gardens, no flowering trees, no newly-iced St. Alphege. It was a street that began shabby, and soon grew shabbier.

Stepping more proudly, swinging the doughnuts, Mr. Alban muttered: "These are the localities we need. The worse the better." And a moment later, as though he had kindled it, he saw a small red flag waving on a doorstep. It waved violently, expressing the rhythm of a series of heartfelt yells, and the hand that waved it was the hand of a very small boy. A stout woman was sitting on the doorstep, she had one arm around the boy and was trying, in a tolerant and rather inattentive way, to stop him yelling.

Just as Mr. Alban approached, another woman put her head out of a window of the opposite house.

"What's up?" she inquired. "What's he howling for?"

"He's thinking of the demo," said the woman on the doorstep. "We'd promised to take him, got him his flag and all. And now he's gone and got pink-eye."

"Poor mite," said the neighbour.

"Couldn't have taken him, you know. Ten to one he'd have passed it on to all the other kids. So Dad and Freda and Walt, they've gone, and I've stopped home."

"Oh well," said the neighbour, "you won't be sorry for it, with your feet."

The stout woman looked up at the sky. "It's a lovely day," she said regretfully. The little boy gave another yell, and a sudden flourish of his flag, which dislodged *Emma* from under Mr. Alban's arm. The stout woman left off looking at the sky, grabbed the boy, drew in her feet, and said: "Sorry, Mister."

Mr. Alban said:

"Don't mention it, comrade."

A feeling of profound annoyance and dejection swept over him. All these demonstrations and pink-eyes, all this worthless, easy-going good nature . . . he heaved an arid sigh as he picked up Miss Austen. But duty called.

"I am glad to see your little boy with our red flag. I hope he will carry it to good purpose, later on."

"Oh yes, he'll go next year all right," said the woman on the doorstep.

"So'll you, I dare say," said the opposite neighbour in an undertone. Mr. Alban disregarded her.

"And not only in demonstrations, I hope. In the revolution."

Now that the child had left off yelling in order to stare at him the street was revoltingly silent.

"Why, indeed, in demonstrations at all? Where do they lead us? Into Hyde Park!"

"Not always," said the intolerable woman at the window.

"Into Hyde Park," reasserted Mr. Alban. "We go there like sheep, licensed sheep, allowed in by the kindness of the police and the ruling class. But does that bring the revolution nearer?"

No one answered his question. The window woman said that she was glad to hear that he found the police so kind, and the child said:

"Want to go to the Park."

"So you shall," said Mr. Alban genially. "It all belongs to you, you know. So do all the splendid houses in Park Lane, and all the sweeties in the shops, and all the . . ."

He had never had a lucky manner with children. As a rule, they did not respond at all. Now, and it was just as bad, this child was going to respond too much, squirming out of his mother's grasp, his eyes fixed on Mr. Alban in confident anticipation.

"Going to the Park," he chanted. "Going to the Park *now*."

Mr. Alban withdrew himself a little, just to make things easier. Throwing off the fairy-godfather he said arrestingly:

"But will you go there under the right leadership? That's the question." And he fixed the woman on the doorstep (he had no hopes of the other) with a compelling glance.

"He'll go there with the right lot, all right," she said rather grumpily.

Meanwhile, several people had collected and were listening to his conversation. There was a shop-boy, and a one-legged man, and a man with a dog, and a woman in a grey tailor-made who had *Social Worker* written all over her.

Turning his back on the social worker Mr. Alban addressed himself to the others. It was a red flag, he explained, which had attracted his attention. It was fine to see a red flag where it ought to be, waving in the mean streets instead of flaunting uselessly along a police-licensed route to Hyde Park. Here the child broke in again, but he got it down. Continuing, Mr. Alban pointed out that this May-Day business was a sop flung by the ruling class to the proletariat. "One day in the year," he said, "they grant you. But what about all the other days?"

A humorous man who had joined the crowd inquired: "What about Leap Year?"

The ruling class, continued Mr. Alban, weren't the only ones to laugh in their sleeves. For now the workers were being led up the path by a double-faced time-serving equivocating gang who pretended to be heart and soul for the toiling masses, and were secretly pledged to sacrifice socialism to a bourgeois bureaucracy. Yes, he would not deny it. He referred to the so-called Communist Party.

"What's going on in Moscow at this moment?" he demanded.

The intolerable woman said:

"May-Day."

"I can tell you," said Mr. Alban. "May-Day in Moscow is as much dope as May-Day here. A procession of deluded window-dressers parading before a grinning oligarch. But what's behind it all? Where's Trotsky?"

The boy with the bicycle said: "Mexico, ain't he?"

"And why is he in Mexico?"

The intolerable woman said: "Couldn't make Norway hot enough for him," and simultaneously a well-informed voice at the back said something about lung-trouble.

"Driven out," exclaimed Mr. Alban. "Driven out."

This was better than reading *Emma*; and yet not so much better (since at this moment his debased craving to do so was powerful and unappeased) that he did not feel a certain heroism of duty. Comparing Miss Austen and the woman at the window, who could deny that he was choosing the sterner path? He looked round on his audience. It was becoming quite sizeable, large enough to make him feel the helpfulness of a platform. He began to edge himself towards the doorstep. The woman sitting there wriggled to one side. He went up the steps backward, holding his hearers with his eye.

"And what about the Moscow Trials?" he asked. "Where are the Old Bolsheviks, the friends of Lenin, the defenders of socialism, the men bred up in the revolutionary tradition? Where's Tomsky? Where's Zinoviev? Where's Bukharin? Dead! And the British Communist Party stood by and smiled."

"Just like them," said the woman at the window. "Always the boys for a joke, aren't they? Larky lot, the British Communist Party."

All this time the woman who was so obviously a social worker stood there with her gaze wandering up and down him, a cogitating expression on her face. He was beginning to think better of her. Even the bourgeoisie may sometimes (though rarely) see the light.

"Year after year," Mr. Alban went on, standing dauntlessly on the upper step, though from that vantage point he had just noticed a policeman pause at the end of the street, "year after year that Stalin has pursued his ruthless wriggling way to power. To trample out the beacon of world revolution, to substitute for our glorious fighting tradition a . . . a pullulating bureaucracy . . . that's his object! Day in, day out, sleeping and waking, he has worked for this end, throwing dust in the eyes of the workers as he goes. Day in, day out, he has pursued this policy, this has been his only thought. And yet the so-called Brit——"

"Nonsense!" exclaimed the social worker. "Do have some regard for psychology. People simply aren't made like that. Do you mean to tell me that during the last ten years Stalin has not once spent five minutes watching a kitten?"

Rage made Mr. Alban dumb. Kittens? *Kittens?* Red herrings!

"Or Trotsky either, for that matter," said the social worker.

Mr. Alban clapped his hand to his forehead and glared. In another minute he would lose his audience. He must say something annihilating at once. But his wits, scattered by that fool of a woman, did nothing but go round and round, debating whether it would be more advisable to say that Trotsky often watched kittens, or that Trotsky had never looked at a kitten in his life.

"As a reader of Miss Austen," the social worker continued, "you really should have more regard for human nature. I see you have one of her novels under your arm. Which is it?"

And in an affable way, as if he had had the misfortune to have known her for years, she tweaked out the volume and opened it.

"Ah! *Emma*, I see."

"Emma?" said the woman at the window. "Well, I thought it was Emma Goldmann he was walking out with, but it's Emma Austen. Like as two peas, I dare say."

The social worker stood there reading bits to herself. The boy with the bicycle looked over her shoulder, and read aloud:

Though now the middle of December there had yet been no weather to prevent the young ladies from tolerably regular exercise; and on the morrow Emma had a charitable visit to pay to a poor sick family who lived a little way out of Highbury.

The man who had spoken about Leap Years now remarked that he had a poor sick family in Highbury himself. The social worker flipped over some pages. The bicycle boy broadcast another paragraph.

"I am sorry to hear, Miss Fairfax, of your being out this morning in the rain. Young ladies should take care of themselves. Young ladies are delicate plants. They should take care of their health and their complexion. My dear, did you change your stockings?"

There was a roar of happy laughter. The woman at the window instantly said:

"Well, what's there to laugh about? First word of sense I've heard this afternoon."

Hemmed in on the door-step Mr. Alban constrained himself not to dance with fury; and in a moment or two the social worker was handing him back the book, saying in boon-companion tones: "I'm glad you like Miss Austen." Meanwhile the first policeman had been joined by a second, and at the suspicious sight of a book being read in public they had drawn nearer. All of a sudden the child who had been the beginning of all this mischief began to agitate his red flag again, and to cry out:

"Here they are, here they come!"

From the further end of the street came a group of people. They looked hot and merry, and wore red favours and badges.

"There's Freda, there's Dad!" yelled the little boy, and dived through the legs of the crowd and made towards the newcomers.

A minute later the crowd followed, and Mr. Alban was left alone on the door-step, except for the social worker—who was now reading the name on the box that held doughnuts —and the woman on the doorstep, who sat there still, not looking at him and yet keeping an eye on him. There was a great deal of talking and exclaiming, and the foremost man, walking with difficulty, for the little boy was clasping his legs, came level with the steps and said:

"Hullo, Mum. Looks as though you'd been having a bit of a meeting too."

And then, nodding towards Mr. Alban, he said:

"Warm, ain't it?"

Mr. Alban, against his will, had endured a good deal. But to be asked, so genially, if it wasn't warm by a man whose lapel flaunted a hammer and sickle and the hateful initials

C.P.G.B. was the last straw. He leaped off the steps, and slammed his fist into the man's face. The bicycle fell with a clatter, the dog barked, and before you could bat an eyelid the two policemen were arresting the communist on a charge of unprovoked assault, and shaking him briskly. Before Mr. Alban could rise to his feet the social worker had stepped over him and button-holed the senior policeman, requesting him to be so good as to take her name and address.

"I'll lend you my pencil," she added kindly.

The junior policeman, who had been most forward in the arrest, muttered something about interference.

"I'm not interfering. I never interfere."

Mr. Alban opened his jaws to protest against this mendacity.

"I never interfere. Are you looking for your doughnuts? There they are, on the step, and I'm sure Mrs. Watson will dust them for you. You really ought to be more careful of your property, if you are in the habit of going about hitting perfect strangers in the face. You should carry a shopping-bag. You should consider your digestion, too. After forty, battening on doughnuts is a foolish thing to do. But if you must eat them, why don't you buy them at Pumfrey's? They're a halfpenny cheaper than at the Maison Delice, and nothing like so clammy. Believe me, you will never overthrow capitalism while you let yourself be swindled into paying twenty-five-per-cent extra for a French name (actually, it's Mugthrope), and a few fal-lals in a window. Try Pumfrey another time. A most respectable firm, and employing only union labour. Well, as I was saying, I never interfere. Are you ready, officer? Don't lick your pencil, it sets a bad example to your young friend here. Miss Phyllida (I'll spell it, P, H, Y, double L, I, D, A) Nettlefish (N, E, double T, L, E, fish), St. Faith's Hostel, 12 Melina Square. Merely a formality. I'm sure you know me as well as I know you. And when this case comes up you will kindly call me as a

witness. Of course it's a great waste of time, and I am a
busy woman. But if you must go about arresting the
wrong persons the least I can do is to appear in court and
say so."

The senior policeman was understood to remark that it
mightn't come to that.

"Oh yes, it will," replied Miss Nettlefish. "For one thing,
this gentleman here who is so fond of Miss Austen must
be given an opportunity to explain why he hit Mr. Watson
in the face."

The junior policeman began looking round.

"It's no use looking for her, she's dead. She died in
eighteen-seventeen. And, as I was saying, for another, this
habit of making indiscriminate arrests must be inquired into.
Only last month Miss Harrison, one of our best rescue-
workers, was taken up on a charge of loitering. Then there
was that very unfortunate affair of old Mr. Cohen, and the
trumped-up case against Billy Horlick's dog. You can see for
yourself, officer, this sort of thing is bound to end by getting
the police-force a bad name. It's entirely in your own interests, I assure you, that I am going to take all this trouble.
Personally, I believe overwork is at the bottom of it. I have
often said that your hours are too long, and your beats too
extensive, besides all this nonsense about having to keep
buttoned up in the hottest of weather. If all this results in
an inquiry—as I hope it will—we may even get conditions
improved. And that would be well worth any passing unpleasantness, wouldn't it?"

While Miss Nettlefish talked to the policeman Mr. Alban
and Mr. Watson—whom now even the junior policeman had
ceased to shake—began to exchange glances, and later, grins.
Now Mr. Alban advanced, and said:

"If you think I'm going to lend myself as a witness, or a
plaintiff, or whatever you like to call it, you're mistaken. I'll
have nothing to do with it."

"Goodness gracious, man, you mustn't say that! You'll be taken up for contempt of court."

"Do I understand," said the senior policeman hastily, "that you are making no complaint against this individual?"

"And when have I made a complaint?"

"Ah, but he knocked you down," said the junior policeman.

"Why shouldn't he? I hit him first."

"But you're losing sight of the point," interposed Miss Nettlefish. "I shouldn't be wasting a moment on this if it were merely a little matter of knocking-down. We're constantly knocking each other down in Melina Street aren't we, officer? But when it comes to the good name of the police . . . I shouldn't bother about that last doughnut, Mrs. Watson. I can see it's past praying for. Just fasten up the other three for the poor fellow. As I was saying, when it comes to the good name of the police, that is something which concerns us all. Doesn't it, Mr. Watson?"

The hand of the law having quitted Mr. Watson's shoulder he had picked up *Emma*, dusted it, and begun reading it, beginning at the first page. Now he looked up with a rather bemused expression, and said:

"Yes, Miss Taylor—Miss Nettlefish, I mean."

"Exactly. I knew you'd agree with me. And I don't doubt *you* agree with me too, though I don't so far know your name."

"My name is Alban. I don't agree with you at all. Why whitewash sepulchres, when . . ."

The senior sepulchre put his notebook and the pencil into his pocket, nodded to his companion, and began to walk away. After a lingering glance at the communist his companion followed.

"Stop, stop! You can't get away with it like that."

The two policemen strode faster.

"You've got my pencil! Drat the man, he's deaf as well as

blind! Such a nice wife, too. Well, I shall have to go after him. Good-afternoon! I suppose you know Mansfield Park? Mr. Gladstone liked it best of them all, I believe."

She hurried after the policeman, only pausing to advise the errand boy to make haste with that meat, and to exchange a few words with the one-legged man about his daughter's spectacles which needed mending.

The United Front temporarily established between Mr. Alban and Mr. Watson was fast dissolving, but before his convictions swept him out of speaking distance Mr. Alban exclaimed:

"My God, what a woman!"

Mr. Watson closed the book, and handed it back.

"She writes all right, but it seems a bit slow. Still, I dare say it grows on you."

LAY A GARLAND
ON MY HEARSE

IT WAS difficult, short of giving one's whole mind to the subject, to keep an accurate census of the Meridens at Foxholes. Just as one had become accustomed to Teresa and Egbert, Teresa and Egbert would return to Canada and Roy, Geraldine, Rosemary, Peter, and the twins, arriving from the Scilly Isles, took their place. Almost literally took their place. For Foxholes was a smallish house, and when the larger consignments of Meridens were in residence it was nothing for three Meridens to sleep in one bed. In summer, of course, it was easier. All the Meridens were hardy—"Quite gipsies, really," as they said, indicating a row of camp-beds extending down the central path of the kitchen-garden.

So, on the whole, it was safest not to dogmatize about the number of the Meridens. One just said that they were a large devoted family, that though fate and economics had scattered them over the British Empire, family affection brought them back to pay long visits to old Mrs. Meriden. Then one might add how lucky it was that old Mrs. Meriden still had her wonderful old Sarah, what a mercy it was that old Sarah still kept about so well, what a loss it would be when old Sarah no longer kept about—though of course Rosalind helped a good deal.

The very involutions of the Meridens' family devotion made it harder to number them. For instance, should Egbert, Jasper, and Bunny be counted as Meridens, or merely as the Messrs. Twillicoat, Hobson, and Webb whom Teresa, Faith, and Dorothy Meriden had married? I always reckoned them as one and a half Meridens; and the four daughters-in-law, Geraldine, Mary, Mary mi., and Molly, summed up, in my estimation, to three and a quarter Meridens. But then I have always been fond, in a piddling way, of arithmetic. Old Mrs. Meriden spun no such filigrees. They were all her dear children, she made no distinction between the bond and the free. The grandchildren were even more her dear children. The instant they were born she swallowed them whole.

Besides the Meridens, there were the Meriden animals. Each of them had a terrier or two, whether Teresa was in Canada or in Kent her bloodhound was at Foxholes: there were cats, Blue Beveren rabbits, a poultry-yard and the "household pony"—a faithful surly creature who pumped water and went on errands. All these animals had names. Most of the Meridens' inanimate belongings had names also —fantastic names: the umbrella-stand was called La Tosca and the lawn-roller Dr. Johnson. So ready were they with their christening wit that if I were having tea at Foxholes I never took a piece of bread-and-butter without preparing myself to hear a sprightly chorus exclaim:

"Oh look! She's taken Esmeralda!"

But however confused one might be as to the number of the Meridens, one could always be sure of Rosalind Meriden.

Rosalind was the youngest daughter, and unmarried, and always at home.

Always busy, too. Rosalind helped in the house and helped in the garden, and took the dogs for walks, and managed the Blue Beverens entirely, and was marvellous with all the children, and wonderful with old Mrs. Meriden, and the life and soul of the Women's Institute. She also drove the car, and every winter she played her fiddle in the Chorsley Operatic Society's production of a Gilbert and Sullivan. Always at home, and always busy, Rosalind's days, as she said herself, went by in a flash.

Rosalind's flashing days had carried her to the age of thirty, when Mr. Wilcox came to live at the newish bungalow in the Foxholes lane. He was a widower, a red-faced, grey-haired, globular man with a toothbrush moustache and round, goggling, codfish eyes. He sweated a good deal, but if by accident you touched him he invariably felt cold. He had a daughter who was at school, he had a weak heart, he had retired from a Bank in the Midlands to live quietly on his moderate means and breed bull-dogs.

It was certain that Mr. Wilcox and the Meridens should establish contact, the conjunction of bull-dogs and terriers made this inevitable. What no one had foreseen was that, even in the moment of kneeling in the road opposite Mr. Wilcox, each of them grasping the hinder end of a fighting dog, Rosalind should fall in love with Mr. Wilcox at first sight.

Love, as the poet Hogg sang, is like a dizziness. It will not let a poor body go about his business. Walking up the Foxholes lane, holding her bleeding terrier and humming inattentively, Rosalind forgot that she had gone out in order to buy stamps for the weekly letters to the far-flung Colonial Meridens. When old Mrs. Meriden observed on this omission Rosalind forgetting that it was tea-time, set out instantly for the post-office and remained away for nearly an hour. In the spiritless winter dusk she leaned on Mr. Wilcox's gate, staring at his bungalow, at his lighted windows, at his newly planted rose-bushes, emblems that Mr. Wilcox had come for good, that he was not merely a dream; she heard his bull-dogs barking, and smelled his dinner cooking. When she turned away it was with a heavy sigh. An hour ago she had fallen in love, and already it was a hopeless love, and Rosalind had begun to pine.

I fear we all took it for granted that Rosalind should love unrequited. All the Meriden women are cut from the same cloth. Plain as children, even plainer in maturity, in their

late teens they develop a certain carnal freshness and lus-
ciousness: the quality which the French call *beauté du Diable*
and the English, more poetically, bloom. Their eyes are
bright, their lips look moist, and a smell of new milk exhales
from them. After a year or so, their bloom goes off, and the
eyes that had been bright become beady, and the moisture
dries on their lips which remain slack and over-large, and
the smell of new milk decomposes into the ordinary smell of
poor mortal flesh—flesh kept clean, but still subject to the
various discommodities of humanity—varied by stronger fleet-
ing gusts of old dog, garden mould, or Californian Poppy.

So Rosalind, whose bloom had long ago faded, pined. But
being of a very honest disposition, and completely unself-
conscious, she doubled her pining with a perfectly open pur-
suit of Mr. Wilcox. Wherever he might be met, there was
she. If he spoke to her, she flushed with pleasure, and if he
did not speak to her, she spoke to him. As Mr. Wilcox's
heart forbade him to play tennis, Rosalind played tennis no
more, giving it as her excuse that she was too old to run
about: and then she would go and sit by Mr. Wilcox. As
Mr. Wilcox fancied religion, Rosalind became a devout
church-goer, and having failed to persuade Mr. Wilcox into
the Operatic Society she resigned from it herself. After a few
years she began to call him Prospero. His name, actually,
was Esmé.

The bull-dogs were an invaluable pretext, and during the
holidays she also cultivated Mr. Wilcox's daughter Olivia.
Olivia was a stony, shallow little baggage, she was abominably rude to Rosalind, and told every one that Rosalind
Meriden's one idea in life was to marry Mr. Wilcox. This
information was, of course, quite superfluous.

As for the Meridens, they did what they decently could
to detach Rosalind's steadfast attentions from Mr. Wilcox.
For one thing, they unanimously and quite properly thought
him not fit to black her boots; for another, they wished those

attentions to return to themselves. The dizzying nature of love made Rosalind much less satisfactory as a daughter, sister, sister-in-law, and aunt. Almost every night they heard Rosalind crying in her bedroom. They pitied her a good deal, especially for the first few years. As time went on Rosalind's unrequited love, like any other infirmity of long standing, became a matter of course. Even so, the assembled Meridens made a protest when, on Christmas Eve, Rosalind remarked that instead of staying at home to fill the children's stockings she was going down to The Rosery to rub Prospero's legs before he went to bed.

"Nonsense!" said old Mrs. Meriden. The rest of the family froze into a disapproving silence, glancing at Roy Meriden, the head of the family, for a lead. Roy slowly removed his pipe from his mouth and said: "I say, Rosebags. Isn't that going a bit too far?"

"It's only five minutes' walk," she answered. "That's nothing." And leaving them to scramble over the misunderstanding, she stumped out.

When Rosalind had been pining for nine and a half years Olivia Wilcox got married. It was a showy wedding, and she insisted on Rosalind being a bridesmaid. I don't think I have ever seen a more painful sight than Rosalind as a bridesmaid, wearing an arch period dress of shell-pink taffetas and a little mob-cap on the side of her large head. She had made up her face for the ceremony, her first experiment in face-painting. It was so derisively bungled that I could have sworn that Olivia had done it for her. There she stood, listening to Olivia and Olivia's gigolo bandying their vows, with tears streaming down her face, crying as frankly, as despairingly, as she cried in her bedroom at night. Afterwards she got appallingly drunk on champagne, and pursued Prospero about the room with a hired gold chair, begging him to sit down and rest his heart.

A month later she shot like a champagne cork into rapture.

Mr. Wilcox asked her to marry him, asked her if she could ever come to love a lonely middle-aged man. He would have asked her before, he added, but it had not seemed fair to her youth to do so.

With groans of wrath and relief the Meridens gave their consent; and before the week was out the omnivorous placid Mrs. Meriden was prepared to look on Esmé as another of her dear children, only needing the wedding day to be as full-blooded a Meriden as any of the rest. There was to be a short engagement, already there was a diamond engagement ring.

Meanwhile Rosalind went round telling everybody how happy she was and licking up congratulations like a bear licking up honey. It was really embarrassing to see one's half-hearted assentings vanish into that candid maw. I could only hope that when it came to the point she would swallow Mr. Wilcox with the same uncritical egoistic satisfaction.

The wedding was going to be embarrassing too.

For Rosalind was determined upon a very grand wedding, a wedding with every traditional floridity. She was to wear white satin, with a six-yards train and a wreath of orange blossom. Four bridesmaids, two pages, culled from the third generation of the Meridens, were to follow her. There was to be a three-tiered wedding-cake, a marquee on the lawn, heaven only knows how many camp-beds in the kitchen-garden.

A bevy from the Women's Institute was to strew rose-leaves before her, a bishop, raked out of old Mrs. Meriden's past, was to conduct the service, and the dogs were to wear white satin favours.

All this, needless to say, was Rosalind's own devising. But in the mood she was in no one could have stopped her, even Prospero was swept along by her enthusiasm. Indeed, now that she was sure of him, Rosalind became in a way rather inattentive to her Prospero. He was in every way perfection,

and he was hers. With that she dismissed him; all her ener-
gies, all her excitement, surging about the wedding, and the
trousseau, and the honeymoon, and the refurnishing of the
best bedroom at The Rosery.

One evening, when the invitations had been sent out and
replied to, and the champagne ordered, and the wedding-
dress stacked together; when Foxholes was filling up with
relations arriving and wedding presents being unpacked: one
summer evening Rosalind and Prospero went for a lovers'
stroll, and strolled down Foxholes lane.

"This is the very place," she said, "where first we met."

"So it is," said Prospero.

"Poor Henry J. Ford!"

There was a questioning silence, and she added:

"Henry J. Ford was the dog that fought your dog. He
died four years ago. Poor old Henry!"

"I remember it quite distinctly. I thought then, this is a
brave little girl. You were wearing a blue muslin dress."

"No, I wasn't. It was in November."

"Blue serge. That's it, blue serge."

Mr. Wilcox laid his arm round her waist.

"Ten years ago, eh?"

"Ten years ago, Prospero."

Mr. Wilcox's face came nearer.

"And have you loved me a long time?" he inquired
tenderly, "a long, long time?"

Taking a surer hold, discarding a puff of cigar smoke,
Prospero bent down for a kiss. The cigar smoke must have
obscured his vision, he did not notice that Rosalind's doting
expression had changed, even in that moment, to a look of
bewildered incredulity.

"Leave me alone, Prospero! Let go!"

He let go with alacrity, looking to see what threatened
him—a wasp, maybe, or some pin.

"I can't marry you. I won't."

"Rosalind!" Prospero's voice expressed pain.

"No! It's impossible. All these years you've kept me waiting, all these years I've been miserable, every one knew I was in love with you, you knew it as well as they did. But you never troubled to ask me till Olivia was married, till you wanted to make sure of a woman to look after you. You selfish beast, you selfish cold-blooded beast! But I see it now, thank God I've seen it in time! For I would rather die than marry you."

"You can't!" gasped Mr. Wilcox.

"*I can!*

"I can, I can," she exclaimed. "I hate you, I'm revolted by you, I'm done with you. This very evening, the moment I get home, I shall write an announcement saying that the wedding won't take place" . . . she put out her tongue, licked up a tear . . . "and send it to the *Morning Post!*"

A FUNCTIONARY

THE alarm-clock hauled him out of sleep. That was exactly the sensation, and for a moment he supposed that to the rattle of a winch, turned with unbelievable speed, he was being drawn up from a deep well into the light of day.

As he reached the surface he opened his eyes and knew where he was; and the stranger who had turned the winch with such commanding force had vanished, and the alarm-clock was not really so loud after all. Yes, though the room was unfamiliar, he knew where he was, and why he was there. It was the nineteenth of April, 1938; and that was why he was here, his alarm-clock rousing him an hour earlier than usual. He had not carried out an execution in this prison before. A provincial establishment: still, everything was very nice, very comfortable. The furniture was old-fashioned; but the fitted wash-basin flashed with chromium. In one corner of the room his dress clothes were laid out on a rather shabby red velvet armchair, in another corner was the box. Through the healthily opened window came the music of larks.

He jumped out of bed and stood before the window, breathing in the country air and scratching his ribs. His room was high up in the building, it overlooked the cheerful roof-tops, the chestnut alleys blurred with their first green, the spruce new factory buildings, the rolling country-side beyond, where the crops were already colouring the fields. Ah, what a country! Wherever one went there was something beautiful.

Unfortunately the window faced west, so he would not be able to enjoy the sunrise.

But the water that gushed from the chromium tap was very hot, was almost boiling, so though he could not enjoy the sunrise he would enjoy a good shave. A sweet lather, a fine blade, a steady hand. . . . Back from the mirror his small forget-me-not-blue eyes confronted him with the visionary gaze of a man who is shaving, and it seemed to him that there was something peculiarly upright and national in eyes so extremely blue.

When he had finished shaving he stripped off his traditional good old German nightshirt, and began to go through his gymnastic exercises. He extended his arms, he touched his toes, standing with his feet widely planted he swung his body round on the hips, he perambulated the room on tiptoe with a springing gait, he flexed his knees. Every muscle was in order, he felt himself to be sheathed in strength as in some elastic armour.

He attacked the last, the crowning exercise. There was a knock at the door.

"Come in."

He heard a tray being set down, and smelled coffee. The door opened.

"Heil Hitler! Oh, excuse me!"

"Heil Hitler," replied the executioner majestically. "Do not be embarrassed, I beg. The manly body is not ashamed of itself."

In spite of his elegant figure and his uniform the boy had a foolish, nincompoop appearance. It was clear to the executioner that he was the sort of boy who would always be sent about with trays, and that later in the day he would re-enter the prison guest-room with a broom and duster. So now he addressed him with particular heartiness, as though effecting a transfusion of the sturdy spirit he could so well afford to bestow on a weaklier member of the Reich.

"Aha! This is excellent! I have a splendid appetite, I assure you. This country air sharpens one up."

"Yes, it's going to be a nice day," the boy replied, walking around the executioner in order to reach the table by the bedside.

"Look out, look out!"

The breakfast things clattered on the tray as the boy tripped over the box and righted himself.

"I didn't notice it," he said.

The executioner was now aware that he definitely disliked the boy. There was a resonance of scorn in his laugh as he replied:

"Fortunately, you are not called upon to notice it. But that's no reason to spill my breakfast."

"I say, though! Somebody else will notice it, eh?"

"I consider my profession no laughing matter," said the executioner severely.

The boy who had put down the tray now stooped over the box. His breath dulled the polished leather, and that, too, exasperated the executioner.

"There it lies, all ready and sharpened. Like a fiddle already tuned. I say! May I have a look at it?"

"Certainly not! What a thing to ask! I don't carry a peep-show for children."

The wrath in his refusal was perfectly genuine. Somehow the boy's request, in itself quite natural, even laudable, had infuriated him. Irked by being naked in the presence of someone he so greatly disliked he turned away and began to pull on his vest and drawers.

"No, I suppose not. But surely you will give me your autograph?"

A little book with pages of various flower-like tints was opened. The pages fluttered, finally he was offered a blank page of primrose yellow.

"I don't carry round a pen."

A pen was put into his hand.

"And if you would add a few words? . . . How it feels, you know. Your sentiments."

"Sentiments!" exclaimed the executioner. "Why should I have sentiments? I do my duty."

And yet, thought he, sentiments might be permissible. For to be an executioner is a position of heavy responsibility. It might be that one's duties were painful to one, it might be that one was not always in the mood, and naturally one is not always at the top of one's form. Yes, a state executioner might sometimes suffer, just as the Fuehrer also suffered.

He signed his name on the primrose-coloured page, and under it he wrote: *I follow my Leader*.

And that, he thought, should be a lesson to the young fool.

The young fool stood gazing at the ink, waiting for it to dry. The notion that he had administered a snub made the executioner feel more benign.

"I dare say you don't often have a beheading here. No doubt you get quite excited about it."

"It is wonderfully exciting," said the boy. "But for me, especially so."

"Why for you in particular?"

"Well, you see. It's like this. She's my mother."

The nincompoop face flushed, and somehow expanded, and was like some mad flower. It seemed to the executioner that he was pushing it away, as one might push away an orchid whose breath was deadly fever.

When he had got rid of the boy he sat down on the bed and began to scratch. He began to scratch not because he was itching but because he was disconcerted, thrown out of train by the unpleasant shock he had received from that unpleasant boy. And the act of scratching, so homely and natural, would doubtless guide him back to the feeling that all was well.

But the perambulation of nails over shin became a large

and rhythmical gesture, as though, to a commanding music, he was scratching in a parade. He got up, and strolled to the window. The same magnifying illusion infected the movement of walking. Each step became a stride, and standing before the window he had a grandiose sensation of being a public figure, more, a piece of public statuary.

"Come, come, this is nonsense!"

So he spoke to himself. But the words boomed through the small room as though an amplifier were fastened before his mouth.

He returned to the wash-basin. He left the wash-basin and took up a coffee-cup. Everywhere he was following himself about, and was unreal and portentous, as though he had become his own enormous shadow.

Meanwhile he had no shadow, for the room faced west.

It faced west, and was mocked by the view outside. It looked cold and dungeon-like, though actually, thanks to the admirable heating system, it was warm. The executioner drank down a cup of coffee and instantly began to sweat. He ate, and felt sick. He looked at the alarm-clock, and was horrified. He had even more time than he thought.

The boy had interrupted him just when he was attacking his crowning exercise. It was his custom to go through it a dozen times, for that was just the right number, sufficient to loosen up the muscles of belly and shoulder, not so many as to trick the body into the illusion that no particular effort was required.

But he sat on the bed, dipping bread into coffee and not eating it.

Every mother was someone's mother. Indeed, she could not be a mother otherwise. And this mother was the mother of that boy. A coincidence, but nothing more. One could not, after all, go through one's public career without somewhere, sometime, encountering a coincidence.

Certainly the boy was unpleasant . . . a poor weedy specimen, lacking in self-control, just such a son as such a mother would have. Yet the boy's spirit was really quite admirable, the spirit of a true Nazi patriot. Perhaps he need not have mentioned the coincidence about his mother, and yet such a single-souled devotion was really very fine.

So it was really quite unreasonable that he should have received this impression of a horror, of having all of a sudden stared into the face of a mad flower whose breath was deadly fever. And still more was it unreasonable to give himself over to this hallucination of being so very large, so far beyond human dimensions—and still growing larger. Timidly, like a schoolgirl, chastely compacting himself, he shuffled to his feet. For why should he be so foolish? He was just an executioner, and no larger than other men.

Unobtrusively he approached his socks, and devoted his attention to putting them on without damaging them. They were made of black artificial silk, and went easily into a ladder.

The shirt crackled as he lifted it. For a moment, depending from his raised arms, it hung over him like a surplice, a ceremonial whiteness. But a moment later he had got his head out, and it was no more than just a well-starched evening shirt.

He pulled on his trousers, and that was easy, too. They were of good cloth, and cut amply around the seat.

He put on his pumps, and then gave himself to the business of collar and tie. He always carried several ties; for his hands, so large and strong, were not adapted for tying bows. But this time the bow was perfect at the first attempt. There was not even any need to look at it in the glass. He could tell by the feel that it was all right.

A waistcoat is a pleasant garment to put on. Slender and quaintly made, yet it embraces a man's girth and holds him together.

The coat hung on the back of the chair. As he reached

for it there was a shrill rat's cry underfoot. It was the sole of his left pump squeaking, and what could be more ordinary than that, and even belittling? But in that involuntary movement of surprise his body escaped his control. It became once more enormous, insistent, and unreal. And the coat dangled from his hand like a dead crow.

With the force of a Titan he put on the coat. It just fitted him.

But now his vast bulk was no longer distressing. His clothes, so well made and elegant, masked it in suavity; and striding across the room to survey himself in the mirror it seemed to him that just so might some great personage, some very great personage, appear—dressed to attend a ceremonial performance at the opera-house, to sit in the centre of the stage-box among flowers and banners.

If there were music . . .

As though his thought had pressed a button, music, warm and massive, welled up in his ears. And now the room faced west no longer. A thousand lights and a thousand glances were focused upon him, and grandly, superbly, he paced to and fro in time to the music, stepping over the box with a majestic swing of the leg.

Presently he began to hum, and then to sing, his voice blending with, and eventually leading, the rich strains of the full orchestra. The music was the Pilgrim's Chorus from "Tannhäuser." But this little room, brimful though it was of lights and glances, of swelling flowers and swelling music, was only the antechamber. Presently he would step forward into the state-box; and then, in the final glare of lights, in the final roar of acclamation, they would see him, towering, and solitary, and know what manner of man he was.

Outside his door the prison officials had gathered. The noise of the executioner stamping to and fro and singing at the top of his voice made them look at each other questioningly, fretfully, as men do whose nerves are slightly on edge.

"Knock at the door," said someone.

At that moment the door flew open. Out came the executioner, pulling on his gloves, and still singing. He passed by as though he did not see them, and went on down the empty corridor, majestically taking the salute.

The prison governor turned to the prison doctor, and said one word.

The doctor nodded.

"It's quite a common form for it to take," he said. "Increasingly so."

FROM ABOVE

THE sharp light of an October morning emphasized the perspective of Albion Terrace, whose small stucco houses with light iron-work steps descending from hooded doorways to pocket-handkerchief lawns preserved, so Mr. Campion said, better than any other street in London the polite amoral grace of the Regency. Many of the polite amoral Graces of that period had lived and entertained in Albion Terrace; and a campaign to persuade the London County Council to commemorate, with blue and white plaques, the tenancy of some of the better-known light-of-loves, was one of Mr. Campion's favourite dinner-party gambits.

Now Mrs. Campion was standing on her top step, staring vaguely at the sky and shaking a duster without energy. She had pale green eyes, pure as a kitten's, and they looked so much at variance with her small, anxious, sallow face that one had the impression they must have been given her by some rich admirer with more connoisseurship than discretion. She yawned several times, and lowered her gaze. At the bottom of the terrace, just closing the gate of Number 47 behind him, was a policeman; 45 and 43 were empty, and he passed them, but turned in again through the gate of 41 and mounted the steps. And having done with 41 he went on to 39.

"Methodical as the milk," she observed. At the same moment she realized what his errand must be. But instead of doing any of the things she ought to have done, instead of going indoors to turn off the gas, the electricity, and the water at the mains, instead of packing up the spoons or changing into a street suit she continued to stand in the sun watching the policeman's advance.

Presently she could tell from the fragments of conversation that reached her that her guess was indeed exactly right; but even when her own gate squeaked on its hinges and the policeman had come up the steps and was offering his chest to her steady scrutiny she continued to look attentive and docile and to say nothing.

"Are you the occupier of these premises?"

"I am," she answered ritualistically. "That's to say, my husband has just gone off to his office and the charwoman doesn't seem to be coming."

"A time-bomb," said the policeman, "has been located in the Mews. In the interests of public safety it is necessary to clear the Terrace. Only temporarily, we hope. Before leaving, which should be done as soon as possible, it would be advisable . . ."

While he spoke she was folding the duster, and smoothing it.

"But what will you do about my husband? He's coming back to lunch."

"Do not trouble, madam. He will be intercepted."

Her expression was so queerly unconvinced that he noticed it, and added:

"There'll be notices up, you know, or a barrier. You needn't worry about him."

And as her expression remained just as unconvinced as before, he resumed his official standing and said:

"Doubtless you could get into communication with him."

Ready just inside the door were the two suitcases. James had placed them there over a month ago, having packed them himself, a man full of plans and foresight. She ran down to the kitchen to turn off the gas and the electricity and the water at the mains. Then she ran upstairs to change her clothes.

Everything that she passed by reproached her, heaped on her the mute reproaches of the blameless and helpless. She felt as though she were being eyed by countless misjudged and faithful spaniels. *You are leaving us*, blinked chairs and tables and ornaments. *You don't love us any more.*

She stared round the bedroom as she fastened her skirt. She must, she must take something with her, some little portable thing. But what? Obviously, something that James had given her. But again, what? The room was full of things that James had given her, all beautiful, all genuine, and almost all expensive.

She picked up a small white satin pincushion, elaborately puffed and pearled. It was a child-bed pincushion and *Bless the Child and Save the Mother* was picked out on it in small pins, every one of which, James said, was of the period. Once, being in a hurry, she had used two of them. One she had replaced. The other got lost, and the break in the curly capital *C* was like a tiny almost obliterated scar. She stuffed the pincushion into her handbag.

"O God, O God!" she whispered, running downstairs. Picking up the two suitcases she exclaimed more attentively. They were astonishingly heavy. She found that she could now recall some of the things James had been saying during the afternoon he had packed them: that one might find oneself very inconveniently fixed without a hammer and some good stout nails, that a bottle of whisky weighs very little more than a half-bottle, that she would be sorry to lose her malachite box, that Browne's *Pseudodoxia* was a book he had always been meaning to re-read.

She staggered out, and behind her the door closed with a noise like a sighing breath cut short.

Other doors too were opening and shutting, the people of Albion Terrace were in retreat. Here and there from a window left open some bright-coloured curtain waved as though in farewell. Dogs barked and tugged at their leads, an old man went rapidly by in a self-propelling bath-chair that was heaped with parcels. Children, pale and walking stiffly, carried little cases, a cat mewed and lurched in a hamper, some canaries sang loudly in a cage.

"How odd! I have neither chick nor child," thought Dionysia Campion. "Perhaps that is why I feel so heartless."

Two women passed her, and as they passed one was saying: "And when I think that only yesterday I had the chimney-sweep . . ."

The suitcases banged against her legs, and she began to wonder what one does with suitcases containing all that might remain of one's worldly goods. Refugees, she knew, carried suitcases and were never parted from them. More fortunate people hailed a taxi. But while the taxi-man was loading on the suitcases it occurred to her that a taxi was only a temporary expedient. She could not drive about in it all day.

"Where to, lady?"

"I'm not quite sure. I've got to think a little. Anyway, drive me somewhere away from here."

"Quite a lot of people use hotels," he said. "Others seem to like railway stations."

"Just drive, please."

Sometimes she looked out of the window, sometimes she looked at her watch. Suddenly everything became clear to her. She would leave the suitcases at James's club, he could meet them there for lunch. As for herself, she would take a day off, she would go exploring, she would visit St. Paul's.

So much a Londoner that she took London for granted, she had never been inside St. Paul's. The taxi-driver thought it a very spirited destination, and remarked, as they parted, that plenty of time-bombs got nipped in the bud. Stuffing back the child-bed pincushion she agreed cordially. An instant later, standing by the statue of Queen Anne and hearing the whirr of the pigeons' wings overhead, she began to tremble. She mounted a few steps, and then looked upward. The portico seemed to reel towards her, she anticipated the weight of the whole enormous building. A door swung open, she heard sounds of a cough, a voice, a chair scraped along the floor, hammer-blows, all melted and enveloped in one vast melodious echo as though these shreds of living were being simmered down in this soup cauldron whose lid was a dome with a cross on it. She turned back, intimidated.

But London was full of things which she had never been taken to see and which it might be amusing to see alone. There was the Soane Museum in Lincoln's Inn Fields. There were all those Wren churches, many of them must still be undamaged, and James could not have taken her to every one of them, for her demeanour in churches was un-endearing to any lover of architecture since she always be-came absorbed in reading about the dead instead of admiring such things as retro-choirs and proportions. There was Green-wich Observatory, where the Astronomer Royal and his telescope still directed themselves to the more permanent phenomena of the heavens. There was the Physic Garden, and Carlyle's House, and Somerset House, and Bedlam.

And immediately in front of her was a telephone booth. In the taxi it had seemed to her that, calmed by a half-hour in St. Paul's, she would find it less painful to ring up James and tell him he was temporarily evacuated. Tell him she must. It would be heartless to leave him to go back for lunch and learn for himself.

Being so much more assimilable in proportions than St. Paul's the telephone booth seemed cosy and reassuring. Opening her bag she downed the child-bed pincushion and got at the pennies. Perhaps he would be out and she could leave the message with his nice sympathetic secretary.

"Mr. Campion? Yes, Mrs. Campion (It is Mrs. Campion, isn't it?), I'll put you through immediately."

"Hullo, Dionysia."

"James."

"Well? Is anything wrong?"

"James. You'd better lunch at your club."

"Gas gone off again?"

"No. But there's a time-bomb in the Mews, and we're temporarily evacuated. The policeman came just after you'd gone."

After a pause he said:

"My God!"

After another pause he said in an even more remote and ruminating voice:

"Damn."

"James. I turned everything off, and I took your suitcase to the club. I left mine there too. I thought perhaps you could have lunch at the club."

"Oh, all right! But why don't I meet you for lunch? Where are you, by the way?"

"Outside St. Paul's. James, I don't think I *can* lunch with you, not while your home is hanging on tenterhooks."

"That's very sensitive of you. Do you think you could bring yourself to sleep with me tonight?"

"I suppose I ought to see about a room in a hotel?"

"Unless you prefer the Tube, or some dome of many-coloured glass over a Rest Centre."

No wonder he was cross. What on earth possessed me, she thought, to say *your home*? Isn't it my home too? Our bed, our rosewood dining-table, our Adam settee? Deep within her, eating away like the chemical of a time-bomb, an invincible ruthfulness responded and said: No! James's home. James's choice, James's taste. James's wife, who was James's home's caretaker.

For now it could not be denied. The policeman had come to her like some draped angel, calling on her to arise and leave the fleshpots of Egypt. At the most, he had promised an absolute departure. At the least he had bestowed a whole day during which her responsibilities to 11 Albion Terrace would be in abeyance, a whole day in which she would be free to gad whither she pleased. How ridiculous of her to think she wanted to see St. Paul's. Of course she didn't. That sort of wish was merely a copy-catting of James. Her wishes were bounded by the West End and solitude, were quite simple, base, and ordinary.

What she wished was first to have her hair washed and set, her face massaged, her hands manicured. Then she would like a simple, base, and ordinary lunch, macaroni cheese and lemon pie. Then she would like to go to the gramophone shop and try over a lot of records, sitting in a little cubicle furnished with nothing but an easy chair and an ash-tray. Then she would like a cup of chocolate and a hot muffin. Then . . . Then it would be time to hurry through the falling dusk to see what had happened in Albion Terrace. If it had gone James would break his heart. Poor James! Poor James, anyway. In one minute he had had to learn that his home was balanced on the edge of destruction and that his wife was unfaithful to his home.

With guilty alacrity she jumped on a bus; shameless and nimble as any cat running off with the cold pheasant, she ran off to make the most of her holiday. Hourly becoming more depraved, she told the manicurist all about the time-bomb in the Mews, and lapped up the sympathy that followed. At the record-shop too she told the man about the time-bomb, and he agreed with her that music was what she needed, music was the only possible comfort and solace. She played through an album of songs by Debussy, a type of music that James detested, and went out, having bought nothing, humming to herself a vague incantation of whole-tone scale melodies in her husky voice that was like a pastel, for it smudged and never could stay in tune.

The dusk was falling as the taxi neared Albion Terrace. But it would not be too dark to see the notice at the end of the street. She peered out. There was no notice.

"There was a time-bomb here this morning," said the

taxi-man, stopping before Number 11. "But it didn't make it."

This time the child-bed pincushion made its get-away, and fell in the gutter. Dangling it by its white ribbon loop she mounted the steps and let herself into the dark hallway. Two steps farther and she fell over the suitcases.

A door opened, a light was switched on.

"Well, Dionysia?"

"Oh dear, I didn't mean to be so late! I meant to be back in time to do the black-out and light a fire for you if we still had a hearth. Then I couldn't. I couldn't face finding it all ruins and smithereens. Was it awful coming back, James, not knowing what to expect?"

"Not at all. I'd rung up the police-station."

Now he looked at the little white bolster she dangled.

"What on earth's that?"

"My pincushion. I just had to take something."

"Incurable kitsch-cat! What a thing to choose! And did you visit St. Paul's with that in your hand?"

"In my bag."

When he said *St. Paul's* she remembered that she had done nothing about booking a hotel bedroom for the night. But as they were now back in Albion Terrace, with any luck that fact would not emerge.

EMIL

"WE ARE going to take an Austrian refugee," Mrs. Hathaway said to Mrs. Kirkpatrick.

"Really? An Austrian? I believe they are charming. My cousin Linda adores hers. But I can't imagine you without your old Hannah. I didn't know she was leaving."

Mrs. Hathaway explained that this refugee was not coming as a domestic servant. He was an Austrian who had escaped to England last March after the *Anschluss*. "It's a boy," she said, and blushed, for it sounded so ridiculous, as though she were announcing a birth.

Emil Kirchner was rather more than a boy. He was twenty-one. He was an orphan, his elder brother was pro-Hitler. He had a high forehead and curly, mouse-coloured hair and a small mouth. He spoke English fluently. Mrs. Hathaway had imagined that on their first introduction he would bow from the waist and kiss her hand, but instead of kissing it he shook it.

They met in London at the house of a friend of the Hathaways', a woman who worked in an organization called the Friends of Democracy. There had been a tacit understanding that if Mrs. Hathaway did not like the looks of this refugee she could have another. But the idea of picking and choosing among the unfortunate was repulsive to her. She could not imagine herself leading Dora Welsford toward the window and murmuring, "I should like to see another of them." And anyhow, Emil seemed a very pleasant young man.

So Emil picked up his suitcase and they went off together and had some tea, Mrs. Hathaway apologizing that it was not chocolate. And then they went to Charing Cross, and travelled to Ryebridge, and went on by bus to the village of France Green.

The village was looking its best. The converted cottages —converted to the use of the small gentry—seemed to wear looks of gentle festivity, fluttering with clean window curtains and poised with flowers. Even the unconverted cottages, which were much more recent in date and built of red brick, had a certain comfortable glow in the sunset. As they walked along the village street, Mrs. Hathaway, exchanging nods and greetings with neighbours, said to Emil, "That is Mrs. Kirkpatrick—an old friend of ours" or "Major Cullen. He knows Austria, too" or "That's Miss Forrester. You'll like her so much."

And then she was introducing Emil to Mr. Hathaway and feeling as though they were already quite old acquaint- ances. Mr. Hathaway was a bank manager in Ryebridge. He was also chairman of the France Green Parish Council and the founder of the France Green Debating Society. Bank managers in England are usually Conservatives, but Mr. Hathaway was a Liberal.

They had agreed that during the first evening they would avoid asking questions about how and why Emil had left Vienna. It would be better to keep to ordinary topics. It is difficult to keep to ordinary topics with a perfect stranger; even though Emil's English was so good, the conversation flagged and it was a relief when he said, "You have a piano. I, too, am fond of music."

Now I shall be caught out, thought Mrs. Hathaway. They are all so intensely musical, and suppose he asks me to play duets with him? If it were only the slow movements—but when everything gets black with semiquavers I always lose my head.

Emil showed no inclination for duets. Most of the time he played by ear. The things he played by ear were all unfamiliar to the Hathaways, but after a week or two they got to know his repertory. Especially Mrs. Hathaway, who had no bank to manage. The piano was clearly a great solace to Emil, even more so after it had been tuned. He played by the hour: sad melodies and dance tunes with a sorrowful hop in them. Hannah said she expected it was as good as knitting to the poor young gentleman. They all did their best to understand his position.

But it is difficult for people living in their busy, untroubled homes to understand the position of a refugee, unless, of course, that refugee is of a class which cooks or sews or looks after children. As the spring advanced, as the lawn needed mowing and the green peas needed sticking, the Hathaways hoped that Emil would find comfort in nature, but he still preferred art and remained indoors. He preferred art to politics, too. It was almost impossible to get him to talk about the *Anschluss*. Mr. Hathaway was inclined to take a large view. Emil had left Vienna because he disapproved of Fascism. Mr. Hathaway also disapproved of Fascism, more intellectually, if less violently, than Mrs. Hathaway. Surely, he said to his wife, a common disapproval is common ground enough.

Other people in France Green could not leave it at that. Miss Forrester, for instance, examining the daffodils in the border below the sitting-room window, made Mrs. Hathaway quite an eloquent speech about the sufferings of the Jews.

"Actually, Herr Kirchner is not a Jew," said Mrs. Hathaway.

Miss Forrester swept on. "And I said to Mr. Benson, I can't understand it, I said. Surely you, as a churchwarden, should realize what is meant by religious persecution. It's nonsense, I said, and it's unchristian to go on talking of Mrs. Hathaway's Communist just because the poor young fellow is a Jew. What about the Bible? I said. Was that published by the Left Book Club? Oh, I was furious with him! Though I couldn't say to him, as I can to you, that I, for one, am beginning to think there's a great deal to be said for the Communists." She glanced in the window. The music continued. "If I met a Communist," said Miss Forrester slowly and clearly, "I would say to him, we have a great deal in common."

But still the music continued and Mrs. Hathaway was obliged to say, "Actually, Herr Kirchner is not a Communist."

Presently she was rebutting other constructions. One time it was Mrs. Kirkpatrick, who, without saying anything of the sort herself, or even believing it, felt obliged to let Mrs. Hathaway know that the Riddles were going about quite openly saying that the Hathaways were harbouring a German spy.

"There's a lot going on in France Green, isn't there," said Mrs. Hathaway, moved to satire, "that Hitler would give his ears to know about?"

"It isn't so much what goes on," replied Mrs. Kirkpatrick, "as what goes over. After all, we have Imperial Airways flying over us twice a day. And any amount of other planes."

"Well," said Mrs. Hathaway, "if the Riddles have seen Herr Kirchner running out to count airplanes and then running out to the post office to send messages in code, they've seen more than I have. My trouble has been that I can't get him to stir out of doors."

"But you wouldn't expect him to, would you?" said Mrs. Kirkpatrick. "Spies have to conceal their movements."

Mrs. Hathaway began to feel that any movement from Emil, overt or covert, would be welcome. He did not care for gardening. He had no impulse to explore the country-side. Though he played tennis very well, he did not care for playing tennis. Throughout the summer he moped—there was no other word for it. He was polite. He was, when called upon, obliging. He played the piano, he took many baths. His stock of small talk kept up better than the

Hathaways', perhaps because he did not tax it so hard. The only person in the household with whom he seemed to feel at ease was Hannah. He spent a lot of time in the kitchen, helping Hannah with the vegetables and listening to her talk of cats she had known in the past, but even this attachment seemed questionable and might have been due to nothing more than an English summer and the fact that the kitchen was the only room in the house that had a fire in it.

Refugee mentality, said Mrs. Hathaway to herself. The phrase would have been more of a comfort to her if she had not been an honest and compassionate woman. As it was, she suffered a great deal, imagining how she would feel in a foreign land and among strangers. What was going on behind that high forehead? What words of melancholy and disillusionment did the small mouth shut back? She herself could hardly endure a week-end of paying a visit, and Emil had been at France Green for the whole summer and had never once crossed the moral frontiers of the spare room.

"Well, that at any rate is something to admire," she said to her husband. "He's not happy and he doesn't try to be. He doesn't like us and he doesn't pretend to. I call that real integrity. I honor him for it."

Mr. Hathaway looked up from the evening paper. "I don't like the look of things," he said.

Presently Mr. Hathaway convened a meeting of the Air Raid Precautions wardens. As chairman of the Parish Council he made himself unpopular by urging that the France Green fire engine, which dated from 1895, should be overhauled. He got leaflets and distributed them. He laid in stores of brown paper and sticky paper, recommended for making rooms gasproof. He collected sacks for sandbags and made a survey of cellars. He wrote several letters asking for gas masks for the village and, thanks to his importunity, received three. He outraged the County Education Department by suggesting that a trench should be dug in the school garden and was told that such a thing would be out of the question, as it was essential not to spread panic among children. And he called two Public Meetings, which would have been better attended, as those who did not attend them explained, if people were not getting up their potatoes just then.

Mr. Benson, who was also a warden, spoke bitterly about the apathy of the working class. "They're spoon-fed!" he exclaimed. "They expect one to thrust a silver spoon into their mouths. They're born like that."

Mr. Hathaway wrote his fifth application for a supply of gas masks and received a reply saying that they were officially termed gas respirators and would be available in due course. He also spent some time examining into the rumour, put forward by several of the oldest inhabitants, that an underground passage, long lost, ran between the church and Manor Farm.

"Every village in England has that story," said Major Cullen.

Mr. Hathaway remarked that France Green might be the village where the story was true.

Simultaneously with Mr. Hathaway's appeal for volunteers to dig trenches between five-thirty, when the men of France Green ceased work, and sundown, the Rector announced that the church would be open every evening between six and eight for those who wished to pray for peace.

"What's the use of all these precautions?" inquired Mr. Riddle. "I'm a bit of a fatalist, I am."

Aided by Mr. Cobb at the garage, Mr. Hathaway spent the next to the last Friday evening in September trying to construct a siren, and on Saturday he returned from Ryebridge with all the picks and shovels he could buy. This was timely, as on Monday every one began to dig, every one except the women, who were attending First Aid classes, and Mr. Benson, who surveyed the diggers.

Emil dug, too. He dug extremely well. After a little wary observation by the other diggers, he became very popular among them. When it was too dark to dig any longer he produced a mouth organ and the gang marched home with a swagger. The moment dinner was over, he tore down to the kitchen, where Hannah had promised to teach him how to darn sacks. At ten-thirty he reappeared, saying that all the sacks were darned and demanding cartridge paper and red paint. He was still making posters and notices when Mr. and Mrs. Hathaway went to bed, and when they got up next morning Hannah told them that he had made an early breakfast and gone out with his pick and shovel.

Mr. and Mrs. Hathaway were so moved with relief that neither said a word to the other. To have commented on this transformation would have been a disloyalty.

Digging went on through Tuesday and Wednesday. They were making a shelter now as well as trenches. Emil had organized the workers into competitive gangs. On Wednesday the news came that the Prime Minister was going to Munich, but no one slackened for that; and that evening Emil and Mr. Cobb rigged up lighting and the younger men worked on most of the night. On Thursday morning a load of timber was found neatly stacked beside the shelter. On it was a piece of paper with the words, "Mr. K with compts. from an unknown friend."

Emil had flashed into such popularity that when young Jimmy Barnes inadvertently dropped a pick on his foot a shout of wrath and despair went up. The First Aid detachment hurried out with bandages and the stretcher. Emil caused himself to be conveyed in a wheelbarrow to where the children were filling sandbags and worked on with them. At sundown they wheeled him home, refusing to let any one else handle their hero and spilling him twice.

"You must go straight to bed," said Mrs. Hathaway.

"I probably won't sleep."

"You must. Really, you must. You are much too valuable to wear yourself out now. You must be kept in trim for when—" She stopped. The question jumped up in her mind: What would happen to Emil in a war—in a war which would make him an enemy alien?

"For when the curtain goes up, eh?" his high forehead was plastered with mud. The small mouth was open in a brilliant, breathless smile. "I go to bed, then. Thank you very much."

Afterward she went to his room and looked in. He was asleep. Hitherto she had seen only his waking countenance. Sleeping, his face was rigid and melancholy. The corners of the small mouth turned down, the arched eyebrows, doll-like by day, now gave him an expression of agonized bewilderment. She glanced round the room. His clothes, his brushes, his washing things. Nothing else. Not a photograph, not a book. It was a spare room, with a week-end visitor asleep in it.

Downstairs was Henry, checking off the names of those who had been measured for gas masks.

"This awful waiting," she said. "I never thought I'd hope for war. I don't even know if I do. Henry, what *is* one to think?"

"It will be the news in a minute," he answered, stretching out his hand to the wireless. She sat down, nerving herself to listen.

The morning papers carried the headlines: "Agreement Reached, Occupation to Begin Tomorrow, Mr. Chamberlain Flying Back," and in smaller type, "Prague Agrees to Further Concessions." Like a nose-bleeding, a ghastly, warm trickle of relief began to move in her. She realized that for the last twenty-four hours she had been counting on this.

Mr. Kirchner was still asleep, said Hannah. She was taking him up his breakfast. Mrs. Hathaway put a newspaper on the tray. "Don't wake him," she said.

"Nothing to wake any one for," said Hannah. " 'Mr. Chamberlain returning.' Trust him to come back! Grinning hyena—feathering his own nest!"

Presently Mr. Hathaway left for his bank. The breakfast tray went up and came down again. I ought to do his foot, thought Mrs. Hathaway. She went upstairs. The room was empty, the bath water was running. She came down again.

About midday Emil appeared. The Rector was calling. He proposed to hold a special service. He also proposed to give the collection to the Czechs. So he had come to ask if Mr. Kirchner would do another of those wonderful posters of his, announcing both these intentions.

"We owe it to them," he exclaimed.

When he had gone, Emil limped across to the piano. For a moment he stared at the keyboard. Then he turned and looked at Mrs. Hathaway—a look of mournful scornful, listless understanding. "Couldn't we play a duet?" he said.

IN THE HOUR
OF OUR DEATH

LEAVING the nursing home David walked back to his mother's lodgings. As he entered she turned round from the writing-desk with a glance of unqualified pleasure. A second later her expression became overcast, and matched the voice in which she said:

"Darling! How is he?"

He sighed. Then he squared his shoulders, shook his head like a dog shaking water out of its ears, and sat down beside her with his knees apart and his hands on his knees.

"It's terribly, terribly difficult!"

She, in turn, sighed.

On the writing-desk lay several sheets of note-paper written over in a fluent handwriting. On the shelf above it were two pictures in standing frames. One was an ageing photograph of a young man with the panama hat of the 1910's tilted over a long thin face socketed in a clergyman's round collar. The other was a woodcut of a contemporary angel, with a slightly turned-up nose, careless curls, and a square jaw.

The young man between them seemed to be compounded of the two. For he also had a slightly turned-up nose and careless curls, and he also was wearing a clergyman's round collar.

"I know," she said. "Oh, *how* I know!"

"There are times when I just can't believe it's dad. There he lies, full of misery and rebellion. The poor darling!"

She folded her hands on her lap and looked at them. Her breathing became slower and fuller, and in the silence of the room one could hear the faint creak of her corsets, the faint clatter of the cross and the locket with a miniature in it, pinned on her bosom. She parted her lips as though to speak, but closed them again in a resigned curve, and waited.

"He is so tragically, utterly alone," continued the young man. "One just can't get through to him. Why, even God can't get through to him!" he exclaimed, "so no wonder I can't."

Staring at her hands she said:

"Is the pain as bad as ever?"

"They are doing everything they can for him, of course. Psychologically, as well as physically. But there it is, one has to admit it. There are some cases where psycho-therapy just doesn't apply."

"Co-operation," she murmured.

"Exactly, exactly! And the poor darling just won't co-operate. He lies there, watching the clock, waiting for the next inspection. He won't even *listen* for the trumpets getting ready on the other side."

Her glance strayed from her hands, rested for a moment on the unfinished letter:

Poor Cyril is v. much in need of your thoughts just now. The Home is wonderfully kind, and do everything possible. If only he . . .

The young man jumped up and began to stride about the room.

"The tragedy of it all is, he doesn't seem able to see what pain means. He won't accept it. It's all evil to him, unmitigated utter evil. He doesn't seem able to realize it as one of the deeper things, one of the deeper sides of God. Why, he won't even talk about it! It's ghastly to find one's dear father, whom one's trusted so, always looked up to, unable to grasp a thing that even a beginner like one's self can see quite easily!"

"My David! There are some things, we know, that are hidden from clever people and yet revealed to babes and sucklings."

He paused in his walk. His open countenance was twitched into a premature age, became sharp, resentful, arrogant. But once again he squared his shoulders, shook the water out of his ears, and turned to his mother with a piercing smile.

"Then thank God I *am* a babe! I could not have gone through these last months if I had not been utterly sure what God means by pain. How could one? It would be impossible, heart-breaking! But, Mother, what he's missing! His share in the mystery, his grand opportunity of getting to know God's special secret, the whole essence of it all."

He scratched his head.

"What I can't understand is, how did he deal with his death-beds?"

"He always disliked them," she said. "That's really why I did so much of the visiting myself. I felt I simply had to take some of the burden . . . and I think that perhaps in a tiny way I really helped some of the poor things. Especially the lingering ones, when one was brought into such wonderful contacts. And, of course, perhaps it was rather easier for me. That's why it's rather a hurt, just now, when he won't let me go to him."

"*Darling!*" he said. "I understand so perfectly. But he shuts out all of us. Worse still, he shuts out God."

After a little she said:

"Could you talk to him at all?"

"Only airy nothings. Good Lord!" he cried remonstrantly, "to have to make conversation, *make conversation*, at one's own father's death-bed. . . . It's so frightfully absurd!"

The door opened. A smell of Indian tea and buttered toast was diffused. While the lodging-house servant was setting the table they remained silent. Just as she was leaving the room Mrs. Davenport said:

"Thank you so much, Mary. The toast smells quite delicious. I hope Mr. David will leave me some."

Mary breathed hard, expressing her sympathy, and left the room. For a little while yet they remained silent and motionless, she at the desk, he leaning against the window.

She rose.

"We must just go on loving him," she said, and walked across to the tea-table.

MUTTON'S ONLY HOUSE

FOR the inside of a minute one could see the house from the train. Then the woods swept forward like a tongue and licked it up. They were fir-woods, equally efficacious at all seasons of the year.

As a rule the people in the train were local people. If they had felt impelled to say anything about the house they would never have been so forward as to mention it before its owner. But occasionally a stranger's voice would say, "Look! There's a house!" And now she heard a brief discussion between two soldiers as to whether or not it was a house by Lutyens. The army was like that nowadays. Upside-down like everything else.

Leaning forward she said:

"No. It's by Mutton."

"Mutton? Oh, I don't think I know his work. What else has he done?"

"This is Mutton's only house."

The first soldier—they were gunners—said that was a pity, and the second said he had told him it wasn't Lutyens, not niminy-piminy enough.

Jane Mutton's pale eyes turned to the window and the pale December landscape. Her long upper lip policed any tendency to smile. Why feel gratified, why be amused? These young know-alls got on her nerves. Personally she thought Lutyens a very good architect.

It was from the train that she had first seen, ten years ago, the moderate severe sweep of hillside, the hanging fir-woods. And her thoughts, occupied by considerations of a new hunter, opened to admit the query, Why not build a house

there? From then till the second year of the war this railway
view of her house had had for her little more actuality than
a minikin replica of the blue-print's *East Elevation with
Stable Block*. She had known how it would look. From the
moment she gave her mind to building her house she had
known very clearly everything about it; but she had not
given much consideration as to how it would strike the eyes
of travelling strangers two miles away.

Mutton or Lutyens, it looked very well; and never better
than in this wintry light, with the morning sun shining on
the sharp new brick and delineating the bays and recesses of
the stable block. For all that, she would rather be travelling
by car.

But just as she had foreseen her house—unerringly, un-
assisted by architects—and presently, there it was, looking
exactly as she had intended it to look; just as all her life long
she had seen how her life should develop, and duly, it was
taking the shape she had decided on, Jane Mutton saw her
duty in war-time, plain, indubitable, rectangular; and part
of that duty was to save petrol. Local deference, the affability
of local bigwigs, would have granted her all the petrol she
might choose to ask for. "My dear good Jane, of course you
must have petrol. You can't fag in and out of Dunwater by
puff-puff." And implied there was the rider of "at *your* age,
my dear." But though this was quite true, for Jane Mutton
was over sixty, rectangular duty sent her off erect on a
shining bicycle to catch, first the 9.50, afterwards the 8.30,
to Dunwater, the county town.

Seeing everything so uncommonly clearly, Jane Mutton
saw also the pitying entertainment of her friends. She would
have scorned them, these soft west-country hard riders to
hounds, living in houses which they had inherited, evading
every war-time restriction and assuming every war-time
authority to the manner born, if her wary conscience had not
kept her reminded that it is unseemly to scorn people towards

whom you have an obligation you would rather not recall.
Evacuees. At the outbreak of war to take in evacuees had
seemed the common doom, and if any one was marked out
for it, she was, living in her great new house, without even
the excuse of only one inherited bathroom to plead for her.
But then a Labour Councillor in Dunwater began to talk
about making the rich do their share. Class loyalty closed
the ranks, with one accord her friends realized how much
more at home the poor evacuees would feel in cottage house-
holds; and in order to leave no gap in this philanthropic front
Miss Mutton's self-made barracks was defended as zealously
as though it had paid a succession of death-duties.

And having seen all this quite clearly she now preferred
to overlook it. As the train slowed down the two gunners
began to get their traps together.

"And that's all till next time, children," remarked the
plain one, and his companion, who was prettier still now that
he had put on his haloing hat, made a small bow, and said:

"*En attendant le plaisir devous revoir.*"

Cook's Tours, thought Jane Mutton instantly. In her youth,
while the Mutton money was still being put together, the
Mutton family group, with a solid Belfast application to
what's what, had made several Cook's Tours, and young men
like this conducted them.

For no recognizable reason she now said:

"Are you stationed here? Would you like to see over the
house, the Mutton house?"

Signalling with a large hand in a white glove she added:
"Wait a minute, guard."

While the train waited she told them how to get there,
when to telephone, and that they must come on a Sunday.
When the train moved on she found that her heart was beating like the heart of some young girl, a gay and flustered
vibration.

And yet Hospitality to the Forces was one of the things

that Jane Mutton did. Christmas parties. Parties to eat straw-
berries. Parties for convalescents from the Naval Hospital
at Mugdown. Always with games, and with young girls to
help with the entertaining. Her parties went off very well,
like everything else she undertook. They involved a great
deal of trouble, and she did them very thoroughly, and the
moment they were over she began to put things straight
again, folding and stacking the deck-chairs, putting back the
gramophone records, airing the rooms, emptying the ash-
trays, collecting the crockery and carrying it to the white-
tiled kitchen in which Mrs. Burt, who came in daily, looked
so doggedly alien to anything labour-saving.

For another of the things that Jane Mutton had seen so
uncommonly clearly was that a solitary woman, however large
the house she lived in, must not absorb labour in war-time.
Her maid-servants had found themselves freed in order to
join the Services (they had married, however), her cook,
travelling with a battery of saucepans, had been loaned to
the Mugdown Hospital, her garden was made over to the
Land Army, and only the stable cat remained in the stable
block.

"Austerity Jane! We've all decided we simply *must* call
you Austerity Jane," shrieked Mrs. Winter of Winter's
Harrow; and later, on a more private shriek, remarked to
her sister, Mrs. Bulteel of Mugdown St. Magdalen:

"It sticks out a mile. Jane Mutton *enjoys* it! She's hope-
lessly mean, and now she's having the time of her life cutting down expenses."

"Trying to recoup after building that ghastly house," said
Diana Bulteel.

"When I think how Henry wore himself to the bone keeping evacuees out of it! I wish to God we'd sent the Enuretic
Children there, instead of wasting ratepayers' money rent-
ing The Myrtles for them."

For this was in 1942, when Jane Mutton had finally put

herself beyond the pale of comprehension by taking a paid job on the County Administration.

"First of all she lets down the Hunt, then she lets us all down by this nonsense about not using petrol, and throwing away perfectly good servants. And now, while we're all doing voluntary work, slaving in canteens and so forth, she walks in under our very noses and pouches two quid a week as a clerk. There's only one word for it. It's *scabbing!*"

"Darling, *must* you talk like a Bolshie? All the same, scabbing's the word."

Returning scabbily by the 5.20, Jane Mutton watched for her house. It had a way of hiding itself from south-going trains. Twice or thrice she had mislaid it thus, looked too soon or too late, thought how some casual bomb . . . there it was, a pale oblong among the darkening woods. The house by Mutton. Mutton's only house. Only Mutton's house if it came to that, for it was not admired. Cycling against the feline pressure of the west wind she thought about it, about its foundations and about its cost, about the smell of its virginity, about its particular echoes and resonances, about a chimney which had smoked and been put right, about its hidden elegancies of plumbing and lighting.

She put away the bicycle in the stable, had a word with the stable cat, and went in by the back entrance. From room to room she mounted through the house, putting up the black-outs, righting this and that, shaking a curtain to fall handsomely. In the music-room (she was not musical though) she paused. It was a long, narrow room with a coffered ceiling. At one end a glass cocktail bar glittered like an up-to-date altar, an altar in the no-expense-spared style of church furnishing which reflects to the faithful how generously they have contributed. Along one wall hung her collection of modern paintings. They were without exception bright and bad: bright apples, bright acrobats, bright landscapes of blue trees or austere pink ploughland. They basked in the faultless lighting like so many suburban harlots being dined at a Mayfair restaurant.

Then she went downstairs and warmed up the supper which Mrs. Burt had prepared for her, and ate it in the kitchen, where it was warm. After considering for a while she poured out a double whisky. It seemed to her she was getting a cold.

Three days to wax, three days to rage, three days to wane. The cold ran the usual course. It had gone, and she was beginning to plan for the usual Christmas party (games and young girls) when a voice on the telephone asked if we could really come over and see your house. If they wanted to see anything of it they must come early, she replied—feeling suddenly pestered and antagonistic. The voice assured her that we would.

*   *   *

"My cousin Hilary Mutton died in '37."

"Indeed, miss?" Mrs. Burt's tone was respectfully smitten. "They do say that time heals old scores, but it's my belief one never appreciates a loss till it's over."

It was Sunday morning, and Mrs. Burt was helping to give things an extra rub-up. Miss Mutton switched on the Hoover, became deaf to any more condolences. Wandering, I shouldn't be surprised, thought Mrs. Burt.

Jane Mutton had no doubt of it. *Mooning* was her word, supplemented by *doting* and *drivelling*. Here she was, imagining, rehearsing fancy conversations, mooning, in fact, just because two know-all young men had condescended to notice her house. That was quite enough time wasted on cleaning, she said, and Mrs. Burt was dismissed, to muse on what might happen to unmarried ladies even when you might suppose them quite safely over the change.

They arrived about three o'clock, and at once in a business-like way she began to walk them round the exterior.

Their comments, and the remarks exchanged between them, showed them remarkably familiar with the east front.

"Surely you didn't notice all that from the train."

"Oh no," said the pretty one. "Oh Lord, no! We're on a searchlight, you see. And once or twice we've contrived to get a look at you."

It seemed to her deeply romantic that while she lay unknowing behind the black-out their beam had probed through the darkness, nosed her out, abandoned her, and visited her again.

"Are you allowed to do that sort of thing?"

"Actually," said the plain one, "searchlight is pretty damaging. A house has to have composition to stand up to it. Yours does."

While she tasted this he began to ask about Mutton. Now was the opportunity to introduce her cousin Hilary. But she did not choose to take it, walking on to where the pretty one was fondling the stable cat.

"Look, Jim, isn't she grand? A Palladian pussy!"

Jim stalked on, reached the north-east angle, paused, stepped back, paused again. A look of deep contentment flooded his face.

"There's management!" he said. Turning to her he added, "I've been puzzling for days how Mutton disposed of that pavilion."

"How else would you dispose of it?"

"Was he a relation of yours?" asked the pretty one conversationally. "I often dream how marvellous it would be to have a house designed by someone who knew one, and who would put in all the things one wanted. Architects can be so intractable."

The plain one caught her eye and grinned.

"I shouldn't exactly describe this as an obliging piece of architecture, Pinky."

A minute later the suggestible Pinky was describing the

kitchen fenestration as formidable. His plain friend then took him under control, and they stood for some ten minutes before the main façade, Jim explaining to Pinky why Mutton's pediment hit the nail on the head, while Mutton listened, rubbing her hands together, shifting from foot to foot as though in some slow dance.

"Now come and see the inside."

Her tone of voice betrayed her. Pinky with showmanly excitement whispered:

"*It's her*. I know it!"

Then why the hell not say so?—thought the other. Mutton the architect was explicit enough, wore no dickeys. He glanced scowlingly round the entrance. He wanted to look at it, but now that confounded woman who might be Mutton would be getting between him and everything.

The stairs, whose iron balustrading gave them a sort of rigid lightness, rose, encircling a vast newel of air, through the three stories of the house, and finished with a circular balustrade under a shallow dome. But fully to display this she had to switch on the light, for the dome was painted over.

"Circling the square," said Pinky.

"Octagon," she amended.

"How you must damn the black-out," said the plain one.

"I do."

"Getting in the way of all your best effects."

But she swept the attribution aside. She would accept it, but not yet, not till they had seen everything. For everything was hers.

Indeed, she was more conscious of the inside than of the outside. It had cost her more trouble. To build a house one needs only to see it, as she had seen; but colour-schemes and decorations have to be looked for.

Coming indoors the two gunners changed their roles. It was now the pretty one who commented, admired, drew his friend's attention to this and that. Occasionally the other asserted himself with questions about some technical nicety, and in the gun-room he became almost violently enthusiastic about the cupboard fittings; but for the most part he looked at the ceilings, or out of the window, or at her and out of the window again. Experience had taught that it was best to leave the music-room, with refreshments, to the last. She threw open the door, switched on the faultless lighting.

"Oh, I say!" Pinky's voice had a dazzled, a dizzied note. "O my God!"

Impossible for her, impossible for the hapless Pinky either, to brace themselves against it by resenting it as an exhibition of bad manners. It was so patently an exhibition of the heart. The words came out on a sort of remonstrating groan, sombre with disillusionment.

"How marvellous to have tea!" exclaimed Pinky, rallying his Cook's Tourists. "Tea in a cup instead of tea in a mug!"

Immediately they began to talk about army life.

Presently everything was quite normal again, and Pinky, under his invaluable eyelashes, could steal a few glances at the modern paintings. No doubt of it, they did go too far. Poor thing! He could feel for her, for he too, according to Jim, went at times too far also. Would another slice of cake be going too far? Anyhow, he'd have it. Eating helped one over awkward patches, he had learned that in the army; and to be well lined with cake, and, oh, if possible fortified by something out of that glassy Taj Mahal, would strengthen him for the moment when he would have to say, Thank you so much for showing us over your lovely house; for to do so would now certainly fall to him.

Sad for poor James, too, bumped down to earth and now pinned there, thought Pinky fluently, by his idol's much too large feet of clay, his mutton suddenly going cold on him. He mustn't say that, though. That would be going too far. *Revenons de nos moutons.* That, too, must not be said. Watch your step, Pinky! Though sooner or later, any minute now,

James, so prone to fall through his illusions, and always falling so hard, would fall out of and be through with him.

Out again in the cold, with the mist sopping the fir-woods, Pinky remarked that their hostess mixed a magnanimous cocktail. He thought he might venture that. He wanted to say something good about the woman.

"Her taste in drinks is better than her taste in decoration."

The tone was grim, yet cheerful. For the young have great powers of self-healing; and during tea Jim re-established Mutton, an architect who knew his own mind, a fine fellow, and nothing wrong with him except the dire fatality which handed over his handsome house to be bedizened by that Jezebel; which was no fault of Mutton's.

Still on the doorstep whence she had seen them walk away, the house behind her like an empty echoing shell, she listened to their footsteps, and to the complacent *plop-plop* of the moisture falling from the boughs. It was cool and impersonal out here, and here she would stay till she had overcome the impulse to break something, anything, everything. Why all this fuss about an afternoon's fiasco? Why this idiot hankering for approval, for what people nowadays called appreciation? She had built the house to please herself, and it pleased her, and that was all there was to it, and all there need be, and all there would be. There they were, walking away, but still within earshot. Habit and army boots compelled them, already the ill-assorted pair were walking in step, walking as though they were marching. Marching away, *soldiers marching all to die.*

With the relief of a hunted fox that smells a near-by earth she remembered that the things in the music-room could perfectly well wait for Mrs. Burt to clear them away to-morrow morning. She was too busy. She really must get on with the arrangements for the Christmas party. With conscription for young women it was getting harder and harder to scratch up half a dozen presentable girls.

A RED CARNATION

NO OTHER word had been used; the order had run: Prepare to depart for manœuvres on June 20th. And accordingly manœuvres was the word which darted about the barracks, echoed from the walls, was mixed with the clatter of knives and spoons and tin dishes, sounded an overtone on the band-music. Even in one's thoughts one continued obediently to use the word.

But every one knew it meant Spain.

Others had gone, many others. By now there was nothing remarkable or dramatic about going to Spain. It was the soldier's duty to fight the Red menace. Whether one was sent east or west it was the same duty, wherever the compass needle swung there the German soldier must march at the word of command. Wherever those red flames sprang up there the German soldier must go, to trample them out under his strong boots.

Kurt Winkler looked at his boots with new appreciation. Such fine boots, good leather, thick soles! . . . At first it had hurt his feet, wearing such boots; now he was used to them, could not imagine himself without them. It was a pity that one could not take one's boots with one when one's army days were over.

The Spanish Reds actually fought in rope-soled sandals.

The word to be said was manœuvres, but the word in his heart was Spain. And for the fiftieth time he found himself flooded with excitement, with pleasure, with a childish and unsoldierly yielding to romance. Spain! He would see Seville, the orange trees, the bullfights, those girls who made cigarettes. He would walk about holding a red carnation between his teeth.

The blood began to dance in his limbs. He clattered up the stairs, caught hold of Heinrich's arm, plump as a girl's.

"Heinrich! Tomorrow we start for manœuvres, eh?"

"Shut up!"

"Why, good Lord!"

"Well, you pinched me."

Heinrich's voice was sullen, his blue eyes looked flat and dark in his round face, they were like two pools of water reflecting the colour of a thunder-cloud.

"Anyhow—it's serious."

That was true, that was certainly true. Kurt was ashamed of himself. Again, for the fiftieth time, he had let himself be run away with by this childish and unsoldierly excitement. Spain? What was Spain? A battlefield merely, a preliminary battlefield. East or west, wherever the Red menace shows itself, there must the German soldier go, strong, disciplined, practical. Heinrich understood this, he had a serious nature, he thought a great deal. Kurt felt ashamed of his levity.

By the next morning all his excitement was obliterated. The moment of departure, the early-morning, ordinary-seeming lorry ride to the station, all the well-managed masquerade that he had foreseen and whose drama he had tasted beforehand—he hardly realized these things were taking place. His thoughts were absorbed by Heinrich Fiedler, who, in the small hours of the morning had gone to the lavatory and cut his throat.

The non-commissioned officers were furious. At this last moment, when everything was so well prepared, every detail polished and exact, to make a gap in the ranks!—such an act was mutiny, was treachery. Why the hell couldn't he have slit his throat a few days earlier?

Naturally, no mention of this bad beginning was allowed. "Heinrich Fiedler!" The name was called. Then a condemning silence. "Ludwig Mueller." "Present." After that, no more of Heinrich Fiedler

And this, of course, was right. Heinrich Fiedler was not only dead, but disgraced. His memory must be thrown away while the life of the stalwartly-living went on. For all that, Kurt could not remove his thoughts from this astonishing disaster. He travelled through the dislustred day feeling hollow and dumbfounded, feeling as though he were going to be sick. Every now and then he recalled with surprise that he was going to Spain.

On the boat he was sick. Not because of the waves, for the sea was as flat as a mill-pond, but because of the heavy smell of engine oil, because of the overcrowding and lack of the exercise to which, in his soldier's life, he had grown accustomed, and because of the disgusting sensation of having water underneath one, shifting, unstable, unknown, instead of good solid earth. But he was only sick for one day, and recovering from physical misery he seemed to have recovered from Heinrich Fiedler too. He began to think about Spain once more, he fished out his phrase-book and dictionary. He had bought them the day after the news came. On board ship there was an unusual amount of leisure, he began to study.

It was a foolish civilian phrase-book, old-fashioned as they always are. With a sensation of losing his dignity he read the sentences in which the traveller asked the way to the cathedral or paid a laundry bill. The dictionary was more useful, he learned a lot from the dictionary. And at night, listening to the noise of the boat, rocked on the indifferent bosom of the sea, he rehearsed the things he would say in Spain. *Good afternoon. We have come to bring you victory.* That was how one would greet the peasants. To the women one would say, *Have no fear. I am here to protect you from the marxists* . . . or something a little tenderer. Children one would greet with *Grow up into a good fascist and patriot.* Whom else would one meet in Spain? Priests, of course. He could not frame a greeting for priests. Advanced nations know that re-

ligion is all bunkum. Presently he was able to hold most satisfactory imaginary conversations in Spanish.

It was disconcerting when the sergeant tossed his phrase-
book overboard, saying that the less he talked to the inhabitants the better, that good German would be all the language
he would need. Some of the phrases stayed in his mind,
though. He could almost feel them in his mouth, forbidden
sweets. But the dictionary he put obediently away, hiding it
behind his cork jacket.

They docked at night. No one had known that this was
about to happen; after supper they had gone to bed, to be
awakened with the order to stand to and prepare for dis-
embarkation. No one knew, either, which port it was, and
they were not told. Soldiers do not ask questions. Waiting
on the lower deck they whispered among themselves. The
port was Cadiz. The port was Seville. One man asserted that
it was Valencia. Then a peevish voice remarked that the
Reds were in Valencia, and another voice replied, with a
laugh: "All the better. We land, and finish them off."

At last the order came and they began to clatter down
the gangways. The ship rode high; for a moment Kurt had
a view of the city rising beyond the docks. It was twinkling
with lights, a pinkish haze embowered it, like vapours from
a stage cauldron, and it seemed to him that he heard music.

The quays were ill-lit. They seemed unpopulated except
for the soldiers, standing in their ranks like a clipped garden.
One could hear the shuffling of feet, occasionally there was a
hollow clanking noise, followed by a sigh of steam and a jet
of water. The reflection of the gangway lamp spread in oily
circles. Sure enough, floating down there was any amount of
orange-peel.

In Spain, he was now in Spain. It must be Spain, for they
had passed through the Straits of Gibraltar. It was a pity
that they had not been allowed to arrive by day. Still, the
city was awake. In Spain gay life persists all night long, and

presently he would be riding past cafés and flood-lit fountains, and girls would throw flowers from balconies, and he would catch a red carnation and hold it between his teeth.

The order to march was given. They turned into a street winding between tall warehouses. It was cobbled, and had tram-lines. The tram-lines made an endless hallucinating path. After a while the warehouses thinned out, and gave place to factories and yards, and after that they passed through a district of mean houses, where their passage aroused the barking of dogs and thin cock-crowings. It became obvious that they were leaving the city behind. Even into the country-side the tram-lines persisted. An astonishingly cold wind blew across the fields and brought clouds of dust with it. The men began to sneeze.

Dawn was breaking when they halted at a small railway station. The only other building in sight was about a mile away: a large barrack-like place with a high wall around it. Their train was in; and the old-fashioned engine, large and lumpy like a peasant woman, had steam up. There was a coach for the officers, and a hunchback was climbing in and out of it, shaking a feather whisk. Her head was bundled up in a white shawl, her feet were bare. The rest of the train was cattle-trucks.

It was rather wounding to be treated like this; but any shelter was grateful against the cold wind, and when they had settled down in their trucks hot weak coffee was served round. The trucks were clean. Cleaned for us, he thought; for the Spaniards are notoriously a dirty lot. The doors were closed, now the next stage of their journey was beginning. Kurt settled himself where he would be able to observe the country through a crack. But though the engine continued to let off steam it did not start. Rays of sunlight began to pour through the chinks, presently a herd of goats came by, bleating and pattering. They were driven across the rails, and a voice was answered briskly by another voice. They were speaking

Spanish, of course. Fancy waiting for a herd of goats! The goats' cries died away, still the train remained in the station. When at last it got underway the jolt barely roused him from sleep.

When he woke the train was once more at a standstill, and the truck had grown stifling hot. He woke remembering that he had forgotten to take his dictionary from its hiding-place. Knowing quite well that this was so, nevertheless, he began to pat his pockets and rout in his knapsack. As he moved the sweat sprang out all over him.

"Winkler! Don't fidget."

He looked through the crack. All he could see was a bush that had small leaves. It was smothered with dust.

Then the door was unbarred, and they were told to get out and relieve nature. The violence of the sun was like a blow. The landscape extended pale and lifeless, as though the light had stunned it. A line of stony mountains lay along the horizon, they were wrinkled, like a crumple of wrapping paper, and it was impossible to say if they were near or far. Looking again at the dusty bush he saw that it was dotted with small white flowers. A shout of laughter came from his companions. One of them had noticed that the ground was swarming with ants, and a competition to drown the ants was taking place. Farther down the track the cooks were preparing breakfast.

They travelled all day. At intervals the train halted, always in places as bare and pale as the first. Every one agreed that this was a worthless country, and Fridolin Kuh grumbled that such a country might as well be left to the Reds, no one else could want it. The engine-driver sat on the step of the cab with his legs dangling, and poured wine into his mouth, holding the bottle away from his lips. At each halt they egged one another on to go forward and talk to him, but each time that a group began sneaking off a non-commissioned officer would order them back.

After a halt where the railway track ran beside a dry river-bed they travelled for a long time, and dusk gave way to darkness, and the noise of the wheels seemed to alter. Then again they halted, but the doors remained barred. They heard an old-fashioned mechanical piano playing quite close by, and presently a thick tenor voice took up the tune. After the song there was stamping and clapping and cries of approval. Listening drowsily, Kurt found that he could understand what was being said. Spanish was an easy language then, he had learned it better than he supposed, and the loss of the dictionary was not so serious after all.

"Do you hear that, boys? That's some of ours. Sounds good, eh?" He realized that the singer and the shouters were German.

Every one was delighted to think that there were comrades so close, and answering shouts and snatches of song came from the trucks, but at the same moment the train got going again, just as though the driver had done it out of malice.

At last they detrained at a station no larger than the one they started from, and just as solitary. The new road also had tram-lines, and inverted the morning's march from country into mean suburbs, from suburbs to yard and factories. They might have been back where they started from, only there was no sea.

Left wheel! The tram-lines went on, the men turned into a road which began to mount steeply uphill, past a cemetery, past large villas, each standing behind a high pale wall. Looking at the cypresses and the fantastic silhouettes of the balconied and turreted villas Kurt felt that at last he was in Spain. Ten minutes later, as Fridolin Kuh remarked with pleasure, they were back in Germany.

The barrack was a large building in modern style. The Republicans had built it, they were told, to house lunatics and cretins. Now it was put to a better use, swarming with healthy young men, ringing with healthy boot-treads, smell-

ing of healthy meat and dumpling. A garden even had been
laid out for the lunatics, and planted with young trees. This
was now a parade-ground, and the few saplings that remained
were broken and dying. Everything was splendidly managed,
day by day swinging by as though to a march-tune. Even the
sun, rising above the white wall, burning the dew off the
dying saplings, bleaching the sky to a midday pallor, declin-
ing into a coppery mist, seemed to be on parade. In such a
life—short of active service the most congenial a young man
can ask for—Kurt should have been happy. But on the whole
he was not happy. Analysing his discontent, he told himself
that he was bored and frustrated, that nothing short of the
noblest could satisfy him, and that having come to Spain to
root out marxism he could not be happy till he was doing it.
Meanwhile, there were other small rubs and annoyances.
The relation between his detachment and the earlier arrivals
was not good. The first lot were sour and clannish, and
behaved as though they owned the place. There was a good
deal of petty thieving, an unwillingness to share or lend—as
though a sense of being besieged had developed from the state
of being in a foreign country. No one felt very well. You'll
soon get it, the old lot told the new. Sure enough, before long
the new arrivals began to suffer from headaches, shivering
fits, and diarrhoea. In a fit of confidence Karl Heidler, one of
the first lot, told Kurt that this was because of a bunch of
flowers which Corporal Schutz had brought in one evening,
flowers bestowed on him by a young lady. They were bright
magenta-coloured flowers, Heidler said, and carried fever,
though they had no scent. There had been a row, and the
nosegay had been thrown into the furnace; but the fever
persisted.

Only the non-commissioned officers, it appeared, were
allowed to go into the town. For himself, said Heidler, he
wouldn't trouble to go. It was unhealthy, the prices were
exorbitant, and there were beggars at every turn.

"All the same, it would be nice to see Spain."

"You'll see it fast enough," Heidler replied. "There's an inspection on Wednesday."

The inspection was carried out by a Spanish general. He was a short man with a worried expression, and at brief intervals he scratched himself. His staff, who accompanied him, all seemed to belong to one and the same family. They were singularly tall and thin, they had blankly supercilious faces and sagging lower lips. It was not romantic.

Yet romance there must be. All the stories, all the songs, all the movies, stressed the romance of Spain, and they could not all be mistaken. Besides, had not a political lecturer described to them how in marxist Spain the singing and dancing and traditional piety and gaiety had been overwhelmed by squalor and starvation?—whereas this was nationalist Spain. So Kurt cultivated Corporal Heidler, listened to his ailments and gave him aspirins and unwaveringly admired the photographs of Corporal Heidler's birthplace and relations; for Heidler was, as Kurt told himself, the gateway to romance. And at the same time he did all in his power to be made a corporal himself.

At last the gateway—none too willingly—allowed him passage. One of the officers had been given a dog, and the dog was coming by train, and a car must go to the station to meet it. Heidler had been told to drive the car, and Schutz, who spoke Spanish, was to go with him to collect the dog from the station officials.

Ill-naturedly they spoke to him of this, remarking how unfortunate it was that they, who didn't want to go, should be going, while he, who would give his ears to go, must stay behind.

"Destiny is often like that," said Schutz.

"The fortunes of war," added Heidler.

"Only gold," said Schutz, "can overcome destiny. By the way, would you like us to do any shopping for you?"

"No. I don't think I need anything."

Schutz raised his light eyebrows. Heidler laughed.

"No brandies for you to-day, honoured corporal. He does not wish us to drink his health."

"But— But of course, I should be delighted. I should be proud."

"Actually," said Schutz, "I do not feel much inclined to get drunk just now. I have a splitting headache. *I* don't want to jolt down to that filthy station and jolt back with a filthy dog. If Winkler really yearns to go instead of me, why shouldn't he?"

"And leave me to deal with all those station clerks? I can't speak a word of their beastly talk."

"I know a little Spanish," said Kurt.

"H'm. Do you? First I've heard of it. What's dog in Spanish?"

"Perro."

Heidler looked at Schutz. Schutz nodded.

"First-rate! And what's brandy?"

Conversation in a restaurant. Bring me more bread, more butter, one of your best cigars. This coffee is too weak, too strong. This fish is not fresh. The phrase-book had vanished through the port-hole, a loose page, snatched by the wind, fluttering lightly upward, like a bird. Heidler laughed.

"I'll teach him on the way down," said Schutz.

The car was large and low, a very grand car. He sat in the back seat, crouching in order to see as much as possible. By daylight the villas were even more romantic, their turrets roofed with blue or emerald-green or orange tiles, their balconies smothered with brilliant creepers. And that, its magenta blossom colliding with a burst of scarlet geraniums, must be the fever flower.

"There's the bull-ring."

He saw a vast expanse of brick wall covered with posters. Farther on a door in a dark porch opened, a woman in black came out, behind her was a brief revelation of candlelight and gilding. The woman unfortunately was ugly and quite old.

As they neared the station the town became pretty much like any other town, though in front of the station was a row of palm-trees. They could not be very good specimens, though: they were short, and the leaves were scanty, and quite a dull colour. Round about the entrance to the station were quantities of beggars. Some were cripples, some nursed babies, some displayed sores. A monk and some nuns were standing near by, dispensing alms, he supposed. Religion had kept Spain a backward country, yet there was something quite touching in this old-world piety, this old-world charity. As the three soldiers approached the beggars began to shout and scream, the cripples hitched themselves forward; but the religious persons swept imperiously to the front rank and held out boxes. They were beggars too.

"Now we will hear you talk Spanish."

Kurt flushed. He began to doubt the efficacy of the phrase he had rehearsed on his way down. *Un perro. Ferroviaria.* But there should be a verb and he could not remember many verbs. All around were people talking Spanish, and he could not understand a word they said. At least he could begin with saying Good-afternoon. Politeness often makes a good impression. *Buenas me*—that was as far as he got. Schutz elbowed him aside and began to question the porter in a loud voice. Schutz's Spanish he could understand quite well.

The porter was explaining something. He kept on using the same word, suddenly it became clear to Kurt that the porter was telling them to hope. Why hope? What had they to hope for? And where was the dog?

"God, what a filthy country," exclaimed Schutz.

"Why, what's wrong? Surely the Reds are not advancing on us?"

"The train's late. We've got to wait for two hours, he says. Idiot!"

"Just nice time for a drink," said Heidler. "Come on, Winkler. Now you can pay for your ride."

They entered the station café, ordered brandies, and began to smoke. The café was large and nearly empty. It had a bar crammed with every sort of drink. On the walls were patriotic posters, showing the militiamen as monkeys, showing a hairy red hand throttling a young lady with well-developed naked breasts between which a black cross dangled primly. Above the bar was a large clock. Kurt paid for the second round of brandies also.

After a while he suggested that they might move on to another café.

"Why?" said Heidler. "They've got eats here too, if you're hungry."

"Well, we might see more."

"That's a good idea," said Schutz to Heidler. "Let's order something salted, and have beer with it."

Heidler beckoned to the waiter. Schutz gave the order, Kurt paid. He half rose, smiled appealingly at Schutz, made himself look boyish. Schutz smiled back.

"Well, as long as you're back on time. . . . If you find anything worth our attention, come and tell us."

Leaving the station he was again assailed by beggars, by nuns with collecting boxes, and by a little girl in a long skirt of tattered yellow cotton. She pursued him, screeching and giggling. At last he threw down a coin. Afterwards, looking cautiously back, he saw that she had returned to her pitch, and was turning a somersault in front of a nun.

This had been very unpleasant. One could not love such children, children so unchildish. He began to walk slowly, keeping close to the shop-windows, staring at their displays. There was nothing beautiful, nothing out of the way. He would have preferred to walk on the other side of the street, where there was a row of flower-stalls. The flowers were marvellous, not just those red carnations, but really expensive flowers; but the flower-stalls were too near the station, the little girl might come after him again. It was very hot, much hotter than up on the hill. Presently he looked at his watch. Only ten minutes had gone by since he left the others.

One shop led to another shop. His ears became accustomed to the sound of Spanish. Large grand cars tore past, honking continuously. Then he heard a strange noise . . . a fine tinkle of falling water. He looked about, and saw, opening out of the street, a passage, and beyond the passage a little square. He waited till someone else turned down the passage, and then followed.

The square had arcades all round. It was like a cloister, but it also looked Moorish, as of course, it should do. In the middle was a small fountain. The jet of water was feeble and intermittent, it seemed as though something might be blocking the feed. But still, it was a fountain. There were some more palm-trees—no better than those by the station, presumably this was not a part of Spain where palm-trees were at their best—bushes of a dark-leafed shrub, and two stone benches. As there was no one about he sat down. The houses round the square were tall, so tall that all the lower half of the square was in shadow. Only on the upper walls was there sunlight. It shone on a line of washing hanging from one shuttered window to another. Somewhere a canary was singing.

He began to be very happy. This was a moment he would remember all his life . . . a corner of old Spain. And he had found it entirely by himself. It was undoubtedly picturesque, yet no one else had found it. There were no directing notices, no artists, no one paused with a camera, and though there were a few shops under the arcades not one of them showed the slightest preparedness for lovers of the picturesque. Sparrows hopped around, the canary continued to sing, a woman called to a child, two priests walked by, the fountain tinkled. If only someone would begin to play the guitar, everything would be perfect.

He looked at his watch. Over half an hour had passed. Heavens, what a long time he had wasted loitering here, when there was so much more to see! How would it sound if he were questioned, and could only reply: "I sat in a little square watching a fountain"? He would be teased to death.

He sprang up and went to the mouth of the passage, assuring himself that from thence the station was in sight. Then, sure of his retreat, he set out to explore.

At the farther end of the square was another passage. It took him into a narrow street that was cobbled, and shady, and highly picturesque. Almost the first thing he saw was a great hooded archway with carving on it. One would have expected such an entrance to lead into a church, but actually it led into a garage. How on earth could such large cars turn in such a narrow street? After a little thought he became pleased with this mixture of medieval and modern, surely most typically Spanish. A church-porch leading to a garage, that was something one might well talk about, for it was both funny and characteristic. Darkening the next turning was a building, so square, so massive, that it must be a prison. An old prison, a prison of the Inquisition. Even now the few slit windows high up in the blank walls of greasy ancient stone kept their iron bars. People were strolling in and out of the prison, women mostly, then came a party of young girls, walking stiffly, shepherded by nuns. Looking again he saw that the prison was surmounted by a Gothic spire, was a church. Remembering the beggars at the station—there would certainly be beggars at a church too—he turned off into a yet narrower street.

This street was very dull, and he kept on thinking that he would turn back. But he did not do so. A soldier of the Third Reich never turns back. Here there were more people about; women carried red and green peppers or very inferior cauliflowers in string bags, children played cards in the road, an old, old man sitting on a rush chair on a pavement nursed a goggle-eyed baby that must surely be an idiot. The cobbles were covered with dirt and refuse, and for a while he tried to pick his way. Then he saw a group of men watching him, and though none smiled he felt they were laughing at him, so after that he walked straight ahead, keeping in the middle of the road. Presently he realized what a loud noise his boots made. Treading on cobbles between tall house-fronts of stone he was in a stone sounding-box. His seemed to be the only footsteps in the street; the other passers-by were wearing rope-soles, some even went barefoot.

He turned off again. This street was narrow too, stonily echoing. Obviously it was very old, yet it was not picturesque; there was no colour, no incident, no gaiety. Even the children spoke little, darting past him like a shoal of minnows. He had certainly got into a poor bad part of the town.

Then he became aware of a smell.

During his ramble he had, of course, noticed many smells. By the station there had been a smell of boiling shell-fish and hot black clothing. In the little square there had been a smell of cooking in oil. By the church there had been a violent smell from a urinal hollowed in the wall. After that he had traversed smells of garbage, garlic, piss, sour wine, and from the old man nursing the idiot had come a strong smell of cockroaches.

But this smell was different.

Naturally, he had not grown up in a palace. He knew as many bad smells as the next fellow. There was the smell of antiquity: dry-rot, cobwebs, mildewed walls; there was the smell of poverty: greasiness of bad fat, the close woollen fustiness of old clothes; there was the smell of sickness, of bad teeth and bad stomachs, the charnel smell of decay, the smell one commonly calls drains. Nasty as they were, and socially deplorable, yet they had also a certain geniality, they had a flattering fulsome welcome like ageing prostitutes, they re-assured one's sense of being a man, and comfortably at home in the world. Even the stink of decay could give one a queer thrill.

But this smell had not a breath of welcome. It was evil, not base. It expressed a stony antiquity, a poverty beyond food or clothing, an immaterial sickness, a cold-blooded excrement, the excrement of fishes, perhaps, a decay, not of a corpse but of a ghost. It was everywhere, unanswerable as the smell of the sea. It was full of despair and lassitude, and yet it was quite inhuman, and yet it was like a curse.

He felt himself daunted, yes, really quite inexplicably frightened. The flower that carried fever had no smell at all, they said. But a smell like this might even drive one mad, shrivel one into idiocy, into cretinism, like some newly in-vented poison-gas. If he could see any sort of tavern he would buy a glass of spirits. He still had enough left for one drink. And then he would turn back at once. After all, he had seen a church-porch leading to a garage, that was something to tell the others. Very likely they would not even ask him what he had seen.

And still he walked on, thinking that there must be a tavern quite close.

At the street corner a group of women and children were waiting outside a closed door. On the door was a nationalist poster, above it was a crucifix of stone. As he went by they turned, and looked at him. How terribly thin they were, how sickly-looking, how mirthless! Even the children were hag-gard. This was what marxism had done to the joyful, care-free people of Spain. Out of his fear and confusion a correct kindly thought sprang to attention. He was here to defend these miserable beings, to lead them to a glorious efficient future. He raised his hand, and cried:

"*Arriba España!*"

One of the children laughed. Its mother instantly cuffed it. Otherwise there was no sign of response. They looked at him with blank faces. He had the strange feeling that each one of them was looking at him out of a pale stone house with shuttered windows. Then another of the children made a grimace at him, and spat. Presently they turned their backs on him. He was ignored, left alone with the smell, knowing himself hated.

And I am dying on their behalf, he thought dolefully. Till now it had never occurred to him that in coming to Spain to fight he might also have come to Spain to die. But from then till the hour of his death the conviction never left him.

THE LEVEL-CROSSING

SINCE 1927 Alfred Thorn had kept the level-crossing where the road from Wellbury to Kingsfield crosses the railway. Before then he had worked in the goods-yard at Paddington. A rupture ended that employment, and the company, since he was a steady man and no drinker, transferred him to the Kingsfield L. C.

For over forty years a Londoner, and living always in the narrow, noisy, shabbily cosy district of North Paddington, he found it strange to live in the country, that was so bare and calm; and going out at night to set the gates for the passage of the 12.41 up goods train he had almost feared the heavy summer whisper of the trees, the moor-hens squawking under the bridge. With a kind of homesickness he would recall the night turn in the goods-yard, the figures under the raw arc lights, his mates shouting, the soft whine of the wind along the metals, and how once, seeing a train come in with a white crust still lying on the tarpaulins, he had said to himself: It's snowing in the country. And a picture was in his mind, a picture based on a Christmas card: a white landscape, a church spire, a sunset glowing between bars of cloud like the coals in a grate.

With his first winter came snow: so sudden and so heavy a fall that before he could swing back the large gates closing off the road he had to shovel the snow to one side. Some winters it snowed, some not. There was more variation in the winters than in the summers. But the years became pleasant to him, for he had taken to gardening, and the driver of the 11.5 would lean out of the cab to wave a gesture of approval towards Alfred Thorn's well-trenched celery or dark autumnal dahlias.

He was unmarried; but as a level-crossing keeper must have a companion, someone to take his place should he be suddenly disabled, he had brought with him his niece, Alice Hawkins. As a child she had been pretty, and when she went out to her first employment as a kitchen-maid it was taken for granted that in a year or two she would be married, and peeling potatoes for a household of her own. But one morning, pouring kerosene on an unwilling kitchen fire, she set fire to herself. They thought she would die of her injuries, but she lived on, her face so frightfully scarred that no one now could think of a husband for Alice, and never another word came from her wried mouth. From shock and terror she had lost the power of speech.

At first Alfred had found it painful to be companioned by this pitiable creature, from whom the flames seemed to have burned off youth and sex and personality, leaving but the morose industry of a machine. Though her hearing was only a little impaired, words appeared to have no more meaning for her. Only very rarely would she feel the impulse to communicate, and then she would scrawl a sentence on a piece of paper, usually no more than a household request for hearth-brick or a new scrubbing brush. But insensibly a kind of harmony grew up between them, his pleasure in her good cooking and cleanliness complementing her instinct to serve; and his old bachelor habits—the easy-chair always drawn forward at the same angle, the pipe lit at the same hour, the coat hanging from one nail and the lantern from another— giving her a sense of security, of being insured against another disaster. She lived by the trains almost as much as he, and though she would not go to the shop or to church, she would go out, almost with gladness, to work the level-crossing gates.

There was an element of monasticism about their lives.

As the monk charts his days by lauds and matins, vespers and compline, Alfred Thorn lived by the four expresses, the ten locals, the six clanking goods, his being always attentive to the note of the signal that linked him to the organization of the Great Western Railway as the chime of the bell links the monk to the organization of Christendom.

The declaration of war in 1939 imposed many changes on the railways. Duplicated notices came to Alfred Thorn advising him of altered runnings and trains that would run no longer. His life was dislocated. In the last war, too, his life had been dislocated—soldiering had sent him hither and thither, the chiming of high explosive had been the mad time-piece he lived by. But these new days seemed reproachfully empty, empty as the autumn landscape, the bare stubble-fields, the trees growing shabby and furtively casting their leaves. And in the lengthened intervals between the clicks of the signal the noise of the river seemed as loud and intimidat-ing as it had seemed on his first coming.

There were fewer trains; but the traffic across the metals increased. Army lorries, army cars, tanks, and riders on motor-bicycles roared past the level-crossing gates. More and more soldiers were coming into the district—"to be given a lick," said the postman, "before they go over." One day early in October a billeting officer came to the house, asking Alfred if he could put up soldiers, and how many.

"If I sleep on the couch downstairs, there's my bedroom. It's a fair-sized room. But it has only a single bed."

"This will take five," said the officer. "Never mind about the bed. Put it away. They'll sleep on the floor."

On Sunday evening the men came. It was a wet, windy evening, and their arrival seemed to darken the house. The rain dripped off them, their feet scraped heavily on the floor, they stacked their equipment in every corner. Sourly humor-ous, they complained of the delays on their train journey. They had been travelling for eleven hours, and of those hours, nearly five, they said, had been spent in waiting on platforms or in sidings.

"We could have marched it in the time."

"And kept a fair sight warmer."

"Yeah! *He* could have marched it, anyway. Twenty miles an hour's nothing to him—look at the size of his feet."

"It wouldn't have been twenty miles an hour. What's twenty elevens? Two hundred and something. You telling me it's two hundred miles from there to here?"

"Well, how far is it, smarty?"

Out of their fatigue a dispirited wrangle flickered up. Alfred and Alice served them with sausages and potatoes and a great deal of cocoa. One of the soldiers—he was a sharp-faced fellow, they called him Syd—remarked:

"You'll be out of pocket by this, you know. They don't allow you'll feed us."

"We don't often have company," said Alfred.

They were all very young. He felt embarrassed among them. His life during the last years had gone on so quietly, so regularly, that he had not thought of himself as growing older. Suddenly he saw himself an elderly man.

When the meal was over for politeness' sake they hung about a little, lighting cigarettes, staring at the pictures on the walls, the fancy calendars, the enlarged photographs of Alfred's parents, the framed certificate of his Friendly Society, the crayons of dogs and roses that Alice had done at school. Now Alice got up. It was time to set the gates for the 9.37. Thinking of the train, Alfred said:

"I'm going."

But the words were hardly out of his mouth before he remembered her shyness, her deformity. Now she would be left alone with them. The train was late. By the time it had passed and he had reset the gates nearly quarter of an hour had gone by. When he got back to the house the curly-haired boy they called Ikey had sunk to the floor and was asleep with his head propped against Syd's knees. The others were in the back-kitchen helping Alice wash up. Later on, after they had stumbled upstairs, Alfred Thorn remembered the feeling that had weighed on him as he stood waiting for the 9.37. It had been a feeling of shame as for some failure of hospitality. Now he identified it, remembering their complaints of the journey, the many delays, the cold. He found himself speaking aloud. "It's a bad thing."

Alice looked up. She nodded her head in agreement, nodded violently. Her expression was harsh and mournful. They were at cross-purposes, but he did not explain his thought. War, too, was a bad thing, at any rate most women thought so.

Agreeing with the billeting officer he had acted on impulse, worrying afterwards as to whether Alice would suffer, her long privacy laid open to the glances of five strange young men; and he had bargained with his uneasiness, planning to do this and that so that she need not come in contact with them. She had made no comment on the news of their arrival, only writing down a list of extra groceries. When they arrived she began to cook for them as a matter of course.

"My niece is dumb," he had said, that there might be no awkwardness over speeches of thanks.

Ask for their washing, she wrote next morning. And that afternoon she wrote again, sending him to the village shop for sultanas for a cake, darning-wool, oranges, cigarettes, seven pounds of sugar for making apple jelly. At the shop he was told that there were no sultanas and that a pound of sugar was all that he could be spared. When Alice heard this she stood a little while, her face working. Then she put on her hat, the hat she had left London in twelve years before, and went out. What happened at the shop he would never know, but she brought back all she wanted.

She feels like a mother, he thought.

A week later he was thinking: She feels happy. Yet how

did he know it? She manifested no outward happiness. Sombre and reserved, she moved from oven to table, took up plates to refill them, clawed at a tunic that needed mending. They praised and thanked her, and gave her presents: boxes of chocolates, gloves, a potted chrysanthemum brought from the town by the carrier; and she accepted her presents so flatly, so ungraciously, that it seemed to Alfred that such acceptances could only be felt as rebuffs. And yet he knew well that between Alice and the soldiers there was an intimacy that would never exist between the soldiers and himself, though it was with him that they talked and joked, played games and swopped tobacco.

"It's like that in every family," he told himself. "It's always the mother means most to the boys."

They were good boys. Syd and Ikey he thought of as the eldest and the youngest, the Reuben and the Benjamin; for it was difficult to remember that there was less than a year's difference in age between them, for Syd was already lined and sharp-spoken, while Ikey, his long lashes gleaming as he screwed up his eyes in fits of laughter, seemed no more than a child. In between came Joe, Ivor, and Wallie. Nicer young fellows you couldn't ask for. Well-mannered too, and more refined than boys had been in his day. Oh, it was a pity you couldn't look at them without seeing the khaki, without remembering the advertisement that said: *Four Out of Every Five*, and the five pictured faces with the black squares laid across four of them. Then, out of the blue, it happened.

Supper was over and cleared away, and the boys were in the back-kitchen, washing up, and he had gone out for the 9.37. To-night it was almost on time. The trains running so unpunctually had irked him, and watching the clouds of rosy steam fade on the sky he felt a warmth of pleasure, thinking: To-night, they can't laugh at me. I've got the laugh on them. For they had found out his foible, teasing him night after night when the last local kept him dawdling with his hand on the gate-lever.

Out of the dark box which was his home came the noise of the soldiers scrimmaging at the wash-bowl—a splash, feigned cries of horror and anguish, Ikey's wild warbling giggles.

And so unheard he entered the front room.

Ivor sat in the easy-chair and Alice, folding a table-cloth, stood near him. He pulled her down on his knees—a gentle, dreamy movement, the movement almost of a sleeper. With one arm about her waist he held her there; and then, his eyes averted, he began to stroke her face, her ruined cheek and chin. She sat stiff and unmoving, staring in front of her, her red hands quietly folded on the table-cloth. Even when tears began to roll down her cheeks and through his caressing fingers, she did not move her hands.

The first thought went no further than: This is cruelly awkward for me. He wanted desperately to go away. But his duty was clear: he must put a stop to it. There could be no doubt as to how to speak; for a young man pulling a girl down on his knees, a girl ten years older than he and as frightful as a figure at a fair, was one thing only: a thief, an abuser of hospitality.

He walked forward, his footsteps tramping. Still holding Alice, still stroking her face, Ivor looked up.

"I mean to marry her."

As for the words, they might have been the words of any boy caught out, a boy who says, *I mean to give it back, I mean to mend it*. But the voice spoke something quite different, and made the words sound formal and irrevocable, like a vow, or a sentence given in court.

"You don't know what you're talking about. You'll be off to France at any moment now—and she's ten years older than you."

He spoke gloomily, hating the words as he uttered them.

Here was a young man who in a month might be dead, and a woman who since her girlhood had been doomed to a life not much better than death; and because he himself was old, and would soon be death's due, he must needs scold them out of their moment's happiness. From the next room came another burst of laughter. It was more than he could bear. He groaned, and sat down, and buried his face in his hands.

When he looked up they were sitting just as before, only Alice had left off crying. Now she got up, slowly, smoothly, as though all her life she had been getting up off a young man's knee, and came over to him. And presently she, dumb Alice, moved her lips; and a faint hiss came from her as though she were shaping the word, *Please.*

"It's one thing or another, my lad. Either you clear out, or you act square by the girl and marry her."

"I mean to marry her."

Then you'd better act openly about it, and tell the others.

The words were on his lips but he did not speak them, for at that moment the others came in. Joe proposed a game of Rummy, the evening went by like any other evening; and when Alice and Alfred were left alone she straightened the room, made up his bed on the couch, kissed him and went off to bed, just as usual.

The more he thought of it, the worse it seemed. Such a match could only bring misery to both of them—if it came to a match. And if it did not? Going out for the 12.41, the calmness, the serenity, of the moonlit night seemed to throw scorn on his perplexity. The goods-train rumbled past, and with all his being he yearned to throw himself into one of those trucks, to be carried to Paddington, back to the goods-yard, back to his lodging in the cosy, shabby street, back to his former strength and the cock-sureness of youth. But here he stood, old and puzzled, and of no use to any one.

Most of the night he lay awake worrying. He worried about Alice, then his thoughts would wander off to the prob-

lem of who would take her place if she married and left him.
But she might marry, and yet remain with him, and bear a
child. A level-crossing is no place for a child, and if the war
went on long enough, or Alice were widowed by it, the child
would be of an age to stagger on to the track or out into the
road, and be run over. How long would the war go on? How
much higher would prices go? When would the air raids
begin? There was a movement overhead, and in an instant
he was on his feet, shaking with rage. No! There should be
no such doings under his roof. The next minute he heard a
window closed, and the footsteps recrossing the floor, and a
sigh, and a creak of the boards as the closer of the window
settled again to his sleep. Overcome with shame and misery
Alfred lay down also. What would he think next? What had
come over him that he should nurse such suspicions, such
jealousy? And what was to be done about Alice?

In the morning he looked at her narrowly, anxiously.
There was no change of expression in her marred face, no
lightening of her tread, no outward indication of love or the
astonishment of love. Yet somehow from her dull unchanged
face and unchanged mechanical serenity there streamed a
conviction of being loved and being triumphant. As for
Ivor, he was no more and no less than the others: a boy in
a hurry who would be punished if he were late for school.

Sorrow is not so self-sufficient as joy. Alfred Thorn had
meant to deal with his trouble unaided, to say no word of the
matter. But when the soldiers came back at the end of the
day he buttonholed Syd, and took him into the dusky garden.

"Something's happened that shouldn't have. Ivor says he
wants to marry my Alice."

"Does he?"

There was so little surprise in the words that Alfred Thorn
exclaimed in instant furious suspicion:

"Did you know about it, then? Has he been talking
about it?"

"Not a word. But I am not altogether surprised. He's been looking at her a lot."

"Looking at her? What sort of looking?"

"Just looking."

"Oh, well, I don't like it. What makes a boy like him run after a girl like her?"

"She's a very nice girl. She's very kind."

"But she's dumb! And her face. Her face, you know. Those scars."

"Perhaps he likes the scars."

"Likes them? *Likes* them?"

Shaking with anger he glared into the young man's face. But it gave him back no look of irony or insolence—unless it be insolent for a young man to look so calmly on an old man in a fury.

"People do, you know. Some people. It's psychological. For him it might be just the attraction."

"I don't know what you call it. I call it plain disgusting. Morbid, I call it."

"You can't blame the boy for being morbid if he's made that way."

"Oh, can't I? You'll see if I can't blame him."

"Well, Mr. Thorn, you'd be wrong. What you're feeling is something very old-fashioned. Nowadays——"

But Alfred Thorn had turned his back, and was stumping off. Reaching the garden gate he paused, and shouted:

"Tell her I shan't be in till the 9.37."

He went off down the railway track, lurching from sleeper to sleeper.

"Maybe a drink will comfort him," thought Syd. He considered the old man to be stupid, and certainly in the wrong; but he had a responsible nature and felt a soldierly impulse to tidy him. It had been such a happy household till now.

Alfred Thorn, however, was not walking to the public-house. A mile farther down the track the Wellbury branch line came in, and here was a signal-box. A signal-box can be a very comfortable place, standing above the cares of the common world, warm in winter, in summer airy, with a mug of tea on the window-sill. Now he was going to the signal-box for shelter, to take sanctuary in his profession. It was as good as he'd hoped. The tea was strong, and they talked of railway matters, and Vincent Jones sang his song of "Crawshay Bailey had an engine," and laughed, and said that war would never change Wales, and perhaps not change England much either. But the clock hung on the wall, and the reminders of time rang and chirped through the conversation, and too soon it was time to go back for the 9.37.

It was a cloudy night, and cold, with a gusty November wind. The moon had not risen yet. The wind droned in the telegraph wires; though he walked with bent head he could know when he was approaching another telegraph pole by the heavy throbbing that spread into the air. He felt fretted and discouraged. It was hard to leave Vincent Jones, a man of his own age and profession, and return to a pack of soldiers —five young men all banded together against an old man, laughing at him up their sleeves, teasing him about the trains being unpunctual. And so he would wait outside the house till the 9.37 had gone through.

Walking to and fro he had an impression that someone was near by. There were no footsteps on the road, no sounds but the wind crying through the wires and along the metals, and the rustle of trees, and the shed-door rattling. But he cried out:

"Is any one there?"

No answer. One of those boys, he thought, following me out to tease me, on the chance of the train being late. Late it was, too. The third quarter had struck and still it was not signalled. A bicyclist came down the road, his light a low wobbling star, and dismounted.

"You can cross. She isn't signalled yet."

The bicycle was edged through the wicket-gate and wheeled across the track. The rider was young Harry Foley, and as he rode off he cried:

"Good-night, Mr. Thorn. Hope you don't wait much longer. Don't catch cold. There's a lot of the 'flu about."

That's how the young think, thought Alfred. Hoping is easy work for them. But as the minutes went by his grievance faded from his mind, shouldered aside by anxiety at the train's delay. Ten o'clock had struck. Something must have happened. An accident? An air raid?

From cold, from anxiety, he began to walk up the line. A creature of his profession, part of the organization of the Great Western Railway, he set out on the up line, and turning came back on the other. His foot struck against something lying in his way. It was heavy, yielding, human. Dead? No, alive! For it rose up, and tried to run. But in the darkness he caught it, and found himself holding on to a man, dressed in tight-fitting clothes of coarse woollen cloth.

"Now what's this? Who are you?"

"I—I must have been asleep."

"Ivor!"

"Yes, it's me, Mr. Thorn."

The boy was shaking with cold and his teeth chattered.

"Now what are you up to? What were you doing here?"

"I must have fallen asleep. I was waiting."

His voice was senseless, he spoke as though still heavy with a dream.

"Waiting? What for?"

"The 9.37. *Where is it?*" he cried out suddenly. "Oh, damn your trains, they're always late."

"You'd best tell me what all this is about," said Alfred Thorn.

"I can't stick it," lamented the boy. "It's no use. I can't go through with it."

"Now, now," said the old man. "You've got worked up, that's what it is. You're young, and it's hard for you. But you mustn't act so silly, boy. War's a thing one gets used to like everything else. Lots of people come through it, and none the worse. I was in the last war myself, I know what I'm talking about."

"It's not the war."

"Not the war? What is it, then?"

"Marrying Alice. I can't go through with it."

The signal rang. Alfred took the boy by the arm and began towing him along the track-side.

"It's her face. I thought it would help, but it doesn't. From the moment I set eyes on her——"

He paused, shuddering.

"That's right," said Alfred. "You tell it from the beginning."

"In Camberwell—I come from Camberwell—there was an exhibition got up by some Peace people or other. And I went in for a look. I'd never thought about war till then. They had a lot of photos. Photos of people wounded in the last war, and still alive to this day."

His voice rose into a scream. When he began again it was in a whisper.

"The worst of them was a man with half his face shot away. Ever since I've been trying to forget it. But I couldn't. Then this happened, and I was called."

"I said all along it was too young," said Alfred.

"When I saw Alice—she isn't so bad, though, nothing like so bad—I couldn't bear to look at her. Then I thought: Suppose I do look at her? Maybe I'll get used to it. Then I couldn't but look at her. It fascinated me. Then I thought: If I could only touch her face, stroke it, then somehow I could get used to it, forgive it. *For that's what will happen to me!* I know it, I've known it all along."

Now they had reached the level-crossing, and stood by the gate. Touching the smooth cold surface Alfred felt that they had overcome the worst, reached some kind of assurance.

"And she sat so still, letting me stroke her. I couldn't help it, it was like something that would go on for ever. And then you came in, and I thought: "It's got to be like this.""

From far off, through the curtaining wind, came the faint regular pulsing of the engine, a feeling on the ear-drums rather than a sound.

"But it's no use, no use! I can't go through with it. When I begin to realize it I know I can't."

A delicate rosy light bloomed on the darkness. The train was audible now.

"So I came out here to end it all. But the train didn't come. I lay down on the line, I must have dropped off to sleep. We've been hard at it all the day."

The train came thundering on, its full steam-voice armoured in clankings and clatterings. It was not possible to speak and be heard. At last, Alfred could say:

"Well, you can't marry her, that's certain."

As he spoke his hand pressed the lever and the gates swung back, leaving the road clear. A couple of cars went through.

"But who's going to tell her?"

"I can't, Mr. Thorn."

"I don't fancy it either."

In the silence that followed they knew themselves drawn together, sharing for the first time a common emotion, a common uneasiness. Ivor pulled out a packet of cigarettes.

"Maybe Syd could. He's best at explaining."

But Alice did not hear it from Syd. The next day they came in with the news that they were to be sent off for a course of machine-gunning. There was a flurry of departure, and on the morrow, early, they were gone. "I'll write," Ivor had said.

Two days later the letter came. He saw her reading it, a slow task, for she was little used to letter-reading. She folded it up, and put it back in the envelope, and laid the envelope on the mantelpiece under the tea-canister. He watched in an agony of pity and embarrassment. He dared not speak, and she could not. Her face became deeply flushed, and the more hideous for being so.

After a while his honour broke down, and being alone in the room he looked under the canister. The letter was gone.

Early in December new soldiers arrived, and the policeman brought another billeting notice. Awkward with compassion, and speaking almost harshly, Alfred said:

"You've only to say if you don't want them, Alice."

She found her pencil, and wrote:

Let them come.

Did she hope in some obscure romance of her heart that the new batch of soldiers would bring her another lover, and a kinder one? Was she bent on proving to herself that the wound of Ivor was only a surface wound, and healing? It was impossible to say. She looked after these as efficiently, as commandingly, as she had looked after those others, and moved among them firmly, and seemingly content. Alfred thought: She'd rather have them than be alone with me. And perhaps she put their unconsciousness of her tragedy between herself and his knowledge. As Christmas neared she began to make preparations, baking and icing a Christmas cake, buying coloured paper garlands and looping them across the ceiling. Gipsies came through the village selling mistletoe. One of the soldiers bought a bunch and brought it in. She nodded approvingly, and hung it in the centre of the room.

Late that afternoon she went into the garden to fetch the washing. She stood there for some time, staring about her. In her attitude there was something of release and sudden boldness, as though she had come out of prison. Perhaps the wind, blowing her hair and fluttering her skirts, had blown this look on to her. On her return she took up her pencil and wrote on a slip of paper, and handed it to Alfred. She had written the word *Snow*.

For a minute he thought it was something she wanted him to get from the shop, something for Christmas.

"Snow, Alice?"

She pointed out of the window at the calm cold sky and the bare landscape, and nodded her head decisively.

When, a few days later, the snow came, and all the railway traffic was disorganized, she went about with a queer look of triumph, and began to treat him more affectionately, as though her prophecy coming true had reconciled them and put them back on the old footing.